**"What is it, Jade?"
Kaeden asked with patience
and lots of distance.**

"That night, what happened between us—"

Kaeden held up his hand. "Just let it go, Jade."

She stepped forward. "That's just it. I can't let it go. If I could I would, Kaeden. But I can't let it go. I can't forget. I can't help feeling like it was the best ever."

Kaeden released a heavy breath as he watched her.

"You don't understand, Kaeden," she stressed. "Before that night I hadn't been intimate with anyone in over a year, but I forgot all of my restrictions, all of my inhibitions with you. I'm still trying to figure it all out but all I do know is that once you touched me, it was over and there was no going back, Kaeden."

Kaeden stared at her, and something about the look in his eyes thrilled her.

Jade was going for it. Life was about risks, and when it came to Kaeden she was willing to take the risk. She was listening to her soul.

Books by Niobia Bryant

Romance

Admission of Love * +

Three Times a Lady #

Heavenly Match * +

Can't Get Next to You < >

Let's Do It Again

Count on This < >

Heated + §

Hot Like Fire + §

Make You Mine #

Give Me Fever + §

Mainstream/Women's Fiction (Trade)

Live and Learn ~

Show and Tell ~

Message from a Mistress

Mainstream/Urban Fiction (as Meesha Mink)

Desperate Hoodwives

Shameless Hoodwives

The Hood Life

Anthologies

You Never Know/*Could it Be?* (novella)

"Caramel Flava"/*Den of Pleasure* (short story)

KEY
* # Connected Books
+ Books set in Holtsville, SC (Hot Holtsville series)
< > Connected Books (The Dutton Sisters series)
§ Connected Books (The Strong Family series)
~ Connected Books

GIVE ME FEVER

NIOBIA BRYANT

Kensington Publishing Corp.

http://www.kensingtonbooks.com

DAFINA BOOKS are published by

Kensington Publishing Corp.
119 West 40th Street
New York, NY 10018

All Kensington Titles, Imprints, and Distributed Lines are available at special quantity discounts for bulk purchases for sales promotions, premiums, fund-raising, and educational or institutional use. Special book excerpts or customized printings can also be created to fit specific needs. For details, write or phone the office of the Kensington special sales manager: Kensington Publishing Corp., 119 West 40th Street, New York, NY 10018, attn: Special Sales Department, Phone: 1-800-221-2647.

Dafina and the Dafina logo Reg. U.S. Pat. & TM Off.

ISBN-13: 978-0-7582-3142-0
ISBN-10: 0-7582-3142-3

First mass market printing: May 2010

10 9 8 7 6 5 4 3 2 1

Printed in the United States of America

*This is my tenth full-length romance novel
so this one is for all my readers—
especially the ones who have been with me since
Choe and Devon fell in love in* Admission of Love.

I thank y'all so much.

Prologue

"After you."

Kaeden Strong held open the front door to Donnie's Diner. His secretary and the sole employee of Strong Accountings, Felecia Craven, smiled briefly at him before she stepped through the door ahead of him. He paused briefly in the doorway to quickly remove his rimless glasses and wipe away a smudge. As soon as he placed them back on his angular face, Kaeden spotted a bright yellow Jeep Wrangler park across the street.

"Mr. Strong, thanks for taking me to dinner . . ."

The rest of Felecia's words and the light touch of her hand to his arm barely registered as every muscle in his body froze when the driver's door opened and Jade Prince stepped down onto the street. The short-haired, dark-skinned beauty had a very thick, curvaceous figure that could stop traffic.

She definitely made Kaeden pause. *Mercy, mercy, mercy,* he thought as he took her in as she strutted across the street in a pair of jeans shorts, a white tank, and gold high-heeled sandals. Her deep and dark skin gleamed like the sweetest and most decadent chocolate. Her short and curly hairstyle brought out her high cheekbones and deep-set eyes.

Jade was the epitome of a brick house. The old Commodores hit came floating into his head as each step showed the muscles of her thigh tense.

"The lady's stacked and that's a fact, ain't holding nothing back."

He swallowed over a lump in his throat.

His heart hammered.

His hands filled with sweat.

As she pressed one foot to the curb in front of Donnie's, the fruity and sweet scent of her perfume floated to him. The same scent had taunted and tantalized him many a Sunday during church services.

Jade smiled briefly at Felecia and then him before she came to a stop in front of him.

Kaeden fought the urge to reach for his dreaded inhaler.

"Um . . . excuse me," she said politely in a husky voice that made him wonder if she could sing.

"Oh. I'm sorry. Sorry." Kaeden stumbled over himself as he quickly pressed his body back against the door to allow her entrance.

"That's okay," she said kindly, briefly touching his arm as she breezed past him into the restaurant.

Dammit.

This woman really did it for him in *every* way possible . . . and she had absolutely no idea.

Chapter 1

Kaeden Strong refused to spend another evening alone.

Okay, he wasn't talking about female companionship, although that would be nice. Doubtful . . . but nice.

Stretching his arms high above his head, he sat back in the leather executive chair. The office of Strong Accountings had closed hours ago, and Felecia was gone for the night. The facts and figures of his clients were beginning to swim before his eyes and did nothing in the way of offering him company.

Lately the loneliness of his life was really getting to him, especially with each of his brothers falling in love one by one. He knew there was no way in hell that he was next. He favored his brothers in looks, but he didn't have the strong build or even stronger confidence that drew the women to his siblings. He was no virgin and he had relationships, but he was in the midst of one helluva dry spell. The handsome but nerdy accountant with glasses and a boatload of allergies wasn't as appealing as strong and cocky farmers.

Kaeden was well aware that he was the black sheep of the Strong family. It was a role he adapted to since childhood. When he graduated from Walterboro High School, he attended Clemson, earning his bachelor of science in accounting and then his MBA. All of his brothers went straight to working on the farm full-time after school.

Adjusting his rimless eyeglasses, Kaeden rose from his seat and grabbed his tailored pin-striped suit jacket from the back of his chair. Usually he would gather up his files and work at home while he ate a TV dinner and watched television.

"Not tonight," he promised himself as he strode out of the renovated brick home he used for his offices in Walterboro. The street lights were on and darkness had long since claimed the skies.

Kaeden unlocked his shiny new BMW 750Li, tossed his suit jacket on the rear seat, and folded his slender six-foot frame onto the Nappa leather seat. If he could be as successful with women as he was with his business, he would have a significant other in his life. His last relationship had ended after only three months because she couldn't take how much he worked. Felicity thought he was not available enough and Kaeden thought she was too needy.

Kaeden came to a stop at a red light. Seconds later a yellow Jeep Wrangler cruised through the intersection.

Jade.

His heart pumped. He wondered if he would ever get used to the dark-skinned beauty. Ever since the first day she'd walked into Holtsville Baptist Church two years ago in that form-fitting pink dress, the woman had his head spinning. And not once in the last two years had he worked up the nerve to even start a conversation with her. Disappointment and rejection were not his faves. The men of Holtsville flocked around her like bees to the sweetest nectar, and he knew there was no way a woman like Jade would want to be with a man like him.

She was completely different from any woman he had ever dated. More beautiful. More sexy. More curvaceous. Less conservative. More . . . everything.

Pushing away feelings that were more akin to a boyhood crush than anything, Kaeden steered his vehicle down Highway 17 headed toward Holtsville. He wished he could put his windows down, but it was just early May and the pollen count was still high enough to send him into a full allergic fit. He'd been through enough of that as a child. It had been hell watching his brothers and his little sister playing outdoors, watching them through the windows.

As he turned his vehicle off the main highway onto a long and curving winding road paved in asphalt, Kaeden soon was able to eye his childhood home. The brick two-story structure with plenty of glass windows was enhanced by manicured lawns with topiaries, bushes, and flowers galore—all carefully selected because they were least allergenic.

Kaeden shook his head at the memory of the landscapers completing rebuilding and replanting the gardens once his parents learned they were so detrimental to him. Yes, he was the black sheep, but his family had always made sure he felt completely loved.

Parking in front of the house, Kaeden hopped out and jogged up the steps to the front door. He frowned to find it locked. His parents hardly ever locked the door, and he had long since turned in his key once he moved into his own place. He rang the doorbell and even knocked twice. They weren't home.

Grabbing his BlackBerry from his hip, he quickly dialed his dad's cell phone number.

"Kael Strong."

"Hey, I'm standing on your front porch. Where are you two?" Kaeden asked as he jogged back down the stairs to his car.

"I decided to take my beautiful wife out to dinner. Is something wrong?" Kael answered in the strong and deep voice that his sons had inherited. The voice only hinted at the strength he maintained as the head of the Strong clan.

"Just looking to catch a home-cooked meal," Kaeden lied as he climbed back into his car and started it.

"Not tonight," his dad joked.

"Ha ha ha, Pops," Kaeden drawled. "Talk to you later."

Kaeden reversed his vehicle into an arc before driving up the paved drive back to the main highway. "Even my parents have a damn life," he muttered as he steered his vehicle back up Highway 17 in the direction of Summerville. After over forty years of marriage and five kids, his parents were still affectionate, still fiery, still in love. That's what he wanted for himself.

He made a left on Raccoon Lane, slowly taking the

long and bumpy unpaved dirt road until he pulled in front of an impressive, two-level brick home. Kaeden parked next to Kade's new Yukon Denali. A night of good food cooked by his sister-in-law Garcelle and playing with his tween-aged niece Kadina was just the distraction he needed. He jogged up the stairs to the large porch, knocking twice on the door. He waited a bit and then knocked again.

The door jerked open and Kaeden frowned at the sight of his 6′5″ brother standing before him in boxers.

"What up, little brother?" Kade asked, sounding out of breath.

"For one, your boxers are on backward, playa," Kaeden teased.

Kade smiled broadly, showing almost every white tooth in his head as he shrugged. "You know how it is sometimes."

"Oh," Kaeden said in clarity.

"Kade, estoy empezando sin ti!" Garcelle hollered from inside the house.

"What did she say?" Kaeden asked in curiosity.

"I told your brother I was starting without him," Garcelle said suddenly in her still-prominent Spanish accent, appearing in the doorway wrapped in nothing but a sheet and a beguiling smile.

Kade laughed as he wrapped his arm around her and easily picked her up to press his lips against her smooth neck.

"Bye, Kaeden," Garcelle said sweetly, waving over Kade's strong, broad shoulder as her husband stepped deeper into the house and used his foot to close the door in Kaeden's face.

He fought the urge to be jealous of his brother's happiness as he jogged down their steps and climbed back into his car again. Kade had found love twice in his lifetime. First with Reema, whose unfortunate passing had sent his brother spiraling into a life filled with mourning, and then with Garcelle—a fiery and sultry woman who helped him learn to live and love again.

Kaeden started to just go home to his own town house, but the thought of another lonely night forced him to head over to his brother Kahron's. Knowing the chemistry he always witnessed between Kahron and his wife Bianca, he didn't want to run up on another scene of seduction. He grabbed his cell phone and dialed the cell of the brother that he favored so much.

"If only I could pull all the women Kahron used to," he drawled, slowing down to pull his vehicle on the side of the road out of traffic.

"Whaddup, bubba."

"Where you at?" Kaeden asked.

"We're dropping KJ off to his PaPa Hank and then I'm driving with Bianca to Knightsville for a horse about to foal."

Bianca was a veterinarian who operated her practice on her father's horse training farm. Kaeden's involvement with the various farms his family operated only went as far as handling the paperwork and paying the employees, but he knew horse foaling could take all night.

"I was gone drop by for some family QT," Kaeden began as he watched for a break in traffic to swing his vehicle back down Highway 17. "But I'll catch you guys another night."

"A'ight."

Kaeden dropped his cell phone onto the passenger seat. His sister Kaitlyn was off on one of her misadventures being twentysomething and carefree with her other spoiled friends. He knew his brother Kaleb—the ultimate bachelor—was already at his usual after-hours hangout, Charlie's, playing whist and drinking beer. Not in the mood for that, he steered toward home.

Kaeden lived on the outskirts of Holtsville near Summerville in a new subdivision of stately townhomes. He steered his vehicle down the various turns and curves and was home in less than fifteen minutes. As he parked his car in the driveway and walked across the yard, he felt the urge to make love. He shook it off. Although he was in his late twenties, sex was not the all of his desires.

"Thank God," Kaeden drawled sarcastically.

Once he was inside, he paused in the doorway, wishing his wife was in the kitchen cooking dinner and that his kids were running to jump into his arms. It was a home of great style and substance. A home that was a testament to his business success. A home that was ready to be filled with family and love.

Jade finished her five-mile jog on the treadmill, grabbing her hand towel to blot the sweat from her chest before she stepped down onto the floor. She picked up her water bottle, placing it to her lips before she tilted her head back. Once her thirst was quenched, she stepped forward to study her figure in the full-length mirror covering the entire rear wall of the gym.

She turned this way and that in the white fitted tank top she wore with lime green shorts with a white trim. She frowned a little. It wasn't that she hated her body, especially considering she had been overweight up until she discovered dieting and exercise in high school. In total irony, the chubby kid shed the fat and revealed a brick house body that drew men to her far more than she wished—and not just because she had a friend. No matter how much she exercised, her assets weren't going anywhere and neither were her proportions. Full breasts, small waist, wide hips, thick thighs.

Just like her mom—sexy divorcée Deena Rockwell-Prince, who was forty-three but looked and acted every bit of thirty . . . or younger. Being just seventeen years younger than your own mother had its ups and downs.

In the mirror, her eyes focused on the scene behind her and she rolled her eyes at four men standing together watching her like a hawk. She locked the cap on her water and turned to walk to the steam room. Unfortunately, her admirers were in her path.

"Whaddup, baby girl?"

"Damn, you fine as hell."

"Whoo-oo-hoo!"

"'Cuse me," she said politely in that husky voice of hers as she edged between equipment and a tall, buff brother in red who looked like a walking steroid commercial.

Whap!

Jade froze as her eyes widened in pure shock and disbelief. One of them had slapped her bottom as if she was walking the strip during Black Bikers Week. Jade whirled on them, and she knew from the smirk on the face of the light-skinned brother looking like the poor man's version of Boris Kodjoe that he was the culprit. She eyed him boldly as she placed her hands on her hips and placed one size nine Nike sneaker in front of the other to reach him.

"Oh, oh, Jay," one of the men warned playfully.

Jade reached out and grabbed his crotch so quick that she caught him completely by surprise. "What's the matter? Don't you feel complimented by me touching your body without permission?" she asked as she squeezed a bit. "I'm just showing my appreciation."

"Dayummmmmm!" the other men roared in unison.

"Now . . . let's both play hands off." With one last jiggle, Jade released him and turned to walk away, desperate to wash her hands.

She was glad to be out of range of the oversized juveniles. She took a quick shower and then wrapped a towel around her body to enter the steam room. "Thank God," she sighed, glad that it was empty as she pressed her body against the steam bench and inhaled deeply and slowly.

She knew time was not on her side because she had an early day tomorrow, but for now she was going to enjoy this small luxury.

Jade knew she looked like a video vixen who wanted to be pampered and treasured, but at heart she was—and would always be—a fiercely independent tomboy. She hunted. She fished. She rode horses. She rock climbed. She liked to go camping. She was *all* about the outdoors.

It seemed only natural for her to start her own business as an outdoor tour guide. Wild-n-Out Tours was her baby and the brainchild of her co-partner, fellow guide Darren Jon. It had been costly to begin the business with purchasing liability insurance, buying the equipment, office space, and used vehicles for transportation of groups, but things were finally beginning to pay off. Thankfully they were able to acquire a small business loan and get lots of help from family. For the first year they mostly operated their services on the weekend, but in the last six months they decided to expand because of the warm weather and increased business. They both were finally beginning to feel good about their decision to leave their factory jobs and join together to blend their mutual off-hours outdoor adventures into a viable business.

She smiled a little at how their business friendship had recently blossomed into them casually dating. So far everything was good. She wasn't looking for a full-blown relationship, but it was nice to have someone to chill and go to the movies or out to dinner with.

With regret, Jade took one last deep inhale and a leisurely stretch before she rose and left the steam room. She wasted no time dressing in her khaki capris and shirt before throwing her dirty exercise clothes in a bag and heading out the gym.

"Night, Jade," the receptionist called out to her.

Jade waved and smiled. She was a regular—at least twice a week—and she was sure everyone at the small gym knew her well. Outside the gym she tossed her bag into the rear of her brightly colored Jeep Wrangler that she lovingly called Sunshine.

As she easily shifted the gears of the six-speed manual transmission, the night air breezing against her body felt good and she was glad she had taken the black soft-top off. She had the Wrangler wide open in the wind because she was so ready to get home to the little cottage she rented from the twin brothers who owned Jamison Contractors. The brothers—who both were sexy as all get out and happily married—had completely renovated their grandparents' cottage and Jade had jumped at the chance to rent it when she decided it was time to move out of her parents' house.

As soon as she reached Holtsville's town limits, Jade slowed her vehicle down, not wanting to get a speeding ticket. Holtsville, South Carolina, was the epitome of small-town America, and Jade loved it. There were under a thousand people living in Holtsville compared to the over five thousand people living in nearby Walterboro. It felt like everyone knew each other or at least knew someone that knew someone else. True, sometimes the gossip of the closely knit townspeople worked her last nerve, but she loved the forest in her backyard, the charm of the small Main Street area, and the fact there was nary a traffic light in the whole town. She loved the laid-back pace. The sound of animals talking in the nighttime. The star-filled nights. The natural smell in the air after rain. Country fairs and festivals.

She'd take country living over city living in a heart-beat. She was born and raised up in Holtsville. She would enjoy the rest of her years there as well.

Jade slowed down, making the left by the lone one-pump gas station in Holtsville. Usually if she made it home in time she would stop and sit on the porch with Cyrus Dobbs, the grizzly silver-haired owner who was more false teeth than anything.

Soon she was turning onto the cement-paved drive-way of her little two-bedroom cottage. She paused and smiled at how warm, cozy, and inviting it looked. The porch light was on above the built-in swing. Her col-orful flower beds perfectly accentuated the wood of the cottage and the black of the shutters and front door.

Pulling forward some more to park in the front yard, Jade grabbed her keys and her bag. She was walking up onto the wooden stoop of the cottage when a car whizzed past and the driver tooted its horn. Jade just threw up her hand in greeting, not even bothering to look and see who it was. In the country, everybody greeted each other in passing.

As she stepped into the house, the scent of her per-fumed body spray still hung in the air. She hit the switch to turn on the living room lights and quickly walked around the room lighting the dozens of scented candles she adored.

She loved the little cottage. It was small and intimate. Just enough room for one.

Jade had just snuggled into the corner of her caramel

microsuede couch to eat the rest of the salad she made last night when there was a solid knock at her front door. Frowning, she eyed the clock above the stone fireplace. It was going on ten o'clock.

Still chewing, she rose from the chair to walk over to one of the two large windows flanking the front door. She frowned at the sight of Darren standing on her stoop. *He could've called first*, she thought, feeling intruded upon.

Jade stepped back to open the door. "Hey, what are you doing here?" she asked, leaning on the door as she looked up at the tall and dark-skinned man who had the muscled frame of a gladiator.

"Damn, I'm glad to see you too," he said with mock sarcasm in a voice that sounded deep enough to shake the rafters.

Darren stepped forward quickly and bent his tall frame to capture her lips with his own. He lifted his head just enough to lock his eyes with hers. "I couldn't go another minute without seeing you," he whispered against her lips.

Jade turned her head and coughed to keep from laughing. He meant well, but Darren had yet to learn that his soap opera lines just didn't work on her.

"What happened with the rock-climbing trip?" she asked.

Darren pushed the door. "Business emergency, so they rescheduled."

Jade nodded in understanding, holding out her hand as he took a step forward into the cottage. "Darren, I still have the trail walk in the morning, so I'm headed to bed," she told him with a kind smile.

His grin spread like warm butter on toast. "I'm just in time, then."

"To kiss me good night and then head back home? You're right on time."

Darren leaned against the door frame and stared down at her with an intensity that actually made her smile. It wasn't that she was not physically attracted to Darren—he was a handsome man with a body—but she wasn't ready to welcome him into her bed, especially not tonight.

Balancing on her toes to raise her five-foot seven-inch frame higher, she gave him a warm peck and solid pat of her hand on his chest—a solid "good night, see you tomorrow 'cause you ain't sleeping here tonight" pat.

Darren smiled but Jade saw the regret in his eyes. Fortunately he let it drop and turned with one final wave to leave. She stood in the doorway until the lights shining in her wide-set black eyes diminished as he reversed out of her yard. With one final blow of his horn he was gone.

Jade walked out onto her stoop and leaned against the wooden beam to look up at the crystal clear night sky. It looked like the best HDTV. The stars shone brightly against the inky black night, and she felt such peace and serenity.

Chapter 2

Kaeden was the last of the Strong clan to arrive at Holtsville Baptist Church. He parked as close to the church as he could and dashed inside. He paused in the doorway to the sanctuary to find it as crowded as an Easter Sunday.

The door opened and the sweet scent of the oncoming end of spring wafted in.

A hand touched his arm softly. "I guess you and I better have a little prayerfest right here to get a seat, huh?"

Kaeden's entire body stiffened as Jade leaned around him to look into the sanctuary. His mouth opened but no words came out, so he just forced a laugh that sounded nervous. His heart was pounding so fast and so hard that he felt like he just ran a marathon.

"Looks like I got lucky too," she drawled when several single men rose to their feet, waving her over. She smiled at him before she moved past him to walk into the sanctuary to take a seat.

His eyes dipped low to watch the movement of her buttocks in the fuchsia wrap dress she wore.

"Uncle Kaeden," his niece Kadina whispered loudly.

Kaeden jerked his eyes away guiltily. He looked down as his preteen niece grabbed his hand and pulled him behind her to make room for him on the pew between her and her dad, Kade.

His brother Kaleb turned around on the pew to eye him. "Did you just walk in here with Jade Prince?" he whispered in total shock.

Kaeden accepted the fan Kade passed down to him from the usher, ignoring his sibling.

Kaleb sucked his teeth. "Man, please. What I'm saying? You couldn't pull that. Hell, you couldn't handle all that."

Their burly father popped him in the back of his prematurely gray head. "Turn around," Kael warned.

As morning worship service began, Kaeden leaned back against the pew to chance a look at Jade. Her eyes were focused forward, but he was able to look at her full on. As much as he hated to admit it, his brother was right. There was no way he could pull a woman like Jade Prince. No way in the world.

"Uncle Kaeden, pay attention," Kadina admonished him as she lightly patted his hand in a mothering fashion.

Humoring his beloved niece, Kaeden Strong did as he was told.

Jade felt eyes on her.

She turned her head in time to catch one of the

Strong brothers turning his head forward. It was the nerdy one. The accountant. The same one who was standing in the vestibule when she arrived to church. She let her eyes rove over his profile.

The other Strong men were a sexy set, with their fine and defined features that were made all the more appealing by their prematurely graying hair. That salt-and-pepper mix perfectly matched their bronzed caramel complexions. Even the nerd was cute with his glasses. He just didn't have the same swagger as his siblings. Everyone in Holtsville joked that the Strongs had twins separated several years by birth. They said Kaeden looked just like Kahron, but Jade begged to differ.

Kahron was strong in build and Kaeden was very slender.

Kahron was well aware that he was sexy as shit, and Kaeden gave off the impression that he just wanted to be invisible. Well, to her anyway. Even those glasses, though stylish, were not the right size for his slender face.

Jade bit her bottom lip and tilted her head to the side. *Maybe with contacts . . .*

"You sure are looking good, Sister Jade."

Jade made a face at the smell of bad breath barely covered by Listerine. She said a silent thanks that her head was turned or she was sure that her nose hairs would've been singed. "Thank you, Mr. Lionel," she managed to say while holding her breath.

* * *

"Man, that's one fine woman," Kaleb said in pure appreciation of the thicker female form.

All decked out in their suits, Kaeden, Kahron, and Kade all turned to look in the direction their brother was definitely intently staring. Jade Prince was walking down the brick church steps.

Kaeden couldn't agree with Kaleb more.

"Do y'all see the hips on that woman?" Kaleb asked as he watched her cross the yard to her Jeep. "Lawd, I could just spread those big legs and—"

"Respect the church ground, man," Kaeden snapped in irritation, truly more annoyed at his brother speaking that way about Jade than anything else.

Kaleb looked confused. "What?"

Kahron and Kade just shook their heads, laughing at their youngest brother, who was by far the wildest.

"Oh, so y'all wouldn't tap that?" he asked in disbelief.

In a New York minute, Kaeden thought, finding himself unable to participate in their usual banter on women when Jade was the focus.

Both Kade and Kahron threw their hands up. "We're married," they said in unison.

The sound of clapping behind them made all the men swerve around. Bianca was standing there in a pale yellow pantsuit with a smile on her full lips. "Good answer, gentlemen," she said with a pointed look at her husband and her brother-in-law.

Kahron pulled her tall frame to his side and kissed her cheek. "You're all the woman for me," he told her, his voice low in his throat.

"Oh, I *know* that," Bianca said with confidence. "But even I can admit that woman is fine."

The men all laughed.

Kaeden lagged behind as they all turned to head to their vehicles. He shoved his hands into the pockets of his slacks. Through his spectacles he watched Jade's Wrangler go driving by.

The Strong family Sunday dinners were tradition. Lisha Strong used to prepare the meal alone—with minimal chopping by her daughter Kaitlyn and her granddaughter Kadina. But now that two of her sons had married, she had two daughters-in-law to help lovingly prepare their families' meal. They laughed. They joked. They shared stories. And they cooked one helluva meal every single Sunday.

Kaeden stood in the entryway to the kitchen, watching them cook and joke around. He smiled as he remembered the Sundays helping his mom while his brothers would ride horses and explore the hundreds of acres of land encompassing the Strong ranch. He probably could cook a macaroni to put any woman to shame—even if he had no clue how to rope a steer.

"Kaeden? Why are you just standing there?" Lisha called out to him.

Suddenly four pairs of eyes were on him. Kaeden shrugged as he pushed his hands into the pockets of his pants and strolled into the kitchen.

Garcelle, Bianca, his sister Kaitlyn, and his niece Kadina all smiled at him.

"Where are the rest of the Strong men?" Bianca asked as she used the side of her wrist to push her riot of curls off her forehead.

"On the porch talking horses and cattle," he drawled, hating that he wished he knew more about the family business than the financial aspects. Although his brothers were a far cry from the typical cowboy with the tight jeans, plaid shirt, and Stetson, Kaeden had always secretly dreamed of working alongside his brothers on the ranches.

"Kadina, go and tell the men dinner is ready," Lisha said, wiping her hands on a hand towel. "Ladies, please start to carry the food into the dining room."

"I'll help," Kaeden offered, unbuttoning and rolling up the sleeves of his crisp white shirt.

"No, I need you to help me, Kaeden," Lisha told him.

Kaeden nodded as he placed his hands on his hips. "What's up, Ma?" he asked.

"What's wrong with you, son?" Lisha asked with concern as she watched him closely.

Kaeden shifted his eyes from hers. One thing that made Lisha Strong a good mother was her ability to miss nothing—good or bad. He shrugged.

"One thing that makes us a family to reckon with is the fact that we are all in this together—"

"No matter what role we play," Kaeden finished for her with a smile.

"You got it." Lisha picked up a huge dish of her homemade peach cobbler. "Now let's go eat. Your father has a big announcement."

Kaeden took the cobbler from his mom's hands.

"This should be interesting," he said as he followed her into the dining room.

Kaeden sat the cobbler on an available spot in the center of the six-foot wooden table before sitting between Kaitlyn and Kaleb.

"Good food. Good meat. Good Lord. Let's eat," Kael said loudly as soon as everyone was seated.

Kaeden's mother shot him a hard stare.

He winked at her before he grabbed a serving spoon and scooped a heaping portion of macaroni on his plate.

Their father was a churchgoing man but not an overly religious man—thus there would never be sweeping blessings of the food from Kael Strong.

"I am starving," Kaeden announced as he eyed the heaping bowls of fried chicken, collard greens, candied yams, macaroni and cheese, rice, and the still hot and steaming peach cobbler.

Kaitlyn elbowed him. "So am I, Specs, so . . . am . . . I," she said, reverting to her childhood nickname for him.

"You eat like a man," Kaeden told her. "One of these days you have got to gain weight."

"*That's* an understatement," Kahron drawled from across the table.

Bianca rose from her chair to pile a plate high with food. "Only dogs like bones. Real men like meat on them bones," she said, sitting down and placing the plate in front of her husband. With a sly smile she added, "Like myself, and Garcelle, and Lord knows, Jade Prince. Right, fellas?"

Kaeden choked on the lemonade he just sipped from a frosted glass.

Kahron focused on watching Kadina feeding his two-year-old son KJ.

"Heck yeah," Kaleb answered in a heartbeat.

"Right, Kade?" Garcelle asked, her Spanish accent as prominent as the voluptuous curves of her frame. There was a twinkle in her bright eyes as she cut her eyes up at her handsome husband.

Kael chuckled as he ate, obviously enjoying his sons being ribbed by their wives.

"Jade is not all that," Kaitlyn said with attitude, pushing her jet-black dyed hair back from her face.

"Yeah, right," Kaeden muttered in disbelief.

He looked up to find all eyes on him.

"I thought Felecia was more your speed, big brother," Kaleb joked.

"Trust and believe. . . . I am ready, willing, and able to handle whatever woman I have in my life," Kaeden said firmly, completely fed up with his brother's teasing.

"All right, now," Lisha Strong said.

"Since Jade is the center of our Sunday conversation, this is as good a time as any to tell everyone about my surprise," Kael said.

Kaeden focused his attention on his father, just as curious as everyone appeared to be about the news . . . and very happy that Jade was no longer the focus.

"Next weekend my sons and I are going camping," Kael announced.

"We are?" they all asked in unison.

"Y'all are?" the ladies asked as well.

Kaeden was completely disappointed because that surprise had absolutely nothing to do with him. He returned his attention back to his food.

"Don't worry, Uncle Kaeden, I'll come stay with you that weekend," Kadina offered.

"Oh no, Kaeden, you're going too," Kael said around a mouthful of food.

Kaeden looked up and his eyes fell directly on his mother, who gave a conspiratorial wink. He knew that his mom had a hand in his addition to the camping trip. The thing was, he wasn't quite sure if that was truly a good or a bad thing.

Jade stretched her arms high above her head as she walked out onto the wraparound porch of her grandfather's house. He was sitting on the top step with his elbows on his knees as he looked up at the sky. His naturally wavy jet-black hair was pulled back tightly into a bushy ponytail. Jade smiled softly as she fondly remembered the many hours she'd spent, as a little girl, on this very porch standing behind him brushing his hair as he sat on that same top step.

"Hey, old man," Jade teased as she walked across the green painted porch to sit down beside him.

Esai Rockwell knocked his bony shoulder against hers in greeting. "Peanut?" he asked, motioning toward the cup of boiled peanuts sitting on the step between them.

"No thanks, Pappy," Jade said with a shake of her head. "I'm still full of the rabbit stew you cooked."

"Your favorite," he said.

"Yup," Jade agreed, leaning over to rest her head on

his bony and broad shoulder in the white long-sleeved T-shirt he wore.

Pappy was a man of very few words. Always had been.

Jade couldn't imagine anyone she adored more than him. Her father had recently remarried a twenty-year-old, and her mother was a flight attendant who was hardly ever in town. Since she was three years old, spending the weekends at her grandfather's had been her greatest joy. Although her parents waited until she was eighteen to divorce, the signs of failed marriage had been there long before.

"Heard from your mama?" he asked about his ex-daughter-in-law.

The thought of her mother immediately brought a smile to Jade's face. "She's in Los Angeles and then she flies to London."

"Ms. Jetsetter," he mused, tilting his head back to toss a peanut into his open mouth.

Jade nodded. She missed her mom but completely understood that after the shock of her father leaving her for a younger woman and divorcing her, Deena was finally enjoying her new freedom and her new job. Her mom married early, had her only child early, and divorced early, but she was trying to catch up on a late start of her independence.

"How's the business?" he asked.

"It's going okay. Mostly because of a lot of local support. Like Darren's taking Mr. Strong and his sons on a camping trip this weekend."

Esai looked surprised. "Those farmers need a guide to go camping?"

"That's what I thought, but we're not looking a gift horse in the mouth."

As Jade did give in to dig a handful of the moist and salty boiled peanuts into her hand, she suddenly thought of the nerdy one and how she'd caught him staring at her in church.

It was a very odd and random thought.

Chapter 3

Kaeden shifted his bespectacled eyes away from the flat-screen computer monitor as his secretary Felecia walked into his office after knocking briefly. "Yes?" he asked, his mind really focused on finishing up the weekly payroll for one of his clients who owned a car dealership.

"I made chicken and dumplings for supper last night. Well, it's just me, so I had plenty left over and I thought we could have it for lunch . . . together," she said.

Kaeden actually wasn't ready to take a lunch break when he was so close to being done, but Felecia was already beginning to unpack a picnic basket he'd just noticed she was carrying. His stomach grumbled as she set a steaming bowl in front of him. He had to admit that Felecia was one helluva cook, so he knew the dish was good.

"Chicken and dumplings on a Tuesday night?" he asked, smiling as he gave in to the call of hunger and cleared the few files piled on his desk.

Felecia waved her hand dismissively. "Took me no time at all. The dumplings are from scratch too."

"It smells good, Felecia," he told her as she set utensils and napkins in front of him.

"I know," she answered with confidence before walking out of the office to return moments later with two glasses filled with ice.

Moments later one of the glasses was in front of him filled with cold sweet tea from a thermos in her basket of goodies.

"Enjoy," she said, rather low and husky in her throat.

Kaeden looked up at her before clearing his throat and looking away. He and Felecia briefly dated for a couple of months a few years ago, but Kaeden ended it because there hadn't been a bit of spark between them. A wet match could generate more of a flicker of flame. She was a beautiful and stylish woman with her caramel complexion and reddish brown hair. She was a sweet churchgoing preacher's daughter who could cook like an old woman. A true lady. A good girl.

They just didn't click to him, and so he moved on.

Several months ago when she walked into his office wanting to apply for the position of his secretary, she promised him she was there for a much-needed paycheck and that was it. Lately, though, he just wasn't sure. He would have to be a blind fool to miss the fact that Felecia Craven wanted more from him than a paycheck.

He focused his attention on enjoying the food as she eased her tall and slender frame into one of the chairs in front of his large cherrywood desk.

"Your family ready to go camping tomorrow?" she asked as she took a sip of tea from her glass.

Kaeden nodded as he chewed. "Thank God I was able to talk them out of pressing me to go. Can you imagine me in the woods for four whole days?"

Felecia laughed. "Yeah, right? *You* camping. Puh-leeze."

Kaeden paused and frowned.

"It's good, right?" she asked, changing the subject.

Kaeden nodded. "You can burn. Reminds me of my mama's cooking."

Felecia smiled sweetly. "Now, you're not saying I remind you of your mama?" she asked in her lilting Southern accent as she licked the gravy from the fork and crossed her legs slowly.

Kaeden's eyes dropped down automatically to take in the move, but instead of enticing him, it made him feel awkward. "Listen, Felecia, it feels like you're flirting with the whole fork lick and . . . Sharon Stone leg cross and . . . everything. We both know that's inappropriate," he said in a firm voice that he hoped sounded like an employer talking to an employee.

Felecia tossed her head back and laughed as she waved her hand at him dismissively. "Kaeden, please stop being paranoid. If I wanted to date you again, I would just ask you out. I don't play games."

Her attitude was so blasé that Kaeden actually felt bad about accusing her. "Felecia, I'm sorry—"

The bell over the front door jingled. Felecia daintily wiped the corners of her mouth with a napkin before easing up out of her seat. "Duty calls, boss."

He watched her cross the carpeted floor and maybe

it was just him, but was there an extra jiggle and shake of her hips and shoulders as she walked. He didn't doubt that she could arouse him and that he could finish the deal, but he would just be using her as a method of release and Kaeden didn't do booty calls or one-night stands.

"You'll have to make an appointment, Jade, Mr. Strong is at lunch—"

Kaeden nearly choked on the sweet tea he was swallowing. Jade was here! He quickly used napkins to swipe away the splats of tea on the top of his desk before he tossed the napkins and the paper plate of unfinished food into the trash. "Felecia, please show her in," he called out, already wondering what Jade wanted with him.

"No," she stressed in a loud voice. "You're at lunch and Miss Prince is making an appointment to come back at a more convenient time."

Kaeden rose and came around his desk to walk across the room that once served as one of the three bedrooms of the converted town house. He stepped across the hall into the living room that was converted into the outer office.

Jade was dressed in a white strapless maxi dress with aviator shades in place on her face. She brightened up the entire room. "Hello, I'm Kaeden Strong," he said, even as his heart raced in his chest.

Jade pushed her shades up onto the top of her head as she turned to face him. She extended her hand to him. "I'm Jade Prince—"

Felecia quickly stepped between them, causing Jade's hand to dart into her stomach.

Kaeden's angular jaw clenched as he placed his hands on Felecia's shoulders. "Thanks, Felecia, I have it," he told her. His hands instantly dropped when he felt a shiver go through her body before she moved to take her seat at her desk.

Jade eyed them both oddly before she extended her hand to him again. "I wanted to speak to you about handling the books for my partner's and my business, Wild-n-Out Tours."

Kaeden grasped Jade's still-outstretched hand warmly as the scent of her fruity perfume surrounded him. Her grasp was soft and strong all at once. "I've heard of it. In fact, my father and brothers are going camping with Darren in the morning," he told her.

"Actually Darren—my business partner—can't make it, so I'm leading the tour," she said as the silver cell phone in her hand vibrated and she looked down at it. "I have to take this. Excuse me."

She walked a few feet away and Kaeden's gut clenched like a bowling ball had connected. Jade was leading the camping trip.

"A woman going camping. What, is she gay? Well excuse me, K.D. Degeneres," Felecia drawled under her breath sarcastically.

Kaeden ignored her as Jade closed her phone and walked back to him. The way that cotton was clinging to her thighs was truly distracting, and Kaeden had to force his eyes to stay locked on her face.

"I actually have to go, something came up, but either myself or Darren will call and make an appointment to meet with you," she said, a smile on her full lips.

Kaeden nodded. "Sounds like a plan," he said.

Jade gave Felecia a smile and turned to leave.

"I guess I'll see you in the morning," he called out behind her.

Jade paused in the doorway.

Felecia jumped up to her feet.

"You're going?" they both asked.

Am I crazy, he thought. "Oh yes, I wouldn't miss it for anything," Kaeden said, sounding far more confident than he felt.

Jade sighed as she sank lower beneath the steamy and sudsy depths of the cast iron claw-foot tub. The lights were off and the scented candles of various shapes and sizes were lit. The soft sounds of her favorite mix of R&B played softly. A frosted goblet of white sangria sat on a small stool by the tub waiting to be sipped, right alongside her cordless phone, which was ready to be ignored. It was the complete scene for relaxation for one.

This was Jade's routine the night before she did a tour and the night after she returned from the tour. It was great for relaxing her physically and mentally.

She slid one leg down the length of the other, enjoying the silky feel of the almond-scented oil she added to the water. The movement caused the lips of her core to connect and she felt a delicious thrill of awareness shimmy over her body.

"At least I know my punany still works," she mumbled to herself as she draped one of her legs over the side of the tub.

Jade hadn't indulged in the opposite sex in at least a year and although she enjoyed going out on dates with Darren, she hadn't discovered the little "do me" urge with him yet. She was far from a prude and she would have never guessed she would slip into the role of the born-again virgin.

It was sad to admit that her mama was getting more than she was. Jade smirked as she reached over to pick up her goblet of white sangria with slices of green apples, oranges, pears, and peaches. Just one glass to help relax her.

Jade tilted her head back and used her tongue to wrangle a peach slice into her mouth. "Hmmmm," she moaned in pure satisfaction.

Her cordless phone rang, completely breaking her peace and serenity. Opening just one eye, she looked at it sitting up straight on top of the stool. Darren's cell phone number displayed on the screen. "Not to-*night*," she sang, before she closed her eyes and sunk lower into the water.

Darren flipped his cell phone as he sat in his pickup with his green eyes locked on the soft glow of light from the small window on the side of Jade's small cottage.

She was in the bath. He knew it.

Darren smiled as he reversed his truck out of the yard from behind her parked Wrangler. Ever since he first laid eyes on Jade Prince walking into the factory where he worked, he had been determined to get to know her and to claim her.

They went from coworkers to friends to business partners over the years. As far as they had progressed in the last three years was "dating."

With one last look back at her house, Darren made his way home well aware that patience was a virtue.

The entire Strong clan was spending the night at the ranch since the men had to be up by three in the morning for Jade to pick them up. Kaeden had to admit he was enjoying everyone being under one roof, especially since there was no chance of getting a spanking for the things they did. The entire clan was lounging over drinks on the porch, but Kaeden had sought the company of his niece and nephew.

Kaeden smiled broadly as his nephew giggled in glee when he tossed him up into the air and caught him.

"Did you used to toss me up like that when I was a baby, Uncle Kaeden?" Kadina asked loudly, the earphones from her iPod snugly in place as she lay on the floor also watching television.

Kaeden straddled chubby KJ on his knees before he reached down and flicked one of the earphones from her ear. "No, because you would cry, but you did like when I would bite your neck."

"Bite my neck!" she squealed before she giggled.

KJ laughed as well before he clapped his hands and leaned forward to press his forehead against Kaeden's mouth—his signal that he wanted to be kissed there. Kaeden immediately obliged.

"Thank you, Un-cle Kae-den."

Kaeden loved his niece and nephew. In fact, he was usually the one to spoil them (a la Kadina's iPod). Any time he could spend with them was time well spent as far as he was concerned—especially since Kadina was growing up so quickly before their eyes. Gone was the cute little kid with the curly afro puffs to suddenly be replaced by a blossoming preteen with bangs and a long ponytail who liked boys more than dolls.

Kadina sat up and removed her other earphone. "Uncle Kaeden, are . . . you . . . sure you should go camping?" she asked, her face clouded with doubt.

He his back a smile as he let a squirming KJ climb down off his lap to the polished hardwood floors. "I'm sure. Why?"

"Because if you're bitten by the wrong thing you'll swell up like a tick about to pop," Kadina told him, her tone completely dry as she gave him a "you know I'm right" look.

He definitely been there and done that before. There was the bee sting of 1986, the ant bite of 1992, and the wasp incident in 2001. Kaeden shook his head at the memories. "I'll be careful," he promised her.

Kadina fell silent with her bright eyes locked on him closely, even as KJ waddled over to her and then unceremoniously plopped down onto her lap. "Jade Prince sure is pretty," Kadina said slyly.

Kaeden tensed and then forced himself to relax. "Yeah . . . I guess. She a'ight."

"Pee-pee, Dina. Pee," KJ said, jumping up to his sneakered feet.

"Kadina, you better get him to the bathroom," Kaeden warned.

She sat her iPod on the leather ottoman in front of the big-screen television as she hopped to her feet. She grabbed KJ's hand. "No chance you like Miss Jade, is it, Uncle Kaeden?" she asked with a twinkle in her eyes.

"Un-cle Kae-den and Jade," KJ said, even as he pinched at his zipper and squirmed.

Kaeden leaned back in the chair to look up at his far too wise—and nosy—niece. "Curiosity killed the cat, little girl," he told her.

Kadina swung her little cousin up onto her hip. "Don't worry, Unc, your secret is safe with me," she promised with an impish smile before she rushed KJ to the bathroom.

Felecia bit the gloss from her bottom lip as she hung up her phone and dramatically flung it to the foot of her four-poster bed. Kaeden wasn't home and his cell phone was going straight to voice mail. "Good heaven," she said aloud to herself, knowing her scheme to trick Kaeden into skipping the camping trip had just scored a big fail since she couldn't reach him.

"What woman in their right mind would send their man in the woods with Jade Prince?" Felecia wrung her hands anxiously. They would be gone from early Thursday and not returning until late Sunday night. There was no way on God's green earth that she wanted *her* Kaeden to go, that's for sure, but what could she do about it now?

When Kaeden had ended their relationship before it

even really began, Felecia had been disappointed, but she never harbored any ill will for the man because of his honesty. In fact, it made her like and appreciate him more. When she was flipping through the newspaper and happened upon his ad in *The Post & Courier* for a secretary, she took it as a sign from the Lord that Kaeden was the man for her after all. She wasn't looking for a job; she was paid a nice salary serving as the secretary for her father's church in Charleston.

Felecia hopped up from the bed to her feet. She was a woman on a definite mission. Her life's plan had been mapped out since she was in high school. Stay out of trouble. Get good grades. Graduate from a good college.

So far so good.

The only two things left were to get married and then have some babies.

Felecia released a heavy breath and slowly walked to her closet. She focused her eyes on the ebony chest sitting pushed back against the wall. She stooped down to slowly open it. Inside lay stacks of bridal magazines, fabric swatches, sample invitations, and party favors. Every detail of her wedding was planned to the littlest detail—even her dream rings. The entire bridal works.

The only thing the future bride needed was a willing groom.

"*Mrs*. Felecia Strong," Felecia said aloud, *completely* loving the sound of it.

Chapter 4

The sky was still inky black in the wee hours of the morning as Jade drove one of the Wild-n-Out passenger vans up to the front of the Strong ranch. She was pleased to see her group was up, ready and on the front porch awaiting her arrival. That was definitely a good sign.

"Thank God," she said, parking the black van next to a row of ATVs.

The last camping expedition she'd led started off rocky when several of the group members arrived two hours late. Those same people turned out to be loafers who made the entire experience hella bad for Jade and the other group members who truly wanted to glean something from the trip. They mistook her role in the trip as a servant. Bad mistake.

She was hoping these twenty-first-century chocolate cowboys would be less stressful than the businessmen from Columbia trying to be outdoorsmen. She was happy for the business, but sometimes people just had to know when to stay in their lane. Switching up could be hazardous.

"Humph." Jade had never been so happy to see the last of people.

A full week of whining men who were afraid to get dirty had worked her last nerve, but she took it in stride with a smile.

She forced herself not to draw the comparison between those men and Kaeden Strong. His father and brothers all owned and operated farms. The man had to know something about the outdoors.

Jade hopped out of the driver's seat of the van. "Mornin', everyone," she called over to the men and women on the porch as she walked to the rear of the van to open the doors for them to store their bags. Hopefully if they stuck to the checklist she gave them, everything should fit. The last thing she needed was unnecessary cargo to deal with.

The camping gear she supplied as part of the package was already secured to the rack on the top of the van. She had a full tank of gas. She'd already spoken to Darren, who was on his way to lead a hunting trip in Spartanburg. She had their waivers all signed. Every person was registered with the state park and alerted to their presence on their grounds—an extra level of security for a woman who at times led men on outdoor excursions. Jade was ready to rock and roll.

She shoved her hands into the back pockets of her snug denims as she smiled warmly at the loving embraces the men gave their wives, who were still dressed in their nightgowns and robes. Kaeden and Kaleb made their way over to her carrying their backpacks and sleeping bags.

"Ready to answer the call of the wild, fellas?" she asked them.

Kaleb whistled as he eyed her. "Yes, by God, I am," he said with clear intent.

Jade fought not to roll her eyes. "Alrighty then, keep it moving, Casanova," she told him with a smile and a firm slap of her hand against his shoulder.

"You know, in other . . . situations, you wouldn't have to prompt me to move. Oh, I get the job done and well."

Jade let her eyes roll, not even bothering to fight it. She turned to the one with the glasses. "Kaeden, right?"

"That's me," he said with a smile.

Jade was completely taken back by the dimples in his cheeks and the brightness of his straight teeth. *He has a nice smile*, she thought, shifting her eyes up to peer through those dorky glasses of his. The only thing she saw was twin reflections of the moon.

"Maybe we can set up that appointment now without all the drama," she teased as he stepped forward in his jeans and long-sleeved black T-shirt to set his bags in the van.

Kaeden pushed his glasses up as he smiled down at her. "I'm sorry about that."

Jade reached out and touched his hand lightly and quickly. "Oh, no, no, it's okay. Your wife was just marking her territory."

"She's not my wife or my girl," Kaeden said so quickly that his words ran together.

"Really? You two look cute together." Jade turned her attention to the other Strong men walking up to the van.

"Are we crazy?" Bianca asked as she stood alongside her mother-in-law and sister-in-law on the porch in their nightgowns and robes.

The three women all eyed Jade as she chatted with their husbands. Someone would have to be blind to not see how beautiful and sexy the woman was—even in jeans, boots, and a long-sleeved fitted tee. On top of it everyone in Holtsville knew she really was a nice and friendly person who was always quick to smile.

"Ella hace que la mayoría de las mujeres parecen hombres," Garcelle said.

Lisha and Bianca both whipped their heads around to look at her with confusion clearly shown on their faces. "Huh?" they both asked.

"I *said* she makes most women look like men," Garcelle said.

"Ladies, listen, I am not married to nor did I raise whoremongers," Lisha told them. "We have good men and we're in trusting marriages. Right?"

"Right," Bianca said.

"Sí," Garcelle joined in.

The men waved before climbing into the van through the sliding side door. Jade closed that door behind them and then walked around the van to slam the rear door closed.

"Don't worry, ladies, they're in good hands," Jade called over to them. "Bye."

All three ladies fixed stiff smiles to their pretty faces as they waved back at her. "Bye," they said in a singsong fashion that was as fake as their smiles.

Two hours later the sun had finally begin to rise, turning the sky from inky black to a deep shade of lavender with streaks of gold. It truly was a beautiful sight, but Kaeden was too busy fuming from his seat at the rear of the van to notice any of it.

Kaeden truly felt like he could strangle his brother Kaleb. Not enough to kill him, but just enough so that it hurt his little brother to talk.

Kaeden frowned deeply as he pierced the back of his brother's prematurely gray-haired head with his eyes. He was up front in the passenger seat sitting next to Jade.

Kaeden was hoping to use the trip as his chance to get to know Jade better and to look for cues that Jade would want to know him better. *If Kaleb would shut his big mouth.*

He gritted his teeth as Jade laughed at something Kaleb said. He opened his Jordan Banks mystery book but he found it hard to focus on the words. Jade's earlier words to him echoed as if she had yelled them into the Grand Canyon.

"You two look cute together."

He hoped Jade wouldn't relay that sentiment to Felecia.

"All right, gents, we're here," Jade said as she pulled the van into a parking spot inside the state park. "If you could load up your backpacks while I finish our registration, we're going to hike from here to one of the trailside campsites along the Edisto River."

As Kaeden followed his family out of the van, he again wondered if he was crazy to agree to go hiking and camping. The idea of him participating in such activities was not logical, and he usually operated on the side of logic and common sense.

"Ready, son?" Kael asked as he slapped Kaeden soundly on his shoulder.

Kaeden took the backpack his father handed to him and caught sight of Jade striding out of the ranger station toward them. The woman took his breath away. "Ready as I'll ever be," he said, determined to make the very best of this trip as he patted his pocket to make sure he had the case holding an emergency shot of epinephrine.

"She sure is a pretty gal, ain't she?" Kael asked.

Kaeden felt his father's eyes on him and he shifted his eyes off Jade. "That's pretty obvious."

Kael shifted the straps of his bulky backpack to a more comfortable position on his broad shoulders. "Sometimes opposites do attract, son," he advised his son with a wink.

Kaeden said nothing. Was his attraction to Jade that obvious? First his niece and now his father?

Once they divided all their supplies, the men followed Jade onto the trail. Each step seemed to take them deeper and deeper into the forest until they were surrounded by varying shades of brown and green. Squirrels skittering past, the leaves rustling as birds swooped in and out amongst the trees, and the sounds of the river running all blended together into a wilderness symphony.

Kaeden wished he could enjoy it. He sneezed loudly, nearly causing his glasses to fly off his face.

"Bless you," Kahron said.

"You all right back there, little bubba?" Kade called back to him.

He pushed his glasses back up on his face and swatted at something crawling against his cheek. "Just fine," he called back, completely lying as he felt the back of his throat itching and his eyes watering behind his spectacles.

They walked single file along the trail, and Kaeden brought up the rear. Keeping up wasn't his problem. He actually was in pretty good shape. He didn't want to let on to Jade that the outdoors definitely wasn't his shtick. He'd rather be back at his town house under the cool comfort of his central air watching sports or playing Literati online.

"All right, fellas, welcome home," Jade declared as they came to a sand-packed clearing among the trees.

"Wow," was all that Kaeden could say.

The riverside campsite was even more primitive than he imagined—and he had imagined the worst.

There was a large stone fire ring in the center of the cleared area, and twenty feet away was a lone building he figured was an outhouse. The sound of the running stream was very calming, but Kaeden figured water drew insects.

Jade removed her backpack. "We can set up camp here. Just situate your tents a few feet back from the fire ring. The smoke will help keep away the bugs."

As Jade ran down the rules and regulations for camping at a state park, Kaeden dug his can of insect repellent out of the side pocket of his backpack. He made sure to spray his exposed hands and neck.

"One of you want to help me gather firewood?" Jade asked as she pulled a small case out of her sack. She opened it to reveal a small but sharp hatchet.

"Jade, Kaleb and I will go chop firewood," Kahron said, using his sleeve to wipe the sweat from his angular face before he slid his aviator shades back into place.

"Yeah, don't be silly. Let the men handle this." Kaleb reached for the hatchet.

Jade raised a brow and moved it out of his reach. "Oh. Okay. So I'm supposed to say 'thank you, kind sirs' and let the men go off to do the manly work while I stay behind and . . . and . . . what? Cook up the vittles?"

Kaeden paused in removing his pop-up tent from its case. He eyed Jade and smiled at the defiance clearly shown in her eyes. The woman had spunk.

"Now, that look reminds me of my wife," Kade said with a dimpled grin as he ran his fingers through his large silver curls.

Kael laughed. "Mine too."

"Hell, mine too," Kahron added.

"Look, gentlemen, you paid me to do my job. Let's put aside the old Southern gender-role crap and *let me* do my job." Jade eyed each of them sternly and then gave them a brilliant smile.

For Kaeden, that smile made the dark and damp woods seem like a tropical paradise.

* * *

Campsites were always so cozy and inviting to Jade. Once they set up camp she had led them farther up the Edisto River to a spot she knew from past experience was great for fishing. After hiking and fishing all day, it felt good to return to the campsite and light the fire.

Jade honestly didn't think anything was more picturesque than the glow of fire amongst the dense trees, particularly with the moon glinting off the running stream.

Since there was only one fire ring, Jade had staked her own tent not far from the men. A part of her guide duties was cooking the meal—unless her clients wished to fix it themselves. Kahron cleaned the fish and Kade agreed to fry them along with baked beans on the side.

Jade dropped down into her little pink camp chair outside her hot pink tent. The fire was crackling and the smell of the fish frying in the pan was divine. Her stomach grumbled loudly, but she wasn't at all ashamed. They had all worked up an appetite.

Well, almost everyone, Jade thought, cutting her eyes across the stretch of packed sand to Kaeden's tent. She could tell from the light on inside the tent that he was scratching like crazy. She shook her head and tried not to laugh at the sight he made.

Jade was normally a good-natured, fun-loving person and there weren't too many people who truly annoyed her . . . but Kaeden Strong had been irking the hell out of her nerves *all* day.

He was a grown-ass man—a good old-fashioned Southern man—who stunk at fishing. He didn't know how to bait a hook and his line always got tangled in his reel when he threw it.

Between that and the clear signs of his dang on allergies, he reminded her way too much of those businessmen from Columbia. The man had no more right to be on a camping trip than a newborn baby. He was an intelligent man with a reputation for taking care of business skillfully, but when it came to the outdoors, Kaeden Strong needed to stay indoors.

Jade closed her eyes and listened to the sounds of the men joking as they moved around the camp. It was the sound of family . . . and it sounded good.

"You look awful lonesome over here."

Jade leaned sideways and opened one eye to find Kaleb standing over her. With his muscular build, he nearly blocked out all of the illumination from the moon. "Looks can be so deceiving," she told him, closing her eyes and returning to the darkness.

When moments passed and he still hadn't budged, she frowned. "Kaleb, please, are you still standing over me?"

"Enjoying the view."

Jade released a heavy sigh that was filled with annoyance. Not the "he's cute and I'm only playing like he is working my last nerve" type of annoyance. True "please get out my face and leave me alone" annoyance. Men like Kaleb were all caught up in the physical and couldn't care less if she knew how to count to five.

"Kaleb, you're my partner in whist!" Kael hollered over to him from his spot at the picnic table.

Jade didn't bother opening her eyes as she held her hand up and wiggled her fingers good-bye.

He just chuckled before she heard him walk away.

Jade was glad because she really didn't want to have to hurt Kaleb's feelings. It was the gospel truth that he was not at all her type. He had a handsome face, but his overly muscular build *was* not at all her type. In fact, the taller and leaner frame of his brothers was more to her liking.

Jade opened her eyes and looked over at Kaeden's tent. *The poor thing is still at it*, she thought.

She rose to her feet and grabbed her backpack from the ground by the entrance of her tent. She pulled out a small sealed Ziploc before she made her way over to Kaeden's tent.

"Kaeden, can I come in?" she asked, stooping down by the zipped-up entrance.

The laughter and joviality at the picnic table immediately ceased and Jade looked over her shoulder to find all the men gazing over at her in open curiosity. "Get your minds out the gutter, gentlemen," she told them, holding up the baggie to show them.

As if, she thought, as Kaeden unzipped the tent. Just as the flap opened she saw him slide his glasses back into place on his face. She felt a moment of disappointment. She would love to see what he looked like without them. *Simply for curiosity's sake, of course.*

"Listen, here's a paste my grandfather swears by for insect bites," she told him, noticing the open Jordan Banks book and an inhaler atop his sleeping bag.

"Thanks, I must have sugar in my blood," he mused with a smile as he took the outstretched baggie from her hand.

"Wow, look at your arms," she said, reaching out to touch the many swollen and red bumps. "Put the paste on and let it sit for at least ten minutes. I promise the itching will stop. It works."

Kaeden opened the Ziploc and used his finger to start smoothing the paste onto the bites. "Thanks a lot," he told her.

"No problem." Jade rose to her feet and walked back over to her camp chair.

Kael walked over to the fire to check the pot. "Food's ready," he said, spooning beans onto paper plates and topping them with crispy golden pieces of fried bass.

Kaeden exited his tent and Jade tried not to chuckle at the sight of the white patches of paste drying on his arms. She dropped down into her chair with a yawn and a leisurely stretch.

"Here you go, Jade," Kael said, handing her the plate.

Jade smiled at the older gentleman who reminded her of her grandfather. "Thank you, but I'm too beat to eat," she told him.

"You go ahead and turn in, we're just going to eat this fish and play cards."

"That sounds good to me, but don't be up too late. We're leaving early," she told him as she rose from her chair and knelt down to crawl into her tent. "Night, fellas."

The men all wished her a good night as Jade zipped

her tent up snugly. She turned on a small lantern and settled onto her side on the puffy sleeping bag. She smiled as she pulled her own copy of the Jordan Banks book from her backpack. She *loved* Jordan Banks's mystery novels. She owned them all and always pre-ordered the newest releases.

She read until her eyes began to feel heavy. In the dreamy seconds before she fell into a deep sleep, Jade was quite surprised that an image of Kaeden Strong in his tent reading the same book came to her.

Of all the things for her and Kaeden to have in common.

Chapter 5

"Kaeden . . . Kaeden. Wake up."

He lifted his head up from the sleeping bag as Jade crawled on all fours into his tent. His breath caught in his throat at the sight of her gloriously curvy figure in a pale peach sheer teddy that did absolutely nothing to shield her nakedness from his eyes. The full chocolate globes. The hard thrusting nipples. Her wide hips. Thick thighs.

Jade was the very epitome of woman.

His heart hammered as he leant up on his elbows. His dick hardened in a rush and tented the top of his sleeping bag with ease. He had to lean to the side to get an unobstructed view of Jade.

She licked her glossy lips as she rose up to straddle his legs. "Hungry?" she asked in a soft and raspy voice.

At the sight of the soft chocolate swells of her breasts above the rim of the teddy, coupled with *hard thrusting nipples and the plumpness of her clean-shaven mound pressing against the sheer material, Kaeden steamed up so much his glasses fogged over.*

Jade laughed seductively as Kaeden snatched them from his face and flung them from him. She brought her hands up to massage her own breasts as she writhed her hips like a snake.

"Got milk?" Kaeden joked as he folded his hands behind his head and lay back to enjoy the show.

Jade fisted the end of the sleeping bag to tear it away from his nude, chiseled physique before she wrapped her hands around the full, curving length of his steely erection. "Do you?" she asked cockily, with a lick of her lips.

Kaeden clenched his buttocks and arched his back from the floor of the tent as she stroked the length of him with swift but fluid motions. "Mooooooo," he said playfully, mimicking a cow as she milked him.

He reached for her. His hands stroked her breasts and teased her nipples before easing down to grasp her hips and massage her thighs. "You feel just like I knew you would," he told her in a ragged voice. Her skin was as soft as satin. Her breasts were soft and fleshy. Her thighs were firm.

"Jade," he said into the heat of the tent. His voice was filled with reverence and passion.

She stretched her body down along the length

*of his with his hard heat still within her tight,
stroking grasp.*

*Kaeden shivered as she pressed her body
against his. "Damn, your body feels good."*

*She nodded with her face pressed against his.
"Um-hmmm, inside and out," she whispered
against his ear with a hot lick of his earlobe.*

*"Whoooo!" Kaeden hollered up to the
rounded top of the tent like a wolf . . .*

"Kaeden . . . you okay in there, son?"

Kaeden gasped as his eyes popped open, completely
startled from his delicious dream. He lifted his head
up. His dick was still hard as time and tenting the
sleeping bag. His arm was curved away from his body
as if he still held his dream girl.

It was all a dream. A damn good one, but a dream
nonetheless.

"I'm up," he hollered as he stretched the length of
his six-foot-one frame and pushed downward on his
hardness with *both* his hands.

Kaeden didn't dare to leave his tent until his erection had eased. He knew they were hiking up to another campsite along the trail so he started to pack up,
feeling really silly crawling around his tent with his
dick sticking out between his legs like an arm. He sat
back on his hindquarters with his hands on his thighs.
"Today will go better. Think positive. Put out positive
energy. Positive things will happen."

Laughing a little as he remembered struggling to
right his body before he fell off the bank into the river,

Kaeden pulled his cell phone from the back pocket of his jeans. He wanted to call Felecia and check in, but he barely had a signal.

Kaeden pushed his BlackBerry back into his pocket before he left the tent with his backpack in tow. "Morning."

Kade stretched his six-foot nine-inch frame with a smile. "Damn, little brother, clear your throat."

Of all the brothers, Kaeden had the deepest voice of them all. His was the most like his father's: deep, echoing, resonant. Kaeden chuckled. "Don't hate."

Kahron strode from between the trees dressed in nothing but jeans, hiking boots, and a black beater tee that showcased the tattoo on his biceps. "Good morning," Kaeden told him as he removed the stakes before he quickly folded down his tent. He was a firm believer in reading instructions, so although he never in his life even touched a tent he was a complete whiz at handling *this* tent. Thank God.

"Anyone have a signal?" Kade asked, looking down at his cell phone. "I'm ready to talk to my wife."

"Not me," Kaeden·told him.

The other three men reached for their devices.

"No need," Jade told them as she stepped off the dirt-packed trail with a large plastic bag in her arm. "When we hike farther up the trail there's a long break in the trees, and that's the best area to get reception."

Kaeden looked over at her and noticed the edges of her short hair were damp and slightly curling. Her smooth complexion was even fresher looking and completely free of makeup. He wondered briefly if she had walked back to the campground's public showers a couple of miles back.

That made him think of her nude and sudsy. *Getting hot.*

And then *that* erotic vision made the blood coursing through his body want to race straight to the long and heavy length of his penis. *Getting hard.*

"Whoo!" Kaeden started jogging in place and air boxing to fight off the erection.

Everyone paused in what they were doing to eye him oddly, including Jade. "Just a little morning workout ritual of mine," he lied.

His impending erection eased and Kaeden cast one last look at Jade as she began to help break down the camp. He had the distinct feeling that Jade thought he was a bumbling fool. That hadn't been the goal of him coming camping.

In truth, he wanted Jade Prince—what he knew of her he liked—and although the woman made him feel like an awkward high school nerd trying to gather up the courage to talk to the pretty, popular cheerleader, he was going to use this trip to at least try to have his dream girl in his life.

He was taking a chance going for a woman like Jade, but life—the best life—was always about reaching for the stars.

Kaitlyn sighed in unadulterated pleasure as she wiggled back in the vibrating massage chair while a nail technician worked absolute magic during her deluxe pedicure. She firmly believed in a woman treating herself to the little pleasures in life. A mani-pedi. A luxurious splurge on shoes by her favorite designer. Weekend trips to sunny places with turquoise water. Chilling at her favorite bar for drinks with her best girlfriends.

"Now, ladies, isn't this a better way to spend a Friday than moping around the ranch worrying about the men?" Kaitlyn asked.

At their silence, she leaned forward to eye her mother and her two sisters-in-law in their own pedi-cure chairs. "Right?" she prodded again.

"Right," they answered, not at all sounding like they meant it.

Kaitlyn just leaned back in her chair and closed her eyes. That's why she was enjoying living life to the fullest and not even thinking about falling in love. There were too many men, too many dates, and too many fun times to be had to spend any time moping about missing a man!

Felecia sat cross-legged on her floor beside her chest. She sighed and tilted her head to the side as she updated her wedding portfolio. Since she'd closed the office early for the day, she spent her time watching *Whose Wedding Is It Anyway?* and gotten some new ideas for her own dream wedding.

Picking up her cell phone she tried to call Kaeden, but his cell was still out of range. She thought of Kaeden—*her* Kaeden—in some secluded forest with Jade Prince, and her hands curled into tight fists filled with tension. But she forced herself to relax. Kaeden and Jade were as compatible as oil and water.

Just two more nights and he'll be back. Still, she wanted the trip over and Kaeden back in her grasp where she could snatch him up for good.

"Where are they camping, the dang on Bermuda Triangle?" she snapped before dropping the phone onto the carpeted floor.

She opened her folder and smiled at the advertisement of a bride and groom with her head and Kaeden's taped on top of theirs.

She firmly believed that to achieve it she had to believe it!

Jade hitched the wide straps of her backpack higher on her rounded shoulders as she led the men single file along the trail. They had hiked and fished away the morning. It took longer than usual because the men wanted to stop and fish anywhere along the trail that struck their fancy. Everything about the hike exhilarated her. The fresh air, the scent of the earth beneath their feet mingled with the sweetness of the wildflowers blossoming among the trees. It always amazed her how the woods could be serenely quiet even as they were filled with the backdrop of nature.

"Jade, don't you think that little grove is the perfect spot for making love?" Kaleb asked near her ear.

Jade rolled her eyes. *Now, why this Negro have to interrupt my peace?*

"We're going to camp right up ahead on the left,"

Jade hollered back to the men, completely ignoring Kaleb, who was giving her a serious migraine.

"We can set up camp quicker if you and I share a tent," he offered.

Jade whirled on him but had to force herself to count to ten to keep from shoving him into the lake. Forcing a smile, she pushed all of her frustration into making a fist that pressed the tips of her short nails into the flesh of her palms. She just hoped *he* laid off or *she* was going to lay her fist square against his jaw. Seriously.

"Okay, fellas, we'll camp here for the next two nights, and for anyone interested, there are some really beautiful and interesting wildflowers just a little bit deeper into the woods going toward the north," Jade told them as they began to set up camp.

A deer went flying past amongst the trees. Kahron shook his head as he pushed his shades atop his head. "I shoulda brought my shotgun and we'd be having deer meat for dinner," he said dryly.

"Hashed down with onions and peppers with that brown gravy spread over white rice," Kade added with a lick of his lips.

"The ten point I killed last season was the best-tasting deer meat I had in a while," Jade added as she grabbed her water jug and unscrewed the top, tilting her head back to take a deep sip.

"You hunt?" the men all asked in unison.

Jade knew she was no ordinary woman, and she liked that about herself. "I've won shooting matches at the county fair," she told them with just a bit of swagger in her tone. "Sorry, men, but I don't do stereotypes."

"With my wife's temper, I don't need her learning to shoot a gun," Kade joked as he raked his fingers through his moist silver curls.

"Sure she doesn't already know how?" Kael Strong drawled.

The men laughed in agreement as they continued setting up camp.

Jade quickly erected and staked her own bright pink pop-up tent a few feet back from the fire ring. She sprayed a fresh layer of bug repellent on her legs and arms since she was wearing khaki capris and an orange T-shirt. "Ready, fellas?" she asked, looking up just in time to see Kaeden take a small toke from his inhaler.

Jade frowned before she walked over to him. "Are you having a hard time breathing?" she asked him, lightly touching his back. "Is the hike too much? Do I need to keep a close eye on you?"

Kaeden jumped like she'd surprised him. He turned and looked down at her. "You need to keep a close eye on me?" he asked, his baritone tone sounding amused.

Jade crossed her arms over her ample chest and tilted her head to the side as she looked into his eyes through the glasses. "Yes," she stressed.

Kaeden laughed a little before he bent his tall frame suddenly and swung her up into his arms easily.

"Hey," Jade yelped in surprise as her hands shot out. She was afraid he would drop her.

"Don't let these glasses fool you," Kaeden told her

low in his throat, the cool breath from his mouth breezing lightly against her chin.

Jade's breath caught in her throat.

Her heart slammed against her chest.

A shiver raced from her head to the tip of pink-painted toes in the hiking boots she wore.

In that one instant her body acted like Kaeden Strong was Denzel Washington.

Whoa.

"The pump helps me breathe when my allergies act up," he explained, his eyes still locked on hers.

Jade's face was just inches from his. One of her hands rested lightly against his chest. Beneath her hand his heart was beating just as hard as hers.

"What you doing over there, little brother?" Kahron called over.

"She *is* hard as hell to resist," Kaleb added.

Jade scrambled and jumped down from his arms. "You guys ready to fish?" she asked, sounding normal even though her heart was still racing.

"Let's go catch some fish, because it looks like two of my boys want to catch you," Kael teased as he closed his tackle box.

Jade arched an eyebrow as she turned away from Kaeden. "Only thing is, Papa Strong, I am not throwing out any bait," she said, firmly hoping to get her point across.

Hours later Kaeden could hardly believe that he'd even gathered up the courage to swing Jade up in his arms. In that instant the idea flew into his head and he just reacted. No question. No thoughts.

And it felt good having every inch of her soft curves in his arms.

He wished he could explain what about Jade Prince drew him in until he was breathless. They were as different as night and day. She longed to be surrounded by the outdoors while Kaeden found being around nature troublesome. She was sexy as hell and knew it while still being comfortable enough to take on tasks better than most men. He had barely a drop of the swagger his brothers possessed.

Even though he knew he wasn't her type—he knew they had nothing in common—the more he found out about her, the more he wanted her.

She was funny and bright. Adventurous and courageous. Friendly but quick to put anyone in their place.

Jade was an enigma.

Taking his bespectacled eyes off his rod and the line floating across the water, he leaned back a bit to look past Kaleb sitting beside him down the long stretch of bank for Jade, but he didn't see her.

Bzzzz.

He used one hand to reach for his BlackBerry, looking down at the wide screen.

INCOMING CALL:
Felecia
(843) 555-0001

He answered. "Hey, Felecia."

"Well, hello, stranger. How's your trip?"

"It's going great," he lied, even forcing a smile as he dropped his reel to swat a mosquito that had just landed on the back of his hand and then used the back of his hand to wipe his running nose.

"Make sure you wear your insect repellent. Do you have your inhaler? Are you eating well? When are you getting back?"

Kaeden held the BlackBerry from his face and frowned as he looked down at it. "I'm good. I know it's Friday, but did anything major come up at the office today?" he asked, clearly steering the conversation back to business and away from Felecia sounding way too much like his girlfriend or wife.

"I'm holding down things for you. We're a team, re-member?"

Kaeden frowned again. "That's good to know," he said vaguely, his focus on a large wasp flying around Kaleb's silver-flecked head. "Enjoy the rest of your weekend. I'll see you at the office Monday."

Kaeden ended the call. "If that miniairplane bites me, you gone have to give me my epi shot," he warned Kaleb.

"Man, stop worrying 'bout stuff like that and just enjoy the experience," Kaleb told him as he rose from his camp chair and strained the muscles in his arms reeling in the line—and hopefully a fish.

Kaeden cast his brother a stare. "That's easy for you to say."

"I think I need the net, big brother," Kaleb boasted as he leaned back and kept on reeling.

"You ain't got nothing down there, son," Kael called down the bank teasingly.

Kaeden grabbed the net and rose from his seat. "That's a big one," he admitted as Kaleb held the line with the squirming bass on the large hook.

"Tonight I want to catch the other fish floating around here," Kaleb told him with a rowdy wink before he used pliers to take the hook from the fish.

"Kaleb, you really need to lay off Jade," Kaeden told his brother in a serious tone.

Kaleb dropped the fish into the bucket. "What?"

"You just called the woman a damn fish," Kaeden snapped. "Straight up you acting like an asshole, always pushing up on her when you know she's not in the mood for you."

Kaleb closed the lid on the bucket and looked up at his brother as he straightened up to his full height. "Yeah, I wouldn't want to act like a caveman and scoop her up in my arms."

"You know what, I can eat that and say I was wrong, but one incident of inappropriateness is nothing compared to your horny ass around here being disrespectful," Kaeden shot back, feeling his anger rising.

"Incident of inappropriateness?" Kaleb barked a laugh. "Man, save that nerdy conversation, man."

Kaeden stiffened his back as his jaw clenched. "Mind this nerd don't whup your ass, little brother," he told Kaleb coldly.

"Hey, what's y'all problem down there?" their father yelled from down the bank.

Kaeden and Kaleb squared off with their noses damn near touching.

"Why you all swoll up and writing a check you can't cash, big brother?"

"Because she's sick of your shit and so am I," Kaeden told him in a hard voice, not backing down one bit.

"You protecting the coochie like *you* got a chance of getting it!" Kaleb said, waving his hand dismissively at Kaeden before he turned to bait his hook.

Kaeden snorted in derision as he too turned away to pick up his reel and rod. "Look like *you* don't have a chance either, pimpin'. That's my whole point."

"Now, I'm sick of both of y'all shit, so both of you sit down before I get up," Kade said from his spot sitting on a stump. He was the oldest, and growing up he frequently took on the father figure role.

Kaleb cast his line into the water. "Man, whatever."

Kaeden sat down on his camp chair. "Whatever."

Chapter 6

Jade was walking from the cleared area where the outhouse sat when she saw Kaeden sitting by the fire reading his book. She paused her steps as she looked down at him alone while his father and brothers were rowdily playing cards at the picnic table. She knew he was close to his family, but in that moment her heart went out to him because he looked alone.

But maybe she was wrong about that.

She'd been wrong about things concerning Kaeden Strong. Like his strength. That seemingly skinny man swept her thick self up in his arms like it was nothing. He wanted to prove he wasn't weak and he did just that.

Crossing her arms over her chest, Jade made her way over to him. "Hi, Kaeden," she said softly, clearing her throat.

He looked up at her over his shoulder. "Hey . . . Hi, Jade."

She bit back a smile at the way the flames of the fire were reflected in his glasses, completely blocking his eyes from her. "Glad to see you out and not cooped up in that tent."

Kaeden laughed as he closed the book, holding his spot with his index finger. "The fire and a ton of bug spray help," he joked.

They fell silent.

"Have you ever seen anything more beautiful?" she asked as she looked out at the scenic view of the lake surrounded by the ebony shadows of lush greenery and towering trees. The sparkle of the moon against the water gave it a glimmer that was almost animated.

"It looks like a screensaver," Kaeden said.

"Or those puzzles we used to do as kids."

"As kids?" Kaeden balked.

"Don't tell me you still do puzzles," she said.

"Okay, I won't."

Oh Lord, he is *a nerd*, she thought. "There is no way I could still work inside a factory without windows all day and miss being surrounded by all this."

Kaeden remained silent although his eyes were still locked on the lake.

Jade licked her lips as she glanced over at him and then briefly at the dirt-packed ground. "Listen, I wanted to thank you . . . for talking to your brother," she said low enough for just his ears.

Kaeden looked at her in surprise.

"I didn't mean to eavesdrop but . . . but I did over-hear your . . . um . . . discussion," she said delicately.

Kaeden looked over at her and Jade looked away, very confused by her sudden nervousness around this man.

"Well, thanks . . . especially since it worked," Jade

said. "Sometimes men can be very annoying when they assume they can say whatever they want to me because of the way I look. It's okay to be sexy and feel sexy, but there is more to me than T and A."

Kaeden thought of his erotic dream and felt guilty.

Jade shrugged and fell quiet. She looked up at Kaeden just as he swung at a gnat flying before his eyes.

"Damn," he swore as he accidentally knocked his glasses off and sent them flying toward the fire.

Jade reached out and caught them. "See, I thought I needed to keep a close eye on you," she teased.

Kaeden laughed as he looked up at her. "Now, that's what got you lifted up the last time."

Jade's eyes locked with his, and where the fire's reflection in his glasses once blocked his eyes from hers, there wasn't one single, solitary thing to keep her from being absorbed into the startling intensity of his chocolate eyes. Warm mocha eyes framed by lashes that curled so deeply that the fine tips seemed to lightly stroke his lids. Deeply dark eyes that made the silver flecks of his closely shaven head seem to glisten.

As her mouth fell open just a little and her heart raced a bit faster, Jade's eyes flickered over Kaeden's slender face. The bronzed caramel complexion made all the more enticing by his prematurely silver hair. The high cheekbones. His strong chin. The supple lips. Just like Kahron . . . but different. Better. The leanness of his feature only accentuated the strong features they shared. Definitely—although surprisingly—better.

Kaeden Strong.

"Jade? Jade."

She shook herself and jumped to her feet. "I . . . um . . . just wanted to thank you . . . *soooo* . . . um . . . thanks, Kaeden."

Jade whirled and headed for her tent. She just wanted—needed—to get away. She wished she had brought along some of her favorite sangria, because she definitely needed a buzz.

"Jade?"

She paused at the sound of Kaeden calling her name. Did he see the momentary lust she felt for him? Did she give out some imaginary clue that in that moment she wondered what his lips tasted like? Taking a deep breath, Jade turned to find him standing behind her.

Jade swallowed past a large lump in her throat as she took a quick step back.

"My glasses," he told her in that deep voice as he looked down at her and smiled.

Jade flushed with embarassment. "Ooops. Sorry," she said, handing them out to him. "You probably have to wipe them off. My . . . palms were a little sweaty."

"That's fine." Kaeden used the hem of his white T-shirt to clean them.

Jade turned and took a few steps, but then she turned suddenly and walked back up to him. "You *really* should consider wearing contacts," she told him before turning and walking the short distance to her tent where she hurried to kneel and crawl in.

Kaeden tried to shift to comfort on his sleeping bag. To him only someone who was half-baked would think sleeping on the ground on something as thick as a slice of bread was more fun than rolling around on a king-sized mattress—like the one he had waiting for him in his bedroom.

Just like all the other comforts he was ready to get back to: taking a steamy hot shower in his open shower with the chrome vertical spa complete with oversized showerhead and four body sprays, watching his huge high-def television, kicked back on his plush leather recliner eating takeout from his favorite Chinese restaurant, and finally crawling into his bed in his climate-controlled bedroom for a good night of sleep. Or making love.

Sweet and tender lovemaking.

Fierce and fiery lovemaking.

With Jade.

His hardness sandwiching the soft curves of her frame as his bed supported their bodies during one furious stroke after the other. He felt his body stir in reaction to just the thought of her. Watching her in church with her makeup and dresses had been enough to stir his desire for her, but seeing her with her hair combed flat, no makeup, and in less casual attire fit for camping—his desire had not lessened one bit. If anything, he wanted her more. He was intrigued by her.

She was beautiful and sexy. That he knew.

But she was also clever, funny, and nice. That he'd learned.

You really should consider wearing contacts.

Kaeden frowned a bit. He didn't exactly get the

reason for the advice, but it was nice of her to even care if he wore glasses or not.

Turning on his side, he reached for his Jordan Banks book. But after a minute ticked by and he still couldn't focus on the main character, Slim Willie, solving another mystery, Kaeden just closed the book and turned off his LED lantern.

Cloaked by semidarkness, Kaeden tossed and turned. His BlackBerry vibrated and the screen lit up but he ignored it because he knew it was Felecia and they had absolutely nothing to talk about at midnight.

Except for the sounds of nature—the hooting of owls, the crickets doing their things, and the loud rustling of leaves as the wood's critters skittered about—the campsite was quiet. Kaeden couldn't sleep. He was hungry but he had been so busy packing emergency medical supplies that he'd neglected to bring along any of his favorite nonperishable snacks.

Their supper of fried bass was long gone. And frankly, he was tired of fish. "I would kill for a Twinkie right now," he muttered in the darkness as his stomach growled.

"Maybe there's something out there I can snack on," he said aloud as he grabbed his glasses from their hard case to slip on before he flung back the cover and unzipped his tent.

The cool night breeze blew in and Kaeden shivered from the feel of it even though he was still fully dressed in his jeans and long-sleeved T-shirt.

"I don't have Twinkies, but I'll share my s'mores."

Kaeden whirled around in surprise to find Jade sitting outside her pink tent by the fire with a book in her lap. She smiled and looked up at him as she held a gooey s'more in her outstretched hand.

"I heard you talking to yourself in there but I didn't want to interrupt," Jade joked.

Kaeden smiled, flashing his white, even teeth. "As long as I don't answer myself, I'm not headed to the mental hospital," he told her as he stepped up and took the sweet treat from her.

Their hands brushed lightly against one another and Kaeden felt an instant spark. As she turned her attention back to her book, he wondered how an attraction he felt so strongly could be so one-sided. "Thanks."

She looked up from her book again. "I was saving those for the last night, but a little sample a little early won't hurt."

Kaeden took a bite of the melted marshmallow and chocolate between two cinnamon- and sugar-coated graham crackers. "Mhan oof ah yawn yoo?" he asked, his mouth filled with the treat.

Jade frowned in confusion. "Huh?"

He swallowed and laughed. "Sorry. I said, mind if I join you?"

Kaeden was reluctant to go back to his tent. The campfire felt good and Jade was awake. Sleeping on the cold, dirt-packed floor. Being attacked by insects. Given up the luxuries he favored. All of that was for him to get close to Jade. There was no way he was going back into that lonely little tent now.

"Actually, I wondered how far along you were in *Death by Midnight*?"

Kaeden looked down at her in surprise before he grabbed an empty camp chair and sat down by the fire.

She held up the book in her lap so that he could see the cover. "You're reading it too?"

She nodded. "The night I brought you my grand-father's homemade itch cream, I saw it in your tent. I *loves* me some Jordan Banks."

Kaeden held his large hands out to the fire. "I have all his books."

"Me too," Jade said excitedly. "I think this one is the best one yet. Slim Willie's investigative skills are getting better, but he is also growing as a person, and I love great character development in a book."

Kaeden looked over at her. "And his character's dialogue is always very realistic."

Jade reached over and grabbed his wrist. "Yes!" she said enthusiastically.

Goose bumps raced up his arms and his eyes dropped down to look at her touch, but she had already pulled her hand away. He felt the loss.

They fell silent but there was an ease between them. Nothing awkward. Nothing stilted. Just peace.

"What are you two doing up?"

Kaeden looked over his shoulder as his father emerged from his small tent. "Eating s'mores."

"And talking books," Jade added.

"A s'more sounds good but I just got up for some water," Kael said. "I left my canteen out here."

"I can make you one, Mr. Strong." Jade rose from her camp chair and walked over to the picnic table to open her small cooler.

"I'm not interrupting?" Kael asked as he peered down to look inside the cooler beside her.

Yes! Kaeden screamed in his mind.

Jade laughed. "Oh goodness no," she said, as if the very thought was silly.

Kaeden gritted his jaw.

"Did I miss my invite to the party?" Kahron asked as he came out of his tent sans his ever-present aviator shades.

Kaeden actually rolled his eyes heavenward in frustration.

Jade squatted by the fire as she loaded marshmallows onto wooden skewers. "I was saving this little treat for y'all last night of camping, but I guess tonight is good as any other night," she said in a cheerful mood.

"Hey, Kade. Hey, Kaleb. Get up, fellas. Jade's making s'mores."

Awakened by Kahron, Kaeden's other silver-haired brothers soon exited their own tents. Kaeden finished eating his now-cooled treat thinking, *My family is a bunch of blockers.*

Jade was glad for the distraction because her new-found awareness of Kaeden was disconcerting to her. When she innocently touched his arm, she had felt a small jolt of electricity.

When I get home I'm going to put on my sexiest lingerie, slip into a pair of "come and get it" pumps, and call Darren on over.

As she roasted the marshmallows, Jade gazed across the flames at Kaeden halfheartedly eating his s'more. *He* is *handsome*, she thought. *It's not like I'm crazy to find him attractive . . . but those glasses, the allergies, the inhaler! I have* got *to be incredibly horny.*

Kaeden looked over at her suddenly. "Your marshmallows are burning."

Jade jumped up as two white globs fell off the skewer and into the fire. "I did this way better earlier when I didn't have an audience," she joked as she slid more marshmallows on the skewer.

"Mine was delicious," Kaeden assured his family.

Jade smiled over at him just as he took off those glasses to wipe them clean. She looked away quickly.

Maybe I should call Darren and get into some really raunchy phone sex. Or text sex?

Jade shook her head as she slid the melted marshmallows between the layers of chocolate and graham crackers. While the men all talked and laughed as if it wasn't the middle of the night, Jade focused on making her group members two gooey treats each.

She side-eyed Kaeden as he reached over to pick up her book from her camp chair. Her eyes took in the fine silver hairs. His bronzed complexion. Broad shoulders. Long limbs. Big feet. *Very* big feet.

Her eyes darted to his crotch between his bent legs. Her cheeks flushed at the noticeable bulge. She jumped to her feet. "Here we go, fellas. S'mores."

Everyone was sitting around the crackling campfire and Jade circled around them offering them a paper plate holding the treats. She offered the plate to Kaleb. He looked up at her and winked. "Thank you, Miss Prince," he said, mockingly polite, before shooting Kaeden a "see there" look.

And she came to Kaeden, whose head was buried in her book. "Kaeden, would you like . . ."

He looked up at her questioningly, kind of squinting his face like he was trying to focus his vision via his glasses. Jade immediately thought of Steve Urkel, Robert Johnson, Bill Gates, and Napoleon Dynamite like a slideshow.

All of her silly notions of wanting to jump Kaeden Strong's bones disappeared . . . just . . . like . . . that.

"Yes, Jade."

"Huh?" she said.

He smiled and reached for another s'more from the plate. "Thanks," he told her.

"No, Kaeden, thank *you*," she stressed with a smile.

He looked confused, but it didn't matter because Jade *wasn't* confused any longer.

Chapter 7

"Do you remember the time Kaeden tried to cut his own hair and took a chunk out of his hairline big as an apple?" Kaleb asked, reaching over to muss Kaeden's head.

"Oh no!" Jade cried out before she laughed.

Kael chuckled as he slapped his knee with one of his beefy hands. "His mama wanted to punish him by sending him to school just like that." He looked over at his son. "But I couldn't do it to you, son, so I shaved you bald."

"I don't know if I should thank you or not," Kaeden drawled in his resonant voice.

The men all laughed and Jade tried hard to hold her laughter in with her hand to her mouth as she looked at Kaeden with sympathetic eyes. "How old were you?"

"Twelve," the men all said in unison.

Kaeden dropped his head into his hands.

"That was about all the mischief Kaeden brought me and my wife." Kael reminisced with a twinkle in his eyes. "He was usually stuck up under his mother in the house while these other pranksters roamed the farm and found any and everything to get into."

"I have severe allergies," he insisted in explanation.

Kade nodded and he leaned forward to brace his elbows on his knees. "That's very true. I must admit I'm surprised we haven't had a Kaeden during this trip . . . yet."

"A Kaeden?" Jade asked, more than curious.

Kaeden groaned and shook his head, wishing his family could reminisce on something or someone else besides him.

Kahron stretched his long, jean-clad legs out before him. "That's a medical emergency involving insects."

"There was the bee sting in 1986."

"The red ant bite in 1992."

"The wasp incident in 2001."

"Oh, and the poison ivy in 2006."

Kaeden winced at each of his brothers adding fuel to the fire. How could he have forgotten the poison ivy he tripped and fell in when he accompanied his brothers and sister on a foolish horse race one Sunday afternoon after church? "Since we're strolling down memory lane, Kahron, why don't you tell Jade about the time you set the whole west field of the farm on fire."

"Whoo-oo-eee. Now that was one helluva whupping," Kahron admitted.

Jade smiled brightly as she eyed them all. "I wish I grew up in a large family," she told them.

"You're an only child?" Kaeden asked, feeling completely mesmerized by the sight of Jade's warm smile.

"Unfortunately. You all are *so* lucky."

"Don't be so sure," Kaeden muttered darkly.

She just smiled at him and reached over to reassuringly squeeze his hand quickly.

Jade was very touchy-feely and Kaeden liked it—even if her innocent touches did arouse him. *Just do it. Just ask her out*, he thought. *Step up to the plate.*

"I haven't seen your mama since your parents' divorce," Kael said.

"She's fine. She lives in Summerville, but she's hardly ever home since she's a flight attendant."

Kaeden found himself staring at Jade's profile and forced himself to look away. *What do I say to her? How do I ask?*

"You look exactly like your mother," Kael told her.

"There's another one of you running around?" Kaleb asked. "What flight is she on?"

Kaeden eyed Kaleb thinking he would cross the line, but thankfully no further jokes came from his lips.

"Well, fellas, this has been a long day," Jade said, rising to her feet in her lemon sweatsuit. "I am going to leave y'all to this and turn in."

Jade stretched and Kaeden allowed his eyes to follow the curvy lines of her body. *She hasn't shown me any inclination that she likes me. Why would I put myself out there to be rejected?*

The look of pure horror on Lisha Strong's face was priceless and her daughter captured it for all eternity on her iPhone.

"There is no way I am putting *that* on," Lisha said, her hand to her chest as she eyed the bright yellow and very sheer catsuit Bianca held up in her hands. "Who would?"

Garcelle bit back a smile. "I have one in every color," she admitted before she bit her bottom lip to keep from giggling. "And trust me, Mama Strong, it was worth every red *centavo*."

Lisha raised a brow.

"Mama, this is the first time you and Daddy have been apart in ages, and I think you should spice it up for him when he gets back tomorrow night," Kaitlyn advised as she reached for another sheer entrapment in Frederick's of Hollywood. "How about this?"

"Be adventurous, Mama Strong," Bianca advised with a soft smile as her diamond hoop earrings glistened from her ears.

Lisha eyed the three of them. "Ladies, please get from underneath my husband and my clothes."

The three younger women just laughed before walking back to the rear of the store. Lisha side-eyed her companions as she reached inside her Coach purse. She turned to the young saleswoman. "Have the black one in a large sent to Lisha Strong at 1001 Cougar Lane . . . and keep the change," she said, easing the hundred-dollar bill from her purse and into the saleswoman's hand.

"Right away, Mrs. Strong."

Lisha closed her purse and made her way to the back to join her daughters. *Humph, they don't need to be all up in me and Kael's business*, she thought with a sly smile. *Like they really need to teach me something. Chile, please.*

* * *

Jade sighed as she dropped her used bath wipes into a Ziploc. The premoistened cloths were as thick and large as washcloths and Jade used enough to cleanse her entire body. It was a great alternative to a shower since they were too far from the public shower to walk to it. Use of any soap near any water source in the state parks was not allowed. She supplied the men with some bath wipes as well until they hiked farther along the trail toward the state campground where the showers were located. She couldn't lie and say she wasn't ready to slip into her tub, sip some white sangria, and just zone out.

Bzzzzzzzzz.

Jade stuck the folded Ziploc into her backpack to dispose of later and picked up her silver cell phone. She flipped it open. A picture of Darren rock climbing flashed on the screen. She answered the call. "Hey, partner," she greeted him.

"Hey, beautiful," he replied. "How's the trip going?"

"It's going great," she told him, pressing her phone between her shoulder and ear to quickly finish dressing in jeans and another long-sleeved fitted tee. "Weather's nice. Trail is clear. Fish are biting. No worries."

"No injuries?" he asked.

Jade unzipped her tent and her eyes fell directly on Kaeden slowly walking from his tent to the picnic table. "Not yet," she said, saying a silent thanks to the Great One above as she eyed Kaeden wince as he sat down on the wooden bench. "How's your trip?"

"Everything is cool here too."

"Good," she told him, switching the cell phone to her other hand.

"I miss you."

Jade paused at his sudden words. "Awwww. Thanks," she said, deliberately trying to keep the mood light.

"I know you like to chill out after a tour, but I really want to see you Sunday night," he said.

Jade opened her mouth to decline.

"We could just hang out at your place and watch a movie," he said quickly, as if he knew her refusal was coming.

Jade knew that once she agreed to starting a relationship with Darren, it meant opening some of her life up to him. Spending time. Going on dates. Compromising when there were things she wasn't inclined to do . . .

"Uh-hmmm. Okay," she agreed reluctantly.

"Good."

"I better get going, Darren," she said. "I'll call you Sunday night when I get in."

"Okay, be safe, baby."

Jade massaged her eyebrows at the tension building there. "Okay, you too, Darren. Bye."

She snapped the phone closed. When her awareness of Kaeden was weirding her out, Jade had considered giving Darren a little bit of her sweetness. *Thank God, I didn't.* She wasn't ready for that yet. Intimacy was huge. It was not a step that she took lightly.

Her eyes fell on Kaeden again and it was hard not to notice that he was feeling some terrible muscle ache. *Sleeping on the ground is tearing Mr. White Collar up,* Jade thought with a shake of her head.

She thanked God for clarity because there was no way a man like Kaeden Strong could *ever* be her type.

Kaeden felt like he'd slept on a cement slab. Wincing, he felt sharp muscle spasms radiate from his shoulders to the top of his square buttocks as he sat down on the picnic bench. "Just one more night. One more night," he promised himself as he reached up to massage his shoulder.

"I'm going to start charging you."

Kaeden looked over his shoulder at Jade standing beside him holding out a small lotion bottle. "Don't tell me. This is another one of your grandfather's home remedies?"

Jade nodded as she sat the bottle on the table. "Better than IcyHot and a bottle of Aleve combined."

Kaeden picked the bottle up. "Any instructions?" he asked, with humor in his deep voice.

"Just rub it on where it hurts, Kaeden," she drawled dryly.

He laughed. "Thanks, Jade."

She gave him a genuine smile. "You're welcome," she said before walking away.

"Listen, I think I'm going to cut out of the fishing today," he announced, rising to his feet.

Kael paused in adding weights to his fishing line to look over at him. "You sure, son?" he asked.

Kaeden nodded. "I'm positive."

Not even the opportunity to be around Jade all day was going to make him sit by the bank all day waiting on a fish to bite a hook. *I'm not getting anywhere with Jade anyway.*

Jade frowned. "What are you going to do all day?" she asked, sounding slightly irritated.

"Read," he answered simply as he lifted his hands to readjust his spectacles.

Jade massaged her temples.

That move didn't surprise Kaeden one bit. "I'll be fine," he assured his father before slowly rising to his feet and pushing the bottle Jade gave him into the back pocket of his jeans. "I might even have Felecia e-mail me some stuff to work on."

"He'll be fine," Kahron said, slipping his shades into place before he picked up his tackle box.

Jade gave him a long look that made him frown and shift his feet in the spot where he stood, before she turned and headed up the small, rocky incline to the trail. "Let's move it out, boys," she yelled over her shoulder.

"We'll be back," Kael said before he turned and followed Kaleb, Kahron, and Kade onto the trail.

Kaeden watched them until they disappeared down the trail, their forms covered by the overgrowth of trees and bushes. He considered putting on the ointment Jade gave him but knew the spot where he ached was hard for him to reach himself.

He settled into his camp chair glad that they had left the campfire lit to help ward off the insects and spent the next two hours reading his book. But in those two hours he came to a satisfying end of the mystery, and that left him with nothing to do . . . and he tried some of everything.

He sprayed on more insect repellant.

He tried his best to kill every ant in an anthill with insect spray.

He fixed himself another s'more that tasted more burned than tasty.

He kicked rocks.

He did anything and everything to occupy his time. Nothing held his interest.

Kaeden was a tech junkie. He loved gadgets. Gadgets that needed electricity or at least Wi-Fi.

He was watching a bird of bright blue color swoop in and out of the tree branches when Jade's words floated to the forefront of his memory: *There's some really beautiful and interesting wildflowers just a little bit deeper into the woods going toward the north . . .*

Kaeden shrugged. "Why not?" he told himself, thinking it wouldn't hurt to try and he could get some really great pictures with his digital camera. "If it's so far that I can't see the camp, then I'll turn around."

Kaeden pushed aside any reservations he had as he took the small incline up to the trail and then walked across it. There was a noticeable break in the trees with a thin footpath. He forged ahead, pausing when he caught sight of a beautiful waterfall in the distance. He lifted his camera and zoomed in for a shot. It wasn't very large, but the sight of the crystal-clear water falling over the side was soothing. He shifted a bit from the path and moved toward it, his curiosity more piqued than any apprehension over being in the midst of a wooded area.

Who knew that snuggled among the dense trees was such a beautiful sight? "That would make a nice postcard," he said aloud to himself, before he stood still and listened to the sound of running water. His state-of-the-art sound machine with the nature sounds couldn't even compete.

Kaeden allowed himself a few more moments of surprising peace in the outdoors before he turned to make his way back. He frowned. He turned in a full circle. His frown deepened. "What the hell?" he asked, his deep voice sounding out of place among the serenity.

He had no clue where he was. *Everything* looked alike. "Shit," he swore, reaching in the front pocket of his jeans for his cell phone. His grip tightened until he was sure he would snap the BlackBerry in half. No signal.

"I should slap my damn self," he muttered, fighting the urge to fling his BlackBerry and camera into the stream in frustration. "What in the hell was I thinking? Seriously. What was I thinking?"

Taking a deep breath, Kaeden walked a straight line to the edge of the trees, hoping it would lead him back to that footpath. It didn't.

"My destination is the camp. To hell with those wildflowers."

After nearly twenty minutes the brush and the trees thickened until he had to use his arms to clear a path before him. He was sweaty and dusty and beyond aggravated. He stopped where he stood and turned, trying to assess whether he should head back the way he came or forge ahead. He turned again, looking for any sign that he was nearing a break in the trees. Suddenly he felt the earth move from underneath him, and Kaeden couldn't help the holler he released as he dropped down a few feet, hitting the ground hard with an "umph" before he felt every rock, twig, and every other imaginable thing on the ground against his frame as he tried to stop himself from rolling.

He hollered out as his head slammed into something hard, and even as he felt his body continue its decline, he also felt himself slip into darkness.

Jade felt anxious.

She didn't know why. She couldn't pinpoint the cause for it. She didn't like it. She couldn't deny it.

Jade bit her bottom lip.

Of course it could be nothing, but it could also be something . . . or someone.

I hate when I feel like this.

Jade's brows furrowed.

"Something wrong, Jade?"

She looked up at Kahron standing beside her as he dropped the fish he caught into the bucket. "Just a little worried about Kaeden," she admitted.

Kahron laughed. "Kaeden's fine. Trust me," he assured her.

"Has he always hated the outdoors?" she asked.

Kahron smiled broadly. "More like the outdoors didn't agree with him," he said, shifting his sunglasses on his face.

Jade's mouth curled up a bit as she looked up at him. "Kaeden always plays with his glasses just like that," she told him.

Kahron's smile broadened. "You noticed that about him, huh?"

Jade shrugged. "I'm very observant about everything. *That's* all," she stressed.

"Yeah, okay," he said.

"Trust me, your brother's cute, nice and all of that, but, he is *not* my type."

"Soooo . . . you think he's cute?"

Jade looked up at him in confusion. "Huh?"

"You said he was cute," Kahron said frankly.

"Are you a rancher or a lawyer?" she snapped, feeling irritable.

Kahron just chuckled as he walked away to cast his line back into the water with well-practiced ease.

And that chuckle that clearly revealed that Kahron found her amusing irked her some more.

"Kaeden's not answering his phone." Kade slipped his cell back in its holster. "I need the lures I left at camp."

"Those lures ain't gone help you catching nothing," Kaleb joked.

Jade jumped to her feet. "I'll walk back to camp," she told them, wanting to kill the two birds with one stone: check on Kaeden and get some seriously needed alone time.

"You don't have to do that, Jade," Kade told her.

Jade waved her hands. "Not a problem," she told him as she headed back down the trail.

Me and Kaeden? Humph. How funny is that? He couldn't even handle all of this if I even thought about giving him some. Probably have a dang on asthma attack.

She would be busy reaching for his dick and he would be reaching for his inhaler. Jade laughed a little at the thought. "Puh-leeze. I'd have his ass grabbing his heart like Fred Sanford."

Her laughter faded as she reached the edge of the camp and saw no signs of him. "Kaeden," she called out as she walked down the decline from the trail to his tent. It was empty.

Jade turned around in a circle slowly as she surveyed the campground. "Where could he be?" she asked aloud as she walked down the length of the bank searching for any sign of him.

What if he's in the midst of one of those "Kaedens" and lying there needing help?

But what if he's just out exploring?

Jade knew she would feel less concerned if it was *any* of the men except Kaeden.

Feeling concern rise in her quickly, Jade strode across the camp. She grabbed her first aid kit. She slipped it and a blanket inside a small backpack that she slid onto her back. *Just in case*, she thought as she moved up the incline to cross the trail. "Kaeden!" she called out as her heart began to beat more furious than war drums.

She eyed the vast wooded area, but most of it was so dense that she saw nothing but varying shades of green. Her eyes lit on the path and she instantly headed for it. "Kaeden!" she called out at the top of her voice until her throat ached.

Her anxious feelings.

Kaeden not answering Kade's call.

Kaeden not answering her hollers.

Something was wrong.

Where was he?

Chapter 8

Jade placed her hands on her hips, breathing deeply as she forced herself to calm down and think. She circled where she stood but she didn't see him so she continued along the path, trying to look for any flash of color among the greenery.

She kept calling his name until she was sure she would be hoarse. The sun was beginning to set and she knew she had no choice but to call the park rangers and alert his family.

"Where are you, Kaeden?" she asked aloud, grabbing her cell phone to call Mr. Strong. It rang just once.

"Jade? Where are you two? We're here at the camp."

You two? Disappointment weighed her shoulders down and she clutched the phone tighter. "Actually . . . I'm . . . I'm out looking for Kaeden," she admitted uneasily.

The line went quiet.

"When I got back to the camp he wasn't there, and I hoped he was back by now," she said, filling the silence.

"You keep looking, and we're going to spread out here and look too."

Jade nodded as she fixed her troubled eyes on a squirrel scurrying past. "I think someone should hang around the camp in case he returns or to alert the rangers if we . . . if we don't find him soon."

"We're on it."

Jade slid her phone into the back pocket of her pants and hitched her backpack up higher on her shoulders before she kept on moving through the forest, searching for any sign of Kaeden. The seconds, then minutes, and finally the hour passed. The sun setting wasn't any help, especially since she'd neglected to bring a flashlight.

Jade was turning to head back when she spotted the last of the sun glinting off the waterfall. She only wished she had time to stop and admire it. She spotted a flash of color down the steep slope. Far in the distance there was just the faintest spot of bright red—the same color of the shirt Kaeden had on that morning.

Without a second thought, Jade carefully worked her way down the rocky and uneven hill, grateful for her hiking boots as she worked to maintain her balance. Her heart slammed into her chest as she made out the outline of Kaeden's frame partially submerged in the stream.

She rushed over, falling to her knees beside him. She dug in and used all of her strength to drag his body completely onto the bank. His clothes were soaked and clinging to his frame. His glasses were gone from his face and there were several surface scratches marring him. She quickly made sure he was still breathing and then inspected him for any broken bones. She gasped harshly at the gash across his forehead. "Shit," she swore as she quickly took off the backpack and removed her first aid kit.

"Kaeden," she called down softly to him as she cleansed the wound carefully. "I knew I shouldn't have left you behind at camp."

Jade entwined her fingers with his as she reached for her cell phone with her other hand. She breathed deeply, forcing herself to stay calm. Kaeden needed her.

"No signal. Shit," she swore again, fighting the urge to fling the cell phone into the stream.

Releasing a heavy breath, she sat back on her heels and looked up at the incline. *Definitely easier to get down it than go up it*, she thought as she squeezed Kaeden's hand. She felt a shiver race across his body and her eyes shifted down to him.

Do I leave you and go get help?

Do I stay with you and wait it out?

The sun was going, and as usual for South Carolina during the spring, there was a slight bite to the air without it.

Jade bit her full bottom lip as she let her eyes flitter over his face. It wasn't the time to notice the strong lines of his angular face. But she did. Tilting her head to the side, she still clung tightly to his hand as she dropped her cell phone to the ground and lifted her hand to lightly stroke his square cheek.

He shivered again.

And so did she.

That confused her because *she* wasn't wet and chilled like him.

Jade released his hand and looked around them as darkness surrounded them. She stood up and walked up the incline, using rocks as leverage, but halfway up her foot slipped. She yelped in pain as she fell and almost rolled down the hill herself.

She steadied herself on her feet and made her way back to Kaeden. She took off her backpack before she knelt down beside him. Jade eyed the length of his tall frame. "I can't leave you in these wet clothes," she said to him softly.

Taking a deep breath, Jade removed the blanket from her backpack before she set out undressing Kaeden. "This is *so* clichéd," she drawled as she removed his boots and wet socks.

Wow. Big feet.

She undid his belt buckle, frowning to see it was Gucci. "Figures."

Jade grunted as she peeled his jeans down his narrow hips and then stood between his legs to jerk them off. She paused, with her body still slightly bent, when her eyes fell on the outline of his maleness against the damp cotton of his boxers. "Well, who knew?" she joked, even as she felt her cheeks warm at the thickness and length of him as it fell across the top of his thigh. *Humph. Mama said skinny men always got big ones.* "He better not be afraid of snakes, *that's* for sure."

Jade diverted her eyes, deciding to risk leaving the boxers on. She worked to free him of his shirt and tee before easing him onto one half of the blanket. Goose bumps raced across his body and she folded the other half of the blanket over his frame—but not before she noticed that although he wasn't massive in build, his frame was well defined and chiseled.

Her heart fluttered like butterfly wings in her chest as her pulse raced.

She checked his pulse again quickly before she grabbed her cell phone and walked around with it high in the air hoping to catch a hot spot for a signal. No such luck.

Jade wrapped her arms around herself as she looked around. Darkness reigned. The moon was almost full. A chill was in the air.

She looked over at Kaeden and could only hope he would awaken so that they could get back to the camp. She laid his clothes out to dry some before she made her way back over to him to find him still shivering. Jade knew she was going to have to huddle close to him during the night to ward off the chill.

Body heat. Pure and simple.

Jade's body warmed from her head to her toes. There were several good-looking men that she'd camped with all weekend, but only this one made her remember that she was a woman with needs. Why?

Pushing aside any thoughts but helping him, Jade removed her boots and vest before she lay down beside him. She huddled close to him on her side, even easing her full and shapely thigh over his legs, her arms over his hard stomach, and placed her head on his chest.

As she closed her eyes, Jade let the steady beat of his heart lull her to sleep.

* * *

Kaeden winced as he stirred awake. His head was throbbing and his body felt like he'd been beaten with a bag of boulders. Then he remembered he'd fought a battle with a rocky incline and lost.

"Hmmmmmm."

Kaeden stiffened at the sound of the very feminine moan. He suddenly realized that a warm and soft body was cushioned close to him. Very close.

He let his eyes adjust to the darkness, and although his vision was slightly blurry without his glasses, he was thankful for the bright light of the moon to help illuminate his bedmate.

Sweetly scented hair just beneath his chin.

A warm face against his chest.

A heated hand on his abdomen.

Soft breasts against his side.

A firm leg atop his.

A deeply curved hip.

Jade.

Kaeden licked his lips as his dick stirred to life in a flash. He felt the smooth skin of his hardness slide against his thigh as it took a stretch in his boxers.

Boxers!

Kaeden couldn't remember how he got from slipping and rolling down a hill to lying in the darkness with Jade cuddled against his side—but he didn't mind it one damn bit. Not at all.

"Hmmmm." Jade moaned again, snuggling closer to him.

Never in a million years did Kaeden think lying on the hard ground could ever feel so damn good.

Still, he tensed as Jade's hands shifted down in her

sleep. He swallowed past a lump in his throat with her hand so close to his member. It hardened more, lifting up from his leg to tent the thin blanket.

A cool night wind blew over their bodies. Kaeden tried to shift more of the cover over Jade's figure. His erection wasn't helping it.

Jade's hand shifted again and his heart thundered wildly as it eased onto his dick. He bit his lip and ignored the throbbing of his forehead as he tilted his head back. He had to awaken her or Jade's innocent touches in her sleep were going to push him over the edge.

He felt her body stiffen against him.

Kaeden looked down at her just as Jade raised her head from his chest to look up at him.

Under the soft, barely there illumination of the moonlight their eyes locked. Their mouths were just inches apart. Their hearts pounded. Something more intensely electric than lightning flashed around them. The slight chill in the air and from the ground they lay upon was beat back by a rising heat. It was unmistakable.

"I'm sorry," Jade said softly, shifting her hand away from his hard heat.

Kaeden was no fool. He put his hand back on top of hers and shifted her hand back to his stiff tool to tightly close around it.

Jade gasped.

Kaeden brought his hand up to cup her face and tilt it up just enough for him to press his mouth to hers.

"Kaeden, we can't," she whispered against his lips, her protest sounding weak even to her own ears.

"Yes, we can," he assured her in that intimate space between their open mouths before he moaned and stroked her bottom lip with his tongue. She shivered against him and Kaeden fought off his surprise that Jade was feeling him to deepen the kiss.

And nothing ever tasted so good to them. Absolutely nothing.

Jade stroked the throbbing hot length of his erection as she returned his kiss with vigor.

And nothing had ever felt so good to them. Absolutely nothing.

Ignoring the hardness of the ground, the chill in the air, and the throbbing of his forehead, Kaeden shifted his body so that Jade was lying on her back and he on his side. He moaned wildly as Jade gripped his dick tightly and sucked his tongue into her open mouth.

He couldn't believe any of this. Was it a dream? If so, he didn't want to wake up.

Jade knew nothing except this man, Kaeden Strong, evoked passion in her that she hadn't ever felt with anyone. No one. Her entire body felt alive from his kiss and his touch. She felt drugged and she wanted more of her fix.

Kaeden brought trembling hands up to slip with ease under her shirt to take one of her full chocolate globes into his hands. The feel of her thick and taut nipples beneath the delicate lace made his mouth water as she cried out a little at the feel of his hands.

Jade broke the kiss to lick a trail from his chin to the groove of his neck, enjoying the erratic beat of his pulse against her moist tongue. "You're salty," she whispered up to him before she shifted down to press her full and plush lips to his chest.

"I'm sorry," he apologized as he fought to control his want of her. He felt near an explosion.

She shook her head. "I like it."

Kaeden roughly jerked her shirt up, exposing her smooth lace-covered breasts to him. "I wish I could see more of you."

Jade gave him one last lick before she sat up and pulled the T-shirt over her head. The chill raced across her body, hardening her nipples further. Kaeden sat up on his elbow, dipping his silver head to hotly pull one of the nipples into his mouth with a deep moan. Jade arched her back and released a gut-wrenching cry of pleasure into the night air.

Her core dictated the night.

She was wet.

She was throbbing.

She was in heat.

It had been *so* long.

She needed this and she was going to get it.

Jade reached behind herself to unclasp her bra, freeing the soft fullness of her breasts for him to do with as he pleased.

Kaeden chose to deeply suck one into his mouth and to massage the other in between twirling her hard nipples between his fingers. He could tell she liked his selection. So did he. "Damn, they soft," he whispered against the moist trail he made with his tongue.

Jade reached inside his boxers to deeply stroke the length of him. "And this right here is so hard," she told him, barely hearing her own words over the furious beating of her heart.

Kaeden moved his tongue against her nipple in a flickering motion and he reveled in the way she brought one hand up to press against the back of his head as she shivered uncontrollably.

"Yes, lick my nipples, baby. Lick 'em," she told him hotly as her core throbbed with a life all its own.

He immediately obliged, going from one to the other in a sweet feast that was more delicious to him than the most decadent chocolate.

Jade released his heat to unbutton her jeans and lifted up her buttocks to ease them down her curved hips.

Kaeden reached out to cup her waist, just needing to keep the physical connection with her . . . afraid that she would reclaim her senses and end the passion ride before they even *really* began.

He eyed her like she was starved as she straddled his hips in nothing but a lime green lace thong. Kaeden could only shake his head in wonder at the sight of her breasts hanging freely with her small waist and wide hips. She was everything he dreamt she would be and more. "Damn, you beautiful," he told her in a low and deep voice that only hinted at the desire he had for her.

She smiled as she wrapped her legs around his and then bent down slowly to let her breasts sway lightly against his face. "Will you do that little tongue thing you did before?" she requested, far too politely for such a heated affair.

Kaeden flickered the tip of his tongue against her

dark nipples as his shaky hands tightly grasped her fleshy buttocks and he worked his hips to grind his hardness against her moist lips. He could feel her juices through her panties and his boxers. She wanted this just as badly as he did. He felt his confidence go up. "Damn, Jade. Damn."

Jade didn't feel the chill. She was hot. She was ready. She couldn't stop her steady fall into desire if she wanted to. Nothing in the world mattered more to her than feeling Kaeden slip every delicious thick inch deep inside her walls—after that, she was more than ready to take over the ride. She leaned back to look down at his handsome face framed by the moonlight. "Condom?" she asked before she bent down to lick hotly at his mouth.

"My wallet," he answered shakily. *We're doing this. We're doing this! Calm down. Don't blow this. Don't you blow this.*

Jade inched forward, leaning down to reach beyond Kaeden's head for his pants in the darkness.

Her globes stroked his face and Kaeden snuggled his face in her warm, sweetly scented cleavage, inhaling deeply of her scent before he licked a trail to her nipple to circle it as he slid her panties to the side and stroked his thumb across her clit.

Jade gasped hotly and her body went weak atop him.

He stroked again.

Her hips jerked.

He stroked again . . . before he slipped his index finger deep inside her to massage against her walls. "Ah," he gasped. Wet. Hot. Tight. Perfect. Just perfect.

Jade pulled his wallet from his wet pants and

blindly searched for the foil packet as Kaeden sucked her nipples like he was starved and stroked his fingers against her slickly wet bud. She shivered as heat coursed over her body. Jade was surprised and pleasured by his skillful tongue as he stoked a fire deep within her that was aching to be quenched.

Sitting up, she regretfully freed her breasts from his mouth to tear the foil with her teeth before she scooted down his legs. She licked her lips at the impressive sight of him: long and curved, thick and hard, straining against the seams of his boxers like it was ready to rip through.

What am I doing? she thought, shifting her eyes up to his.

Panting heavily, with her heart pounding and her pulse racing, Jade had never felt more alive. Never felt more desired. Never felt such an intense craving to be sexually fulfilled.

What if I never feel this way again?

Jade licked her lips as she grasped his dick tightly and held it upright as she sheathed as much of him as she could with the latex. It fit him snugly—almost as snugly as she planned to fit him with her walls. "I can't explain this, Kaeden," she said huskily to him with raw honesty and emotion in her voice. "But I *can't* stop this. I can't. I won't. I need this."

Something clutched at Kaeden's heart as he looked up at her. He reached up to cup the back of her neck and pulled her down to press her plush breasts against his hard chest as he kissed her with all the passion she evoked in him.

Their eyes stayed open and locked as their tongues did a wicked slow drag.

Nothing mattered but their passion. Their chemistry. Their heat.

Jade broke the kiss to bite his bottom lip lightly before she licked a trail to his chin. The hollow of his neck. From one hard nipple to the other. The long ridge running down the deep jagged valley of his abdomen. She enjoyed how each touch of her tongue to his flesh caused him to shiver, moan, and groan.

"You ready?" she asked seductively before she slipped her panties to the side to ease her core down onto him. Inch by inch.

"Are you?" he returned cockily as he jerked his hips upward in one fluid motion and filled her. She gasped and dropped her head to his chest as her fingers clawed the earth.

The breadth of him pressed against her walls and she waited, panting heavily as she tried to adjust to his size as his hand massaged her back and buttocks.

Kaeden bit his bottom lip to keep from hollering out as he felt her throbbing against the full length of him. Taking the lead, he dug his fingers into her fleshy bottom as he began to work his hips clockwise and then counterclockwise.

Jade flicked her tongue out to taste his nipple.

"Ah!" Kaeden gasped loudly.

Jade locked her ankles around his and then rose up to press her hands into his chest. She panted like she was thirsty as she stared down into his face, then she took over and led the ride with small circular motions of her hips. She let out a little moan in the back of her throat with each circle as the strong trunk of his hardness slipped against her throbbing bud.

"Damn, Jade," Kaeden cried out as he felt hot spasms radiate across his abdomen as his climax came on quickly. "Don't make me cum, Jade. Don't make me cum."

Jade ignored him, completely lost to everything but the electricity twirling around them. She bent down, guiding his open mouth to her breasts, and she quickened the pace of her hips. "Cum in me," she demanded.

Kaeden wasn't trying to let this experience end. Not now. He used his hands on her hips to lift her up off his rod with a little pop.

The chill surrounded his inches like a cold glove.

"Get on your knees," he demanded roughly.

Jade eyed him. "Say please," she demanded in return.

Kaeden smiled wolfishly. "Pretty please," he countered in that deep voice of his as he brought his hand up to twist lightly in her short hair. He jerked her head back gently to lick a hot trail up and down her throat.

Jade loved it. She grabbed his chin with one hand and roughly jerked his face up to plunge her tongue deep into his mouth.

"Hmmmmm," Kaeden moaned in pleasure.

Tomorrow she would wonder if the full moon made her crazy to sex a man in the middle of the woods, but tonight she had found her sexual equal in the most unexpected of men.

Jade finally did as he bid, freeing herself from his grasp to get on all fours on the blanket. Kaeden quickly moved to kneel behind her, the tip of his sheathed hardness slapping lightly against her up-turned buttocks. Grabbing the side of her lacy panties, he pulled them with his fist and easily tore them from her body to fling them away.

Jade felt a rush at his aggressiveness. "Slap it," she told him, not even caring that a twig pressed into her knee through the thin blanket.

Kaeden licked the tips of his fingers before he soundly slapped one of her chocolate cheeks, then used his hips to guide his shaft into her swiftly from behind. He released a broken moan.

Jade bit her bottom lip as she quivered. "Kaeden," she cried out, pounding her fist against the grass and dirt.

Kaeden reached up to grab her hair, his arm out-stretched, and slid the other hand around her plush frame to cup one pendulous breast. Pulling her head back slightly by her hair, he worked his hips to send his dick sliding in and out of her wetness like a piston. Back and forth. Swift and strong. He broke a heavy sweat that sent droplets down onto her back and but-tocks like a slow drizzle.

Jade worked her hips in unison with him. One. United. She'd never felt so complete. So whole. As she felt the crescendo of her own white-hot release, tears welled up in her eyes. "Yes. Yes. Yes," she whimpered softly, anxiously awaiting the passionate onslaught.

"Ooh," Kaeden cried out, bending over to rest his forehead against her smooth back as he fought for control. He enjoyed the feel of her fleshy buttocks cupped against him as he brought his hand to her quivering body to slide the length of his middle finger between her moist, thick lips. They cupped his finger as she jerked her hips slowly, sending her bud coursing up and down his finger.

Jade rose to her knees, reaching back to wrap both her arms around Kaeden's neck as she spread her knees wider in front of his. "Kaeden!" she cried out in erotic pleasure as he brought his hand down from her hair to deeply massage her throbbing nipples while he used his other hand to finger her in deep circular motions that sent her spiraling over the edge until she was free-falling into a black abyss of an electrifying climax. "I'm cumming! Don't stop, Kaeden. Don't."

Kaeden buried his face into her neck and deeply bit her neck as she flung her head back on his shoulder and filled the night with her hoarse cries. He continued working his hips, driving his dick up into her as she delivered small, tight clasping pumps that sent him free-falling behind her. He let his own head fall back and opened his mouth to let out a roar that shook the very trees that surrounded them.

Long after, they lay clutching each other as they still trembled in the aftermath of it all, both shaken and moved beyond words.

Never had both felt so sated.

Chapter 9

Jade was the first to stir awake. She was lying atop Kaeden, her head on his shoulder with his arms wrapped snugly around her beneath the blanket they shared. She kept her eyes closed and allowed herself to relish the moment as she inhaled deeply of his scent. It was bittersweet.

She knew once she awakened him and they dressed for their return to civilization, what they shared would officially end. She bit her bottom lip as she finally opened her eyes to the faint orange glow of the sun rising. Last night nothing had mattered. Nothing at all.

In the light of day everything was different. So completely different.

"Morning, Jade."

She allowed herself another few seconds of his warmth before she raised her head to look up at him. "Morning."

His hands shifted from the small of her back to cup her butt. Her skin felt alive and hot where his hand lay. The electricity she would never forget instantly shimmied over her body, along with tiny goose bumps. She felt the length of him stir to life against her stomach.

Not everything is so different.

"How's your head?" she asked, her eyes on the bandage on his forehead as she shifted up from his chest.

Kaeden eased his arms up to lock her into place. "Fine time to ask," he drawled dryly.

That made Jade smile, but she still eased from his embrace to rise to her feet. He placed his arms behind his head as he watched her. Jade tried to cover her breasts and her clean-shaven mound with her hands.

She failed miserably.

"It's a little late for modesty," he mused with the hint of a smile at his lips.

"Kaeden! Jade!"

At the sound of their names being hollered in the distance, Jade quickly gathered up her clothes, ignoring the tenderness of her core. She found her torn panties several feet away. She snatched them up. "We really need to get dressed before the cavalry finds us," she told him, trying to keep things light.

Kaeden sat up and then climbed to his feet atop the blanket.

Jade couldn't help but take a gander at him. She swallowed past a sudden lump in her throat as she eyed the almost literal third leg hanging between his legs. She flushed and fanned herself as she remembered the pleasure that exquisite tool had brought her last night. Turning her back to him, she rushed into her bra and clothes, shoving her torn panties deeply into the front pocket of her jeans.

She felt Kaeden's eyes on her as she quickly rolled up

the blanket to shove back in her backpack. "We really need to get you to a doctor to check you out," she said.

Kaeden slipped on his jeans, leaving them unzipped as he reached out and lightly grabbed Jade. "I didn't prove to you last night that I'm physically fit?" he asked low in his throat.

Jade glanced up at him and then at his bare chest before she shifted her eyes back up to his. "I'm concerned about your head that's above the waist."

Kaeden slid his arms down to stroke the back of her hand. "Last night was good, wasn't it?" he asked her boldly.

Jade ignored the fluttering of her heart. "Last night was last night and this . . . this is today."

Kaeden frowned deeply as he looked down at her. "And that means what, Jade?"

"Kaeden! Jade!" someone hollered from above them.

Jade shifted away from his grasp as she pulled her backpack up onto her shoulders. "We're here," she hollered back.

Kaeden leveled his eyes on her for a long time before he turned and finished dressing. "Why do I feel like I gave you a tune-up?" he snapped.

"Don't act like that, Kaeden, we're both adults."

He snorted as he stepped into his boots. "Act like what? A person who was used for a good fuck?"

"I see them," the voice hollered from above.

Kaeden and Jade both looked up to find Kade looking down at them from the top of the incline.

"You two okay?" he asked.

They both nodded.

"I'm fine. It's just a bump," he said, knowing his older brother's watchful eyes were on his bandaged head.

"Jade, baby, are you all right?"

She stiffened at the sound of Darren's concerned voice. She held her hand over her eyes to block the light from the rising sun as she looked at Darren and Kahron now standing beside Kade.

"Baby?" Kaeden drawled sarcastically.

Jade winced as guilt plagued her. In the midst of the passion, Jade had completely forgotten about Darren or their burgeoning relationship. She never thought she would be one of "those" women, and now two men might be hurt for her actions. "I'm fine, Darren," she said with obvious hesitance.

Kaeden leveled cold eyes on her. "Don't worry, everything is crystal clear for me now," he told her in a hard voice.

Jade started to call out to him but just bit her mouth instead.

Kaeden was definitely in a bad mood. What other man in his position wouldn't be? He frowned as he eyed Jade and Darren at the head of their group, leading them down the trail back to the ranger station at the front of the state park.

The camping trip was over.

And he was clear that he and Jade were over before they even really began.

She had a boyfriend?

Must not be tapping all that right since I had to play the cleanup man last night.

"What's going on with you today?" Kade asked, lagging behind to walk with Kaeden, who was intentionally staying at the back of the pack.

"Nothing," Kaeden answered him shortly.

"Okay, so what happened between you two last night?"

The best sex I ever had while I was used as a dang on maintenance man. "Nothing," Kaeden answered him shortly again.

"Your problems get heavier on your chest when they become your secrets," was all that Kade said before he sped up and left Kaeden alone with his thoughts.

Darren placed his hand on the small of Jade's back and Kaeden's gut clenched in pure jealousy.

Jade eased up from Darren's touch, well aware that Kaeden's eyes were on her. The men had decided to skip the canoeing to get back home and get Kaeden checked out by a doctor. Jade had to admit that she felt waves of relief at that news.

It was completely awkward being in both Kaeden's and Darren's company after last night. After what she and Kaeden shared. That chemistry between them was way bigger than them and it hadn't been about quenching a horny thirst, otherwise Darren would have been blessed with her goodness weeks ago. The way she felt being with Kaeden had been the ultimate.

The ultimate connection.

The ultimate sex high.

The ultimate emotions.

The ultimate everything.

And she hadn't had the strength to fight it.

But she knew what she did last night was wrong. No matter how right it felt.

She glanced over her shoulder and the shoulders of the men to lock eyes with Kaeden as he lagged behind. Sans his glasses, it was clearer to see his fine features and remember the taste of his lips. Her bud double-pumped between her still-sore feminine lips.

He gestured at Darren angrily and then signaled for her to turn around.

Jade did as requested but she knew she had to at least explain that she definitely was not double dipping in the sexual pool.

"Negro, please," Kaeden muttered for the umpteenth time since they'd left the state park two hours ago. He was glad his vision was blurry because he was tired of watching Darren constantly touching Jade during the drive back to civilization.

Several times he caught Jade looking at the rearview mirror. Kaeden knew she was glancing back at him. *Probably scared I'll tell her boyfriend she gave it up last night*, he thought, knowing he was being snide and not really giving a damn.

"I'm sorry you guys didn't get to canoe," Darren said suddenly, turning in the front passenger seat to look back at them.

"Jade said she would reschedule a day trip to make up for it," Kael told him from his seat in the second row of the passenger van.

"Well, I really want my little baby doll here to rest up after that scare she gave me last night," Darren said, looking over at her before he placed his hand snugly on her thigh.

"Trust me, your baby doll got all her rest last night," Kaeden told him. *After that good dicking down I gave her.*

Jade slammed hard on the brakes, sending everyone forward a bit on their seats.

Darren made an odd face as he leveled his eyes on Kaeden briefly.

"Sorry about that, everybody," Jade said with a nervous laugh, her voice skittish.

"You want me to drive?" Darren asked, squeezing her thigh.

Kaeden turned to Kade, who was sitting beside him in the rear of the van. "Who *called* him?" he asked sarcastically, low in his throat.

Kade smiled, flashing his bright white teeth. "Dad thought we should let him know Jade went missing too. Seems like he's cool."

"Humph." Kaeden turned back to look out the window, glad when they pulled into Holtsville's town limits. He was ready to get the hell away from Jade Prince and her business partner/boyfriend.

Before she had even pulled the van to a stop in front of his parents' house, Kaeden had gathered his things and was just waiting for his father and brothers to get out of his way so that he could be free of the van.

As soon as he stepped down onto the ground, Kaeden felt a rush of activity.

"Kaeden, are you okay?"

"What happened to your head?"

"You had us worried sick."

"Thank God you're okay."

The rest of the Strong men stood there with shocked expressions as the women breezed past them to surround Kaeden.

Kael dropped the arms he had open and waiting for his wife to run into. "What the . . ."

"Ain't this a trip?" Kade asked, just shaking his head as he smiled.

Kahron pushed his aviator shades atop his silver head. "We're fine too," he drawled dryly.

Kaleb just laughed as he crossed his strong arms over the wide breadth of his chest.

Kaeden felt bombarded as his mother, sister, and two sisters-in-law each took a turn hugging him close. "I'm okay. I promise," he told them. "Jade took real good care of me. Right, Jade?"

He looked over his shoulder at her still sitting in the driver's seat while Darren helped his family unload their backpacks from the rear of the van.

She locked her eyes with his and some emotion flittered in the mocha depths. "That's right," was all that she softly said.

"That's my Jade," Darren said, walking up to them. *She wasn't your Jade last night.*

"Be sure to see a doctor and get that head injury checked out, Kaeden," Darren told him before easing past them all to open the passenger door of the van. "Y'all have a good day."

Kaeden just stood there watching the van pull away as everyone else waved. *Maybe it was better just having her in my dreams*, he thought, hating that the reality of having her had turned so sour.

"I'm glad that you weren't hurt, Jade. I was so worried about you, baby," Darren said, sliding his hand onto her thigh to squeeze lightly.

Jade started to shift his hand away, but she didn't. Instead she waited, assessing whether his touch could evoke the same electric and immediate response as Kaeden's.

It didn't.

Jade sighed as she steered the van down the long, winding road leading from the Strong ranch. "Where am I dropping you?" she asked.

Darren twisted in his seat to look at her. "Actually, I thought we could go back to your place—or mine— cook dinner, and just chill out," he suggested with a bright smile.

"Oh, Darren, I really am very tired." Jade hoped that would be the end of it. She really wanted to be alone. She had a lot on her mind.

He massaged her thigh again. "I've been up half the night hunting for you, worried that you were hurt."

"Darren—"

"Jade, listen, I'm a patient man, but if you keep putting me off and don't show me you have any real interest in something happening between us, what do you expect me to do?" he asked.

"Darren—"

"Jade, I'm not going to lie. I want you."

Jade pulled to a stop at a stop sign. She gasped

slightly when Darren lightly grabbed her face and turned her so that she was looking at him.

"I want to make love to you," he told her fiercely before leaning in to press his mouth to hers.

Again Jade waited for the sparks. The fire. The electricity.

Nothing. It was nice and sweet. She wasn't at all repulsed. But she wasn't at all feeling the fireworks.

Darren pressed one last quick kiss to her plush mouth and Jade gave him a small smile before she faced forward and drove the van toward Walterboro.

Kaeden hated that thoughts of Darren making love to Jade plagued him for the rest of the day, making him grouchy and irritable. It was good lounging with the entire family and wolfing down some of his mother's home-cooked food, but Kaeden was glad to finally be in his car headed to his town house.

He turned on his XM Satellite Radio to clear his thoughts of those little moans she'd made in the back of her throat when he was sexing her last night.

"I need you to wrap them chocolate legs 'round me . . ."

Vision of Jade's chocolate thighs straddling his hips as she rode him flashed and Kaeden reached out to power off the radio, quickly bringing Eric Benét's song "Chocolate Legs" to an end.

Kaeden released a heavy breath as he turned his BMW into the subdivision. He was just turning the curve into the cul-de-sac when he spotted Felecia's blue Honda parked in front of his house.

Now what? he wondered as he turned onto the asphalt-paved drive.

He climbed out, deciding to leave his backpack in the trunk. He had barely reached the rear of his car when Felecia came rushing toward him.

"What happened to your head, and what's the scratches on your cheek?" she asked in concern, her eyes searching his face. "I knew you shouldn't have went camping."

"I'm okay, Felecia," he told her as she lightly touched his face with her hand. "Did my mom call to tell you I got hurt?"

"No, no. I actually just came by to welcome you home," she said with concern in her eyes. "Oh, Kaeden, do you need anything? Is there anything I can do for you? Just say it."

Kaeden looked down at Felecia, her face filled with concern for him. Waiting on him to return. And although she denied it, he knew she was waiting on him to see that she was the woman for him. A woman who wanted nothing more than to make him happy.

Why chase behind a woman who's willing to cheat on her man?

A woman who ignored you up until last night?

Kaeden pushed aside the pang of hurt he felt at Jade's actions and reached out to wrap one arm around Felecia's waist. He jerked her body close to his and lowered his head to press his mouth down upon hers.

Chapter 10

Brrrnnnggg.

Jade moaned as she rolled over onto her back in the middle of her oh-so-comfy bed with her pink satin eye mask still in place. She sighed. She'd gotten in late last night from a weekend whitewater rafting trip and she had planned to do absolutely nothing all day except sleep—until her phone ringing jarred her awake.

Reaching out blindly, she patted the top of her nightstand until she felt her cordless phone. She snatched it up and hit the large Talk button. "Hello," she said, sounding like a man.

"Rise and shine, Honeybear."

Jade frowned. "Mama?" she asked in surprise.

"Open up. I'm at your front door."

Jade's frown deepened. "Huh?"

The sounding of someone loudly banging on the front door echoed into her bedroom. *Mama.* Jade hung up the cordless before she dropped it back onto the bed.

Jade knew she should be a bit more excited to see her mother, but Deena Rockwell could be so exhausting.

Everything with her was over the top since "The Divorce."

Jade rolled out of bed in her wifebeater T-shirt and striped boy shorts. She snatched off her eye mask as she made her way out of the room and across the living room to the front door. Deena was the anti-Jade. Whereas Jade hated to be looked at as nothing but a sexual object, her mother . . . that was another story.

Jade opened the door.

Deena winked at Jade before she flipped her long, straight jet-black weave over her shoulder, posing in the doorway in her white tube jumpsuit, gold strappy heels, and oversized shades. Jade definitely got her looks and her shapely frame from her mother.

"There's my Honeybear," Deena said, kissing Jade's cheek before she strolled inside the cottage like she was on a runway.

Diva Deena was in the house.

"Hi, Mama." Jade closed the door.

"Come on and wash and throw on a cute outfit. Mother-daughter day." Deena took off her shades before she sat down on Jade's couch and crossed her legs with flair. "I thought we'd go to Savannah for a little shopping and then lunch at the seafood restaurant we both like."

Jade arched a brow and crossed her arms over her chest as she strolled across the room. "No layovers with one of your hot boys? I actually get to spend time with my mother."

Deena pulled her cell phone from her gold clutch purse and proceeded to text someone, using her neon-painted thumbs.

Jade rolled her eyes.

Seven years ago Jade had turned eighteen and her father announced he was divorcing her mother. Later they found out that he ran into the waiting arms and bed of a twenty-year-old he met at his job. Her father leaving wasn't the only change in Jade's young life, because suddenly the woman she knew as her mother disappeared as well. After having a baby at sixteen, getting married at eighteen, and living under the rules of her husband for sixteen years, suddenly Deena Prince had freedom.

Her last name went back to Rockwell.

Her clothes became more fitted and hip.

Her hair was lengthened with an expensive, stylishly cut weave.

Her weekend nights were filled with clubbing.

And her taste in men went from being married to a man twenty years her senior to running through men twenty years her junior—her "hot boys," as she called them.

Deena Rockwell was having *all* of the fun Deena Prince never had.

Jade couldn't recall how many times she'd strolled into a club to find her mother already on the dance floor. Or to have cute guys stroll up to her—to ask if she could hook them up with her mother!

Sometimes, Jade just wanted her mom and not someone who was more like a friend.

Deena snapped her phone shut. "Actually, Hassan canceled, so I'm all yours, Honeybear."

Hassan?

Good Lord.

Jade walked into her bathroom, shutting the door before she undressed and turned on the shower. She busied herself brushing her teeth and cleaning her face as the steam built up in the small room. She studied her reflection, inspecting her unmarried chocolate face. "I am going to have a great day with my mom," she said aloud, placing a huge, bright, and completely fake smile on her pretty round face.

Jade stepped into the shower, inhaling deeply of the steam. Stretching her arms high above her head, she arched her back as she let the spray rain down on her body. She frowned as the fall of the water running down her breasts made the fleshy bud nestled between her lips flutter to life.

Jade's lips pursed. "Ooh."

And that steady thump-thump beat of her core made her think of Kaeden.

"Ooh," Jade sighed again as she recalled the fierceness of his loving as he pulled her hair and rode her from behind.

That night was seared into her memory. She doubted she would ever forget it, no matter how much she wanted to. And she did want to.

Jade adjusted the water so that she could be a bit cooled.

She hadn't seen Kaeden since the trip two weeks ago, and she was more focused on making it work with Darren. They were just perfectly suited for one another. And although she didn't have those sparks with Darren . . . yet, she was sure she would. Okay, she hoped. If they couldn't evoke any passion in a kiss or a caress, how dry would the sex be? Jade shivered at the thought of boring sex.

Truth be told, she had no desire to have sex with Darren, while she was quite sure if Kaeden made half the effort, she would drop her panties in a hot second.

Thump-thump.

"Whoo!" Jade pressed her thighs together to ease the ache.

Jade still hadn't come to the understanding of why on earth Kaeden had attracted her and drawn such passion from her. She couldn't wrap her brain around it. She just knew that they were as different as two people could be.

"No more Kaeden. No more Kaeden. No more Kaeden," she chanted in the same fashion as "I think I can. I think I can. I think I can."

She rushed through her shower, ready to get dressed and into a diversion from the erotic memories that plagued her. She whipped back the curtain and stepped down onto the plush carpet.

She quickly sprayed her damp body with her own mix of baby oil and lemon, orange, and bergamot essential oils. She massaged them in before she towel blotted her skin. It was a trick to help ease the dry tendency of her skin. She just loved for her deep mocha skin to gleam, and gleam it did.

Jade scooped her dirty clothes into the wicker hamper near the tub before she loosely draped the towel around her body and opened the door, releasing the steam in a dozen swirls ahead of her.

"Darren's here."

Jade whirled before she could catch herself, and the

ends of her towel briefly flew up around her. She could tell from the way his eyes dipped that he had caught quite a peek. "Hey . . . Darren. I'll be right back."

Jade closed her bedroom door and rushed around her room grabbing things until she was able to quickly jump into a lace thong and a flowing cotton maxi dress that was strapless and a brilliant shade of white. She barely put on mascara, topped her lips with a pale lip gloss, and slipped on a pair of leather flip-flops before she flew back out of the room.

She made a face at her mother and Darren, who were both laughing like crazy. *Is she telling him all my business*, she wondered.

"What's so funny?" she asked, her eyes darting from him to her.

Deena opened her purse and pulled out a pack of cigarettes. "He was just saying he can't believe I'm your mother."

"Ha . . . ha . . . ha," Jade drawled as she took the pack of cigarettes from her mother's hand. "Now you smoke? What's next? A blunt?"

Deena waved her hand dismissively.

Darren rose up to his feet to lean over and kiss her cheek. "You look beautiful as always, baby," he whispered near her ear.

"I know," she teased, cutting her eyes up at him with a smile.

"We were just headed to Savannah," Deena said, rising to her feet. "Join us. That way I can check out my daughter's man and *all* of that."

"I wish I could, but I have a few errands to run,"

Darren said, stepping past Deena to slide his arm around Jade's waist.

Deena slid her shades back in place and slid her purse under her arm. "Finish up your errands and meet us at the Comfort Zone at eight. Bye, Darren," she said in a little singsong fashion before she sailed out the door.

"Guess I'll see you at eight," Darren quipped before he pulled Jade's soft body to his and squatted down to level his eyes with hers.

Jade wrapped her arms around his neck, tilting her head to the side as she looked back at him with smiling eyes. "I guess we will."

Darren kissed her warmly. "And how long before I see all of you?" he asked as he nuzzled his face against her neck. "Second base was nice the other night, but I'm ready to slide into home."

Jade fought not to frown as she tilted her head back, forever searching for that spark with him. Forever searching and forever coming up empty. She looked into his eyes. "Soon," she promised him . . . and herself.

Darren is the man you are trying to build something with. It's time. Take the lid off the cookie jar. You didn't even know Kaeden's home number or address and he got all up in it . . . in the woods.

Jade shook her head to clear it of her thoughts. "My mom's waiting."

"I gotta run anyway. See you tonight."

She waved him off and grabbed her purse as he left her cottage. "Maybe I should just give him some," she thought as she walked out the door, locking it behind her.

She walked around her mom's cherry red convertible

to climb into the bucket passenger seat. "Mama, you can't order people around like that."

Deena looked at her over the rim of her shades. "When it comes to men, they always do what I tell them to do. Look, listen, and learn, Honeybear. Look, listen, and learn."

Kaeden parked his BMW in front of his parents' house, grabbing the leather Coach briefcase from the passenger seat before he hopped out. He straightened his tie before he slid on his shades and made his way to the barn. The closer he got to it, the more the customary smell of farms surrounded him. He'd smelt worse.

Kade and his father were strict with keeping the farm and its animals clean. As long as Kaeden could remember, his father had raised grazing livestock and used the irrigated area on the land for growing hay and feed grain to feed the cattle and horses. Like their father, Kahron had started his own cattle ranch and Kaleb had ventured off into dairy farming. Now his father was semi-retired and Kade ran the Strong ranch.

He waved to the ranch hands he passed. His father walked out of the barn leading Kaitlyn's all-white stallion, Snowflake, behind him. "Hey there, son," Kael greeted him in his deep voice before he handed the reins over to one of the hands.

"Evenin', Pops. Where's Kade? I have the payroll checks for him to sign." Kaeden frowned as Snowflake unloaded his digested hay and twirled his tail. The smothered pork chops that Felecia fixed for him for lunch got upset in his stomach.

"Kade should be on his way back from town. He rode with Kaleb." Kael accepted the envelope Kaeden took from his briefcase.

"You know you still can sign them."

Kael shook his head. "Nope, not gone step on my son's toes. He'll handle it when he gets back. You staying for dinner?"

Kaeden shook his head. "Nah, I have plans."

"With Felecia?"

Kaeden nodded.

"Hmm." Kael leveled wise eyes on his son. "Think it's gonna work this time?"

Good question. Kaeden shrugged. "Working on it," he said. "She's a good girl."

"You should bring her over some time and let the family meet her," Kael suggested, stooping down to scratch behind the ears of one of the dozen dogs on the ranch.

Kaeden frowned as he shifted his new pair of spectacles on his face. "I don't know if we're to that point yet."

"Hmm."

Bzzzz.

Kaeden snatched his BlackBerry from the holster on his hip. "Hello."

"Hi, sweetie. Where are you?"

Kaeden cut his eyes at his father briefly before he turned his back to him. "I'm at my parents'."

"Oh, I didn't know you were headed there," Felecia said. "Something wrong?"

Kaeden walked a few feet away from his father. "No, I brought the payroll checks for Kade to sign."

"Oh, that's right," she said with saccharine sweetness.

"Tell your mama I said thank you for her recipe for homemade chicken pot pie. She said it was your favorite, so I'm making it tonight."

Kaeden frowned deeply. "You spoke to my mom?" he asked in surprise.

"Yes, I called her today."

"Oh."

"I just wanted to make sure I cooked your favorite meal. Is that okay?"

"No, no, that's fine." Kaeden rolled his shoulders to try and ease the tight tension he felt.

"Well, I closed the office and headed home to start dinner. You're coming straight to my house now or . . ."

Kaeden's rolling motions got bigger. "Yeah. I'll see you in a bit."

"Okay, bye."

Kaeden slipped the device back in its holster as he turned and walked back across the dirt to his father. He raised his glasses to massage the bridge of his nose.

Kael cut his eyes up to Kaeden. "Think it's gonna work this time?" he asked again.

"See you later, Dad," Kaeden called over his shoulder, ignoring his father's chuckle as he started to walk back to the house.

After stopping in quickly to speak to his mom, Kaeden headed out to Felecia's apartment in North Charleston. He was starving and actually looking forward to a good home-cooked meal and just hanging out with Felecia.

Over the last two weeks he was beginning to feel that being with Felecia wasn't just an impulsive, knee-jerk reaction to Jade. He and Felecia were more suited to one another. The thing between him and Jade—that crazy explosive shot of chemistry—was good for the fling they had but would have fizzled out since they had nothing else in common.

Truth? He'd actually thought that he would walk out of those woods with Jade as his woman, and it hurt him that she didn't want the same thing.

But now in hindsight he was all 20/20 that she was right, especially since she already had a man. How could he trust her anyway, especially since he knew that men flocked to her in droves begging for her number, wanting to holler, wanting to claim her as their own?

Wanting to see that gloriously lush body of hers in nothing but a lace thong.

Wanting to have her astride them.

Riding.

Licking.

Biting.

Moaning.

Cumming.

Over and over and over again.

Kaeden's hand tightened on the wheel as he felt his nature rise at the thought of her. "Down, boy," he drawled, not wanting to want her anymore. Mentally the thrill was gone for him. Now he just had to get his body to play catch-up with the updated status.

Right now he was going to give Felecia a chance. That undeniable spark or flame or chemistry—or *whatever*—had yet to show up, but they had other things. More stable things. She was a good churchgoing, home-cooking, typical Southern gal who catered to her man.

He knew that tonight she would greet him at the door in a pretty dress—in heels—with a drink ready for him in her hand and a pleasant, welcoming smile on her face. And from the door everything she did would be about him.

Kaeden settled down in his seat and pressed the gas a bit. In twenty minutes he was pulling his Beamer into a parking spot in front of Felecia's apartment building. He removed his tie, throwing it onto the backseat before he climbed out of the vehicle and walked up the short paved walkway to her front door.

He barely raised his hand to knock before the door swung open. Felecia stepped forward, looking pretty in the print strapless maxi dress she'd changed into. "Hey, baby," she said softly with a smile before handing him a frosted glass of ice tea with a sweet kiss to his lips.

Just like he expected.

Kaeden pushed aside any second-guessing of their relationship as he walked into the apartment and let Felecia firmly shut the door behind him.

Nestled in one of the booths in the front of the Comfort Zone, Jade smiled across the table at Darren. "Let's dance," she told him softly, swaying to the sounds of classic R&B.

Darren rose to his feet and held his hand out to her.

Jade let him lead her to the dance floor at the back of the club. She just laughed at her mama dancing with her latest hot boys recruit, a tall and muscular man of about twenty-five. She didn't really like partying with her mother—that was rule #1 for her once her mother showed up on the club scene—but the Comfort Zone was laid back and Jade was actually having a good time with Darren.

Jade turned her back to him and was surprised when Darren stepped up and pressed the length of his body against hers. She rocked her hips side to side and let her head fall back against his chest.

She hated the way several of the men sat watching her movements like vultures checking for roadkill. Rolling her eyes before she closed them, she ignored their leers.

Darren put his hands on her hips.

Jade brought her arms up to wrap around his neck. . . .

He brought his hand down from her hair to deeply massage her throbbing nipples as he used his other hand to finger her in deep circular motions that sent her spiraling over the edge until she was free-falling into a black abyss of an electrifying climax. "I'm cumming! Don't stop, Kaeden. Don't."

Jade jerked her eyes open as her body flushed in sweet pleasure at the heated memory. Even in Darren's arms, the memory of Kaeden could not be stopped.

The madness had to stop.

Turning in Darren's arms, she caressed his face. "You know, I saw a nice bed-and-breakfast in the historic district of Savannah today," she told him. "Maybe it's time for a weekend getaway."

"Now, that's what's up," he told her with a big grin.

Chapter 11

Jade was thankful for a slow week as she unlocked the rear entrance to their small three-room office on Main Street in Walterboro. She had just come from a quick workout at the gym, showered, and now she was energized to actually work on getting their files out of labeled cardboard boxes and into the file cabinets lined against the wood-paneled wall.

She removed her shades as she set her oversized turquoise tote on the empty desk in the reception area and walked across the room to turn on the lights. "Be nice if we *had* a receptionist," she said into the silence, raking her fingers through the long swooped bangs of her short jet-black hairdo.

Jade had just turned the radio to 99.7FM for her *Steve Harvey Morning Show* fix when she looked up and saw Kaeden's vehicle slow down as it turned into the parking lot of the brick post office.

Her heart slammed against her chest.

It had been nearly a month since the camping trip, and she had barely seen him since. After church, he was one of the first to leave and he would be gone by the time she stepped outside the church doors. She bit her lips as she rose from the office chair and walked to the large window to watch as he climbed out of the dependable but still luxury vehicle.

He's gotten new glasses, she thought, her heart pounding as he strode into the post office in his shirt, tie, and slacks.

Jade pressed her fingertips to her chest as she fought the immediate urge to go to him. Maybe a part of her moving on from that night was not just her and Darren's trip to Savannah next weekend, but to talk to Kaeden.

And in truth, she wanted to see him and at least set things straight.

Following an urge, she walked out of the building. She checked the one-way street for oncoming traffic before she crossed. Her nerves were in a riot and she was scared her heart would literally burst through her chest, but Jade forged ahead.

Kaeden was just walking out of the building as she neared his vehicle. His steps visibly paused as he sighted her. Jade could see the surprise on his face, but she also saw when the surprise quickly changed to irritation.

"Is that necessary, Kaeden?" she snapped.

He shook his keys in his hand as he came to a stop in front of her. "What?"

"The look on your damn face," she snapped again, her eyes flashing. "I just wanted to get things straight between us and you looking at me like I'm bird shit on your windshield."

Beep-beep.

Kaeden deactivated his alarm as he stepped past her to open his car door. "Trust me, you already got me straight," he told her coldly.

Jade grabbed his arm. "Why are you so mad at me?" she asked.

Kaeden turned his head to look down at her through his spectacles. "Because there is more to me than *dick.* You should understand that since there is more to you than tits and ass, right?" he asked, flinging her own words back at her.

Jade flushed with guilt. "Do you have to be so crass, Kaeden? I would've thought that was beneath you."

Kaeden laughed bitterly. "And I would've thought sleeping with two men *shoulda* been beneath you. What's wrong? He ain't tapping that thing right?" he asked her coldly.

Jade fought the urge to slap the hell out of him as his words cut her like a knife. "You know what, you bullheaded, arrogant asshole? Just forget *it* and forget *you,*" she told him before turning away.

"You did that as soon as old boy showed up," he shot at her.

Jade whirled back to face him. "This has nothing to do with him, Kaeden," she told him.

Kaeden stiffened as his eyes shifted behind her. "Then why is he headed this way?"

Jade whirled and her eyes widened to see Darren strolling over to them. *What the hell does he want?* she thought, aggravated at his oncoming intrusion.

"Mornin', baby," he said, stepping up to slide his hand onto Jade's back with his eyes on Kaeden.

"Listen, Darren, could you excuse us for a minute?" she asked, hating his increasing shows of possessiveness.

"No need for that, playa, we're done. Trust me." Kaeden opened his car door with one last long look at Jade before he climbed in. Soon the car purred to life.

"Were you two arguing? It looked like you two were arguing," Darren asked as Kaeden reversed the car out of his spot, threw up a deuce sign, and then drove out of the parking lot. "What was that all about?"

"Just a misunderstanding I was trying to get straight," Jade admitted.

"About the camping trip?" he asked in obvious confusion.

A hundred different steamy flashes of a moonlit rendezvous in the middle of the woods bombarded her.

"Yes, about the trip," she said in half-truth. "Everything's fine, Darren."

They walked back to their office in silence, but Jade could tell that he had more questions. Thankfully he left them unasked.

Kaeden watched Jade in his rearview mirror until he turned the corner and erased her from his line of vision. The woman was effortlessly beautiful . . . but she was not his woman. She was in a relationship with someone else and so was he.

It was for the best anyway.

But was it?

Kaeden knew he hadn't half the female conquests of any of his brothers, but he wasn't a slouch either.

Since high school he always had a steady girlfriend while his brothers played the hell out of the field. There was Keesha in eighth grade. July in the tenth. Mickala in the eleventh. Keesha again in the twelfth. Then Farrah during the college years and Jennifer in graduate school.

He'd had sex with them all and a few more. None compared to that one sizzling night with Jade. Not separately or totally.

Tapping his fingers against the steering wheel, Kaeden steered his vehicle toward his offices across town. His BlackBerry vibrated on his hip and he grabbed it.

"Kaeden Strong,"

"Kaeden, where are you?" Felecia asked.

"On my way to the office. What's up?" he asked in return.

"Nothing. Just hadn't heard from you this morning, that's all. I'm at the office."

Kaeden frowned. "Felecia, listen, I don't need you to check up on me like this. I'm fine. Believe me."

"I know you're fine," she said with a laugh that sounded forced. "I've been calling you and leaving messages all morning."

Kaeden's jaw tensed in irritation as he accelerated forward. First Jade running up on him with the drama, and now Felecia and her third degree. Rolling his shoulders, Kaeden felt tension race from his shoulders to the back of his head. His eyes lit on the turn for Highway 17. "I'm headed down to Kahron's. I'll be in later," he told her.

Their was silence on the line before she reluctantly said, "Okay, Kaeden."

He really needed a little piece of peace right now.

He made the turn toward Holtsville and didn't stop until he was pulling in front of Kahron and Bianca's house. Kade and Kahron were sitting on the porch with frosted glasses of lemonade in their hands.

"What's up, bubbas?" he greeted them, using the common Southern nickname for "brother." Kaeden immediately felt his tension ease being in the company of his brothers.

"We just got back from the auction. What's up with you?" Kade asked before taking a deep sip of his drink.

"Wishing *I* had a big old glass of lemonade," he joked as he climbed the stairs and soon felt the cool shade under the roof of the porch.

Kahron jumped to his feet. "You lucky I have to go inside," he told him before walking into the sizable ranch-style home.

Kaeden let out a long breath as he dropped down into one of the rocking chairs. "Man, it's gonna be a hot summer."

Kade nodded as he squinted his eyes. "Especially trapped in a relationship you don't want to be in," Kade slid out with ease—and far too much wisdom.

Kaeden leaned to the side to eye his older brother through his glasses. "You and Garcelle having troubles?" he asked without one bit of seriousness.

"Picture *that* shit," Kade drawled dryly.

Kaeden fell silent.

"I saw you and Jade that morning."

Kaeden's gut clenched.

Kade leaned over to sit his glass down beside him before he ran the long fingers of his strong hand through his full silver curls. "I found you guys and saw . . . you know . . . you . . . and, um, Jade doing the Adam and Eve thing. So I walked away and *then* I called out for you two. You know . . . I gave you guys a chance to find your clothes and ripped underwear and all that."

"Oh," was all that Kaeden said as the hot memory of him ripping those lace panties from her made his dick throb with sudden life.

"So it's funny to me, little brother, that Jade's boyfriend strolls up almost catching you two and then you take up with Felecia the next day."

The same night, actually.

"Felecia and I haven't slept together."

Kade frowned. "Look, man, I didn't ask for all your business," he snapped.

Kaeden chuckled.

"What the hell is going on?" Kade asked, turning his head to look at Kaeden.

"Nothing. With Jade and me, things got out of hand for one night, and Felecia and I are building something more lasting, you know," Kaeden said.

The words sounded hollow to his own ears.

"First off, you don't do one-night stands. Second off, *you* barely wanted to hire Felecia because *you* broke up with Felecia because *you* didn't want to date Felecia."

True. Kaeden just released a heavy breath.

"Just be careful with playing with people's hearts,

little brother." Kade reached down for his lemonade. "You rebounded to her because you mad or hurt or whatever about Jade having a man. So if Jade didn't have a man and she was wide open for more Strong loving on the regular, you wouldn't pick her over Felecia. Come on, man."

Kaeden shifted his eyes away from his brother and the truth.

"Felecia is a good girl. Jade has a man. Jade and I don't have anything in common but something physical," Kaeden said, listing his argument, annoyed that the very thought of Jade made him feel alive.

"Don't settle. Felecia is a pretty girl. A good girl. But you can have the fireworks and the good girl wrapped all up in one. I have it with Garcelle and Kahron has it with Bianca."

"Felecia is a good match for me," Kaeden insisted.

"Man, Felecia is the type of girl to go all in," Kade advised him. "At least sit back and make sure you're ready for that. Don't lead her on."

Kaeden leaned forward to rest his elbows on his knees as he stared off into the distance at Kahron's farmland.

"You're not *that* guy, Kaeden." Kade finished the last of his lemonade in one gulp.

Kaeden spent the rest of the afternoon with his brothers and his inhaler. He'd left his BlackBerry in his car and wasn't at all surprised to see a dozen missed calls from Felecia when he finally got back to his vehicle.

He called the office, but when there wasn't an answer he tried her cell phone.

"Kaeden," she said in a disappointed tone.

He felt like a child being chastised by a teacher. *Or a child being checked by my mama.*

"I'm headed back to the office now."

"Actually, just come on to my house."

She closed the office early again? he thought. Felecia had been taking a lot of liberties at work since they started dating.

"I already fixed dinner," she told him.

Kaeden really just wanted to go home and chill out for the night. Kade had put a lot on his mind to think about, but he knew if he was serious about building a relationship with Felecia then he had to put in the time and the effort to make it work. "I'm on my way," he told her, turning his car around in the dirt yard of Cyrus Dobbs's one-pump gas station to head toward Summerville. His mind was set on getting there, eating, and then jetting back to his own house. He wanted to get home but he also wanted to talk to Felecia and make sure they were on the same page about their relationship. Slow and steady *might* win the race.

In truth, the memory of Jade was affecting his relationship with Felecia.

Or maybe just revealing the flaws in it.

In about twenty-five minutes he was pulling up to the front of Felecia's apartment building. The curtains and blinds of her first-floor apartment were open. As he climbed out of his car, his eyes locked on the sight of Felecia moving about her living room.

She looked nice in the ruffled white shirt she wore with darn denim slacks.

He walked to the door and just as he knocked, she opened the door.

"Hey, Kaeden," she said with a smile as she handed him a frosted glass of sweet tea.

But Kaeden nearly let the glass slip through his fingers as he eyed the dozen or so people walking out of the kitchen to greet him.

What the hell?

Felecia wrapped both her arms around him and pulled him in. "My family really wanted to meet you," she whispered in his ear, just before a circle was formed around them.

Kaeden couldn't do anything but force a smile.

Chapter 12

The moon was full and so large that it seemed a child could reach, grab, and hug it close to their chest. It was perfectly framed by the dark shadowy outline of the tips of the towering trees and the brilliant sparkles of stars. Definitely a beautiful scene.

But Jade Prince saw none of its grandeur as she tossed, turned, writhed, and moaned in the middle of her bed . . . deeply in sleep . . . and completely aroused.

Jade slid her hand down the length of the leather thigh-high boot she wore after she slowly pulled up the zipper. She placed her hands on her bare hips as she stood tall at the foot of the black satin-covered bed in the center of the woods. Surrounded by the sounds of night and nature, she eased her hands over the smooth, deep mocha of her nude body.

Lying in the center of the bed with his hands and feet lightly strapped with torn cloth,

Kaeden's hungry eyes missed not one single sensual movement.

The slight jiggle of her breasts as she massaged them.

The way her nipples hardened as she teased them.

The goose bumps racing over her curvaceous frame.

The sight of her hands easing over her wide hips and the tops of her shapely thighs.

He had to lean his head a bit to the left to see past his growing erection as it stretched and reached for the night sky.

"See something you like?" Jade asked with a purr as she pressed one foot onto the end of the bed and then used her hand to press her knee back, opening herself to him. With a lick of her lips, she ran her finger across her intimate lips before opening them to expose her core.

"Hell yeah," Kaeden told her, then licked his bottom lip as he wrapped his hand around his shaft and stroked the length of it before he massaged the smooth, thick tip.

Jade laughed softly as she walked around the bed to stand by his side. "You are blessed, Kaeden," she told him as she eyed his hardness and licked her lips as if hungry.

She reached out slowly and stroked Kaeden's thigh. It quivered.

She shifted up until his maleness was in her hands. It stiffened at her touch.

She grabbed him just a bit tighter around the

base and she knew he liked it as his eyes glazed over. "This is mine," she told him with just enough force in her voice to make it interesting.

"Then get what's yours," he ordered her as he lifted his hips to pump his dick inside her fist.

Jade spread her legs and bent down slowly until her open and panting mouth was just above the heated, throbbing tip of his dick. She inhaled deeply of his unique scent before easing the smooth tip against her lips. "Hmm," she moaned as she kept her eyes locked with his.

"Suck it," he ordered thickly.

Jade shook her head and licked it slowly instead, enjoying the smooth feel of it against the tip of her tongue as she enjoyed it like a treat. "Say please," she demanded huskily, enjoying the thrill of their play.

"Please," he begged shakily.

And with a moan she did, slowly taking the thick and lengthy hardness of him until his silvery hairs tickled her lips.

"Aaah!" Kaeden hollered out as his body arched, only his bound limbs keeping him from fully springing up off the bed.

Jade smiled around the width of him as she worked her head up and down. She circled her tongue around the tip before sucking it deeply between her pressed lips.

"Shit," Kaeden swore, tugging at his bonds.

Jade reached down to press her fingers against her own moist bud.

Kaeden watched the move and he gasped in

pure pleasure as her hips jerked. "Untie me," he told her forcefully.

Jade shook her head and deep throated him again.

"Ahhhh!" he cried out, closing his eyes tightly as his muscles tensed as he fought to break the ties.

And they did break.

First the left and then the right.

Kaeden sat up and swiftly picked Jade up by her hips.

She shifted her hands from her slickly wet bud and roughly pushed them against his lips. His head shifted to the right as he captured her moist fingers with his mouth and sucked the juice from them. "Mmm," he moaned, closing his eyes.

Jade straddled his hips, his shiny hardness standing straight up and ready for Kaeden to arch up and fill her in one swift thrust.

"Ahhh!" they cried out.

"Yes, Kaeden. Yes . . . yes . . . yes. . . ."

"Yes. Yes." Jade stirred in her sleep. Her head thrashed back and forth on the pillow as her heart beat furiously and her clit throbbed with a life force all its own. "Get it, Kaeden—"

She gasped. Her eyes popped open. She panted through her open mouth. A fine layer of sweat covered her entire body. Her short nightie was up around her waist. Her panties were shoved to the side . . . and her hands were pressed intimately between her legs.

Jade released a heavy breath as she closed her eyes and shook her head at herself. "Good grief," she muttered, rolling out of bed like she'd discovered a snake beneath the covers.

Why was that one night with Kaeden Strong haunting and taunting her?

The sun was just starting to break through the trees and Jade wished she had a tour or some work to do. There was no way she could sit around her little cottage with nothing but hot memories of Kaeden and one night in the forest. She rushed through a shower, threw on running shorts, a tank, and her sneakers. She went out the door jogging and she didn't stop until she jogged around the long, winding curve to her grandfather's.

I just hope he didn't go fishing, she thought, finally slowing down to a walk as she made her way up the paved driveway to his house.

She smiled to find Esai in the large garden in the backyard. The rows and rows were filled with fruits, vegetables, and plenty of herbs—to cook and to use for his herbal remedies. "Hey there, old man," she said as she walked up to him.

Esai rose to his full height and brushed some of the dirt from his hands on the front of his jeans. "Just who I wanted to see," he said, bending down a bit so that she could give him the customary kiss on the cheek. He called it his own little blessing from an angel.

Jade loved her grandfather to pieces.

"You needed something?" she asked as he moved over to the rinse sink at the rear of the house.

"Nope, I just wanted to see you," he told her with a hint of a smile as he cast her a sidelong glance.

Jade wrapped her arms around herself and watched

him rinse the vegetables in the basket. "I wanted to see you too," she told him when he walked up to her. She wrapped her free hand around his arm as they made their way toward the large wraparound porch. She thought of Kaeden and her face became pensive as she bit her bottom lip. She thought of the dream that sent her running to the safety of her grandfather.

Mmmm . . .

She tripped over her own steps at the sound of her moaning in pleasure echoing inside her head. Her dreams were still chasing her down.

"Something on your mind?" her grandfather asked.

Mmmm . . .

Jade shook her head to clear it. "No, nothing. Well, not really. Kinda. Sorta."

Esai laughed. "Come on. Get it together."

Jade followed him up the steps. *What do I say? I'm dating one guy and feigning for another?* She released a heavy sigh. "It's nothing. I'll work it all out in my head."

Esai leveled his eyes on her before he sat down in one of the rocking chairs and started peeling a tomato with a pocket knife. "The best advice I can give you— even though you're not asking—is honesty is the best policy. Whatever it is, stay honest to your feelings and you can't go wrong deciding what to do."

Jade reached down into the basket and pulled out a long and thick cucumber that was ridiculously similar to Kaeden's . . . *attribute*. Even down to the curve. The bud between her legs swelled with life. *Kaeden* really *is blessed*.

Really.

Mmmm . . .

Jade's mouth opened a bit as she looked down at the phallic vegetable in her hand. *And the things he did to me with that blessing. Have mercy. . . .*

"You hear me, Jade?" he asked.

Jade looked up at him with eyes glazed over from the heated memory and a desire to relive it . . . again . . . and again . . . and again. "Huh?" she asked, completely lost in the heated thoughts.

Her grandfather's eyes squinted as he looked at her. "Something going on between you and Darren?" Esai asked.

Not something. Someone. His name is Kaeden, she thought as she forced a smile to her face. "Nothing I can't handle, Grandpa."

They fell silent as she dropped the cucumber back into the basket and pulled out a tomato for her grandfather to peel for her. "Why don't I cook?" Jade offered, wanting to change the subject. She rose to her feet. "You feel like some grits?"

"That boy likes you more than you like him, Jade," Esai said simply before easing a slice of tomato into his open mouth.

Jade paused in the doorway. *Say what? Say who?* She turned and looked down at her grandfather calmly eating his tomato.

"You have him 'round here behind you like a lapdog," he added for good measure.

"Grandpa, that's not true," Jade protested . . . half-heartedly.

"Sometimes friends should not become lovers."

"We're not lovers," she protested instantly.

"Surprise, surprise," he drawled.

Jade opened her mouth and then closed it, before she turned and walked into the house. As she made her way to the kitchen, she thought about how easy it had been for her to be with Kaeden when she had known Darren for years and dated him for a few weeks.

Kaeden? Lid off the cookie jar quicker than the snap of fingers.

Darren? Cookie jar closed. And tight too.

Her grandfather said that honesty was the best policy—whether with herself or someone else. She knew he was right. It was time for some honest reflection. It was time to deal with her attraction for Kaeden Strong once and for all.

As she pulled eggs and bacon from the fridge, her cell phone vibrated against her hip. She grabbed it and flipped it open in one fluid motion. "Hello."

"Hey, Jade. Listen, I need to talk to you."

She paused in placing the food on the counter. "I'm at my grandfather's. Can this wait?" she asked.

"No."

Jade closed her eyes and used her now-cold fingertips to squeeze the bridge of her nose. "Darren—"

"I'm sitting in your yard," he told her, his voice hard.

"A phone call first would have been nice," she snapped, annoyed at his attitude.

"Well, I'm calling now," he snapped back.

"Negro, have you lost your mind talking to me like that?"

Silence.

"Listen, Jade, it's important, okay? Could you just come down here and let's talk."

"Fine, Darren, I'm on my way." She closed the phone and released a deep breath.

Jade left the house. "Can I hold your pickup, Grandpa? I'll be right back," she told him not even waiting on an answer as she flew past him and jogged down the stairs to hop into his navy Ford F150.

As she drove the short distance around the curve toward her cottage, Jade knew that this conversation was about Kaeden. She just knew it.

He was leaning against his truck parked off to the side in her front yard as she turned her grandfather's truck in. She kept her eyes on him as she hopped out and walked over to him. "Morning," she greeted him as she squinted her almond-shaped eyes against the sun.

Darren shoved his hands into the front pockets of his jeans as he looked down at her. "What happened between you and Kaeden that night?"

Straight. No chaser.

Jade jiggled her keys in her hand. "You want to go inside?" she asked as she turned from him.

"What happened with you and Kaeden that night, Jade?" he asked again.

She turned to face him. "You don't have any right to question me, Darren," she told him in a soft but firm voice.

The look on his face was incredulous. "I have every damn right."

Jade shook her head slowly. "No. No, you don't. Are we married? Are we . . . engaged? Are we exclusive? That's a no, a no, and another no."

"I haven't been seeing anyone else, Jade," he yelled.

Jade took a step back and looked at him like he was

crazy. "I never asked you to do that, Darren. We were just dating, hanging out, chilling, spending time."

"About to go to Savannah and share a room," he added sarcastically as he pushed up off the truck.

"Exactly. We were about to go to the next level but hadn't *yet*, Darren. You just proved my point that you don't have any right to question me."

"What happened that night?" he asked.

Jade released a heavy breath.

"What happened that night?" he asked again, taking a step forward to tower over her.

Honesty is the best policy, Jade.

Not this time Grandpa, she thought, pushing aside his advice. "Darren, just go home," she told him, turning to walk away from him.

She felt the sudden grip of his hand on her arm and she turned to eye first his offending hand and then his eyes. "Get your hands off me, Darren," she told him in a tone that could freeze water.

"Did you sleep with him that night, Jade?" he volleyed, just as coldly.

Jade snatched away from his grasp. "Leave, Darren."

"Yes or no. It's simple."

Although Jade knew she'd done nothing wrong, she still felt guilt flush over her. The look on his face changed from angry to incredulous and she knew something that hinted at the truth shone through in her eyes. She reached out to touch his arm. "Darren—"

It was his turn to snatch away from her. "So I'm 'round here with the dry dick syndrome and you giving it up to some fool in the woods? *That's* how you get down?"

Jade stiffened. "Don't disrespect me, Darren."

He laughed bitterly. "You full of shit," he muttered before he turned and stormed back to his truck.

"Darren," she called out.

Seconds later dirt and pebbles flew as he reversed his truck out of the yard.

Chapter 13

A light breeze from the open window at the end of the hall blew across Kaeden's tall, naked form as he stepped up to the closed door. The sign read:

WELCOME TO PARADISE

Kaeden was more than ready.

He opened the door and his hard and lengthy erection led him inside. He was instantly surrounded by the heady scent of the millions of flowers covering the walls, ceiling, and floors. Nestled among the flowers were plump candles offering a soft glow. And there in the center of it, lying on a bed made entirely of flower petals, was Jade. His Jade.

Divinely nude. Gloriously seductive.

His spectacle-free eyes missed not one detail. Nothing. Smooth deep brown skin. Plump full breasts with her dark and wide nipples pointed to the ceiling. Endless curves. Long legs. Wide hips. And a smile that was taunting and tempting all at once.

Kaeden shook his head to clear it as he felt her allure draw him closer, the softness of the flowers' petals cushioning his feet. "You have something for me?" he asked as he wrapped his hands around his shaft and massaged the length of it.

Jade's smile widened as she slowly spread her legs and exposed her own flower to him with the throbbing bud nestled deeply. "It's all for you . . . and only you, Kaeden," she answered him dreamily.

He licked his lips before he reached down and grabbed her ankles. "Then give it to me," he demanded, pulling her to the end of the bed to spread her core out for him like a buffet.

He was ravenous.

Jade kept her eyes locked on his as she shifted her hand down her svelte body and used her fingertips to lightly pat her moist lips before she spread them to expose the fleshy and throbbing bud like a blossoming flower. "Go'on get it."

Kaeden felt weakened. He dropped to his knees and pressed his face to her thigh to inhale deeply of her intoxicating womanly scent. A deep moan of pleasure and want came from the back of his throat as he dipped his head and licked a trail from her buttocks to her core, where he twirled his tongue deep inside her, enjoying the feel of her tight ridges and grooves.

Jade gasped hotly and sat up as she pressed her hands to his silver-flecked head. When he shifted his clever mouth up to suck her bud, she trembled visibly, her fingers digging deeply into his broad shoulders as she cried out and arched her back.

Kaeden felt a rush as he closed his arms around her thighs and locked her into place. At his will. A prisoner to his passion. A willing prisoner.

"Suck it," she demanded hoarsely as she felt the heat of her desire warm her feet and rise to the pit of her belly.

He moaned as he opened his mouth wide and sucked her like he was thirsty.

Jade squeezed her eyes shut as she felt the familiar and sweet anxiousness flood over her body . . . wanting, craving, needing the release. "Yes," she moaned as she bit her bottom lip and panted for air. "Yes."

Kaeden looked up and pulled his head back just enough to release his tongue and flick the tip quickly against her bud.

Tears filled Jade's eyes. Her hands balled into fists and pounded his back, then splayed against it to stroke him. She didn't know whether to hate him or adore him for the sweet torture he wrought on her.

"I'm cumming," she cried out brokenly. "I'm cumming."

The room spun.

She felt dizzy.

Her heart pounded wildly.

Her pulse raced.

Her body trembled.

Sweat covered her body in a fine sheen that made her body glow against the candlelight.

She was lost to everything but that moment.

Kaeden felt his dick harden and lengthen against his belly as he watched the pleasure he gave her render her weak and trembling while her juices exploded against his tongue and nourished his soul.

She bucked against his mouth. He sucked harder.

She beat him about his shoulders and head. He licked her bud with the tip of his tongue again.

She tried to fight from the tight grasp of his arms. He held her tighter.

Spent. Dazed. Completely satisfied. Jade enjoyed the ride but also felt relief that it was over. Weakened, she fell back onto the bed of petals, causing some of them to rise up in the air around her.

Kaeden climbed onto the bed beside her, his dick sticking out of his body like a sword. He used his hand to guide it against her open and panting mouth. "My turn," he told her thickly before he lightly tapped the thick tip against her lips.

Jade smiled softly before she darted out her tongue to lick that tip. Once. Twice. Three times.

Kaeden's ass cheeks flexed in reaction. His mouth fell open as she captured the tip in her mouth and sucked it deeply. "Ohhh," he cried out, his lips pursed.

Jade laughed huskily. "You ain't ready?" She

tested before she sucked half of the length into her mouth and then circled it with her tongue before flicking the tip with her agile tongue. Kaeden jerked his hips back, freeing his shaft from her mouth as his thighs quivered and his heart fluttered in his chest. "You gone make me cum, girl," he told her thickly.

"There's other ways to get it wet," she told him before turning over onto her stomach and then climbing up to the head of the bed on her hands and knees.

Kaeden watched her, reaching out to soundly slap her plush chocolate bottom. Whap. *The flesh of her buttocks jiggled in a thousand different directions. Kaeden's dick did a push-up at the sight of it all. "Damn," he swore, shaking his head and giving his mouth an LL lick.*

Jade grabbed the floral headboard and rose up to her knees. She looked over her shoulder at him as she used her muscles to make her buttocks dance. "Come on, let me sit on it," she told him.

Kaeden moved to her on his knees until he was directly behind her with his rod standing up— willing, waiting, and wanting.

Jade licked her lips and moaned as she reached behind her to grab the base. She shivered at the feel of his hands lightly pressed to her hips as she guided her tight core down onto him with one swift dip of her hips.

He filled her. Completed her.

They both shivered and tensed until they both adjusted to the feel of one another.

Grabbing the headboard, Jade rose and began to work her hips up and down, locking her feet behind his knees as she rode him.

Kaeden leaned back to look down at the sight of his rod, glistening with her juices, as it appeared and disappeared with each lift and dip of her buttocks. "Damn, Jade. Damn," he swore, flexing his hips.

Feeling playful, Jade slid her core up to the tip and flexed her walls against it before she made the cheeks of her buttocks clap.

"Oh shit," Kaeden said, his eyes locked on the motion.

Jade moaned as she slid down along the hard inches to bounce back against his thigh—before she slid up to the tip, worked her walls, and then jiggled her buttocks. She laughed and did the wicked up-and-down jiggle move again. And again. And again. And again.

"Do it . . . do it . . . do it," he moaned between sharp hisses of pure pleasure.

"Do it . . . do it . . . get it. Hmmm."

"Kaeden. Kaeden? Kaeden!"

Kaeden froze as he was jostled from his sleep with a shake. He opened one eye and jumped a bit to find Felecia bending down over where he sat behind his desk. And he was grateful for the desk, as it hid the aching erection straining against the zipper of his tailored pants. "Huh? What?"

"What did you just say?" she asked, standing up to cross her arms over her chest.

Nothing I can repeat, he thought as he cleared his

throat and straightened his glasses. "Just dreaming," he told her, his erection pressed between his desk and his stomach.

"About what?" she asked him as she sat the files in her hands on the desk in front of him.

Kaeden shifted his eyes out the window to his right as he squinted. His dreams were of Jade. Always Jade. Would he ever be free of his desire for her?

It wasn't at all fair to Felecia, but her strong stance on no premarital sex wasn't helping defeat the dream named Jade.

"Nothing," he told her, opening the files.

Felecia sat down in the chair before his desk, easing the hem of her white linen sundress down over her knees as she crossed her legs. "You are still going with me to my cousin's wedding this Saturday?" she asked.

Kaeden nodded as he signed his name to the documents. "That's the plan. Did you get the dress you wanted to wear?" he asked, happy that the conversation was distracting him enough that his erection had eased.

"Yes, and I found you a nice tie and shirt to match me," she told him.

Kaeden nodded, his focus really on his work. "Okay."

"I love going to weddings," she said. "Maybe we can get ideas for the one we'll have one day. In fact, I would love a wedding on the beach at sunset with fireworks exploding just as my groom kisses the bride. And then we can do the reception on a boat."

Kaeden froze with his pen in midair. He frowned. They were nowhere near marriage in his eyes. He finished signing the documents and closed the folders to hand them to Felecia. "Maybe you should be a wedding planner," he said, trying to change the subject.

Felecia shook her head. "I am saving all my ideas for my own wedding," she told him.

Kaeden glanced up at her briefly, but he looked up again when he saw the dreamy look in her eyes as she looked out the window. He squinted behind his glasses. "Felecia . . ."

She smiled a little as she brought her hands up in front of her like . . . like she was holding something in them.

An imaginary bouquet?

Nah, can't be.

"What are you doing for lunch?" he asked her before he turned his attention back to his work.

"Actually I have an appointment, but I can bring you something back," she said, still sounding distracted by her thoughts.

"I'll just get something from Donnie's when I leave my parents' this morning," he offered as he closed the folders and stood while he slid his BlackBerry into the case attached to his belt.

"I should only be gone for my lunch hour," she told him, rising to her feet as well, as Kaeden grabbed his keys from the top drawer of his desk.

Kaeden paused beside her, lightly touching her face to press a kiss to her cheek before he walked out of his office. "See you later," he told her over his shoulder.

"Okay. Bye-bye."

He left the office and climbed into his BMW. He was soon pulling up to a light when he saw Jade's yellow Jeep already sitting in the left lane. Kaeden's heart clutched in his chest as he pulled up beside her. He tried to keep his gaze straight ahead. He didn't want to know if she was looking at him. He didn't want to know what her reaction to seeing him was. He didn't want to know what color she wore or how her hair was fixed.

He wanted to work on getting Jade Prince out of his system once and for all.

The light turned green and Kaeden accelerated forward quickly. He was proud of himself, but he knew he still had a long way to go.

As he made the right turn onto Highway 17 headed toward Holtsville, he finally slowed down. "No need to get a ticket," he said, flipping the visor down to block the sun.

He turned the music on and tuned out any thoughts of his desire for Jade or his aversion to Felecia's recent wedding talk.

In no time at all he was easing the vehicle to a stop in front of his parents' house. He hopped out and jogged up the stairs, the distant sounds of the ranch work reaching him. "Kaeden in the house," he hollered out as he entered the foyer.

"In the den," his mother replied.

Kaeden dropped his keys on the wooden table in the foyer. He smiled at the sight of his mother on the floor on her hands and knees beside his nephew as the sounds of some colorful kiddie program blared on the big-screen television.

"Now you got down there, but can you get up?" he teased, sliding his hands into the pockets of his khakis.

His mom dropped her head and laughed. "This little one is wearing this old lady out," she told him.

"Grandma's a horsie," KJ said, giggling as he

jumped up to his feet and then tried to climb onto Lisha's back.

Kaeden walked over and swung the toddler up into one arm. "There's plenty of horses around here for you not to have my mama on the floor," he joked as he offered his mother his free hand.

"Tell me about it," she drawled as she accepted the hand and the gentle tug to her feet.

Kaeden just chuckled before he bent his head to kiss her cheek as KJ stuck his chubby hand in the pocket of his burnt orange button-up shirt. "Where's Dad?"

"Down at the paddocks with all your brothers," she said. "How about you take this little one here with you to see the real horses. You'll save your mama a walk."

"No problem," he told her before turning and walking down the hall to grab his keys and leave the house.

As soon as they stepped down off the porch, Kaeden lifted the toddler up onto his neck. He enjoyed the feel of his nephew's hands lightly resting against his closely shaven head as he walked down the dirt-packed yard toward the ranch in the distance.

"Un-cle . . . Un-cle . . . Un-cle," KJ sang.

Kaeden was just in his late twenties, but the feel and sound of his nephew reminded him that he was ready for kids. With Felecia? Something about the idea of that didn't sit right with him. Not right at all.

"What's up, family?" Kaeden greeted the men of his family as he neared the large and spacious paddock where one of the hands was working out a Strong stallion.

"Da da da da da da," KJ squealed at the sight of Kahron.

Kahron smiled, his eyes covered by his ever-present shades. "Hey, Daddy's boy," he said, reaching his fist up to his son. "Gimme dap."

KJ made a fist and pushed against his father's. "Dap," he said, his eyes bright.

The men all laughed, and that caused KJ to squeal with laughter as well as he covered his mouth with both of his hands.

Kael took off his Stetson and wiped the sweat from his forehead, the dampness causing his silver hair to lie plastered to his head. "Go on 'head, Kade," he said, nodding his head in the direction of his eldest child.

Kaeden, Kahron, and Kaleb all looked at Kade, who shoved his large hands into the pockets of his navy Dickies work pants. "Kaeden, did you check the stuff I asked you about?"

Kaeden nodded as KJ placed his hands over his spectacles. "Everything's straight."

"Good. Just got an early word that Lockhart Farm is going out of business and they're going to sell their farming equipment—equipment we all can use."

"Confirmed?" Kaleb asked, shifting his weight on the heels of his dusty Timberland boots.

Kade nodded solemnly. "Unfortunately."

"Me and Randy Lockhart started out around the same time. His boy Juba and him have worked real hard to make it last," Kael added. "Feels like we swooping in like vultures."

Kaleb snorted. "I disagree," he drawled.

"Kaleb and I think the most fiscally sound way to approach this for all three ranches is to buy into the equipment together," Kaeden offered. "That way you're not taking out an unnecessary loan that carries risk and you're contributing equally to the capital needed."

"Sounds like a plan to me," Kahron said with a shrug.

"Me too," Kaleb added.

Kade nodded. "We can ride over to the ranch and look at the equipment."

Kaeden shook his head. "I think we should get an itemized list faxed here. Let's strategize a base price that we're willing to offer and then go to the ranch. We can go up or down based on the condition, but at least we're all in the same ballpark from the jump."

"I agree," Kahron added.

"Then let's go call him and have him fax the list over," Kade said, pushing his tall, sinewy frame up off the wooden rails of the paddock.

"Let's go, then."

"Oh, heck no," Kaeden said as he felt KJ's gas bubbles hit his neck. His mouth fell open in shock and he instantly reached up to take the toddler down. "Boy, you stink."

"Oops," KJ said before bursting into giggles. The men laughed as they made their way back to the barn to the foreman's office.

It was time for business, and when it came to teamwork, no one did it better than the Strong men. Each played his position well and Kaeden was learning that he was just as important to the team as the others. And that's the part that Kaeden loved about being one of the Strongs. It was one for all and all for one, all the way and all the time.

* * *

Felecia took a sip of her tea and honey as she flipped through the newest addition to her bridal magazine subscriptions: *Brides*. She placed a sticky note on the page she'd just read about destination weddings. *Me and Kaeden barefoot on the beaches of Jamaica saying our I dos.* She sighed longingly.

The outer office door opened and Felecia reluctantly took her eyes off a picture of a decorative wedding cake lit by a spotlight. She smiled at the tall and handsome fair-skinned man who walked in. "Can I help you?" she asked.

His eyes darted to the door leading to Kaeden's office. "I need to speak to Kaeden. Is he in?"

"No, he's been in Holtsville all morning, but he'll be back after lunch," Felecia told him, thinking that the man looked like an older version of Bow Wow. "Do you want to make an appointment?"

"No, I'll just try him later." He turned and walked to the door.

"Your name?" Felecia asked.

"Darren," he said over his shoulder before he walked out, softly closing the door behind him.

Felecia shrugged before she grabbed her purse and keys from the bottom drawer of her desk. She grabbed their framed OUT TO LUNCH sign and walked out of the office, locking the door behind her before she hung the sign on the small brass hood on the door.

She walked to the driveway to her car, her eyes falling on the wedding gown lying across her rear seat. She had an appointment that she was going to keep.

Chapter 14

Jade stretched as she rose from her desk and walked across the room to retrieve a bottled water from the small fridge in the corner. She walked into the outer office as she took a deep drink.

Darren had not shown up to the office. He hadn't called, and when she called him he didn't answer.

She sighed. She couldn't lie and say she wasn't worried about him. Things between them had ended so horribly, and she wondered if there was any hope of saving their friendship . . . or even the business.

Glancing down at her watch, she saw that it was lunchtime, and her stomach was asking to be filled. Switching on the answering machine, Jade grabbed her purse and keys before walking out the front door onto Main Street. She slipped her shades on and walked down the street that was the epitome of small-town America with its little shops and businesses dating back fifty years or better—shops and businesses that had once been the shopping center of the town, but had long been challenged and sometimes defeated by the larger retail chains about town.

Smiling at the people she passed on the street, she allowed herself to browse the storefronts. But Jade was only interested in picking up a soda and a couple of hot dogs from the street vendor on the corner by the courthouse.

She strolled past the ice cream shop and came up to the Wedding Salon. She slowed down, eying a strapless wedding gown that sparkled with pearl beads. It was simply beautiful . . . but it was definitely for someone else. Jade was not looking to be a bride. *Not that I have any prospects anyway*, she thought with a humph.

Through the glass window she saw a flash of white in the background. She focused her line of vision inside the bridal boutique. She frowned. Her eyes widened a bit. She squinted them to make sure she was seeing clearly.

She was.

Her hand clutched the strap of her tote tightly as she stood there and watched Felecia step up onto the circular platform in front of a trio of long mirrors . . . in a wedding gown.

"Oh my God . . . Kaeden's getting married," she whispered aloud as her heart raced and pounded all at once.

She stepped back and accidentally bumped into a pedestrian. "Sorry. I'm sorry," she said, turning to quickly head back down the streets to the Wild-n-Out office.

Jade didn't stop until she closed the front door of the

office behind her. She paced the outer office, not quite sure why she felt like pure panic was settling in on her. She forced herself to stop and breathe, slow and easy. She laughed a little but it came out sounding pained. "Okay, wait," she said, brushing her long bangs back from her forehead. "Okay. Last month he's emphatic that he's not even dating this woman . . . and . . . and . . . and *now* they're . . . they're engaged?"

Jade put her hands on her hips and closed her eyes as she shook her head. "Okay. Okay. Wait a minute. You know what. Why am I freaking out? I mean, this is none of my business. Even though I gave him all of this goodness and . . . and he's mad because I am . . . or *was* with Darren . . . but now he's getting married. What. The. Hell!"

Jade scratched her head in confusion as she stood there coming to grips with her feelings.

Her anger.

Her confusion.

Her jealousy.

Her overwhelming sense of loss.

"Okay, Kaeden's getting married. So what? Right?" Jade said aloud, not even sounding convincing to her own ears. "It's not like we dated or anything. This does not affect my life one bit. I don't care. Good luck, well wishes, and whoopee-do to the happy couple."

Jade propped against the desk. Tears welled up in her eyes and she felt like a fool as one lone tear raced down her cheek. She swiped the tear away and blinked her wide almond-shaped eyes to prevent any more from falling.

She never imagined her and Kaeden getting together, but the thought of him marrying someone else didn't sit well with her at all. She barely knew the man, and most of what she'd seen of him during the camping trip had irked her nerves.

But that night they had shared a connection like nothing she had ever known before. Kaeden had touched her body and her soul. It felt like the memory of him was forever implanted within her. But what they shared—the physical connection had been to her complete and total satisfaction.

Needing a distraction, Jade picked up the cordless phone from the desk in the reception area and called her mother. Her cell phone went straight to voice mail. Jade assumed she was on a flight.

She dialed her grandfather. His house phone rang endlessly. Jade assumed he had gone fishing or was in his garden.

She started to call Darren but she left that alone, knowing he needed space.

Jade walked into her office and sat at her desk, trying to focus on their dreaded paperwork. This was the part of the business that she hated. All she wanted to do was be outdoors and not closed in by four walls, behind a desk shuffling papers.

Like Kaeden.

Jade rolled her eyes, frustrated with herself for even letting her mind wander back to him. It seemed like she always thought about that man. Little things. Stupid things.

What is he doing?

Is he thinking of me? That night?

Jade's eyes clouded as she allowed herself to get lost

in the memories. Lost in the passion. Lost in the little world they created . . . if only for that one night.

A vision of Kaeden's nude lean form nestled above Felecia flashed and her stomach clenched in aversion. She shook her head to free it of the image.

She pictured the woman and Kaeden. They made a cute match. Fine. But did he share the same explosive chemistry with his . . . fiancée as he did with her? Could she make him stutter? Could she make him howl to the moon? Could she make him ache like a fiend craving a drug? Could she handle Kaeden the way that Jade knew she could?

Jade smirked. Then she felt childish for her thoughts. Jealousy was a trip.

She didn't love him. She hardly knew him. So why did she still dream of him? Why did the very thought of him give her a thrill? Why was she jealous of the thought of him marrying someone else? Why did her heart ache so terribly?

The Strong men decided to join Kaeden for lunch at Donnie's Diner on the main strip in Holtsville. The men made an impressive sight with their broad shoulders, towering heights, handsome features, and prematurely gray hair. They joked together as they made their way over to a large round table in the center of the small restaurant.

Kaeden rubbed his stomach as he pulled out his chair. "I'm starving," he said, just as he felt someone touch his shoulder.

He looked over his shoulder. His handsome features

shaped into a frown as he looked into the face of Jade's man. "Darren, right?" he said.

"Can I holler at you outside for a second?" he asked in a hard voice, his eyes glittering like glass.

Kaeden was taken aback because the man's eyes, voice, and stance were all cold. And in return, Kaeden's eyes hardened behind his glasses. "Why all the hostility?" Kaeden asked.

"Because you need to stay the hell away from Jade," Darren chewed out as the muscle in his jaw clenched.

Kaeden heard the scrape of chairs behind him signaling that the rest of the Strong men had risen to their feet. But Kaeden didn't need them.

"Let's take this outside. After you." Kaeden followed Darren out of the restaurant, aware of the curious eyes on them as they did.

"I ought to whup your little skinny ass for even *thinking* about touching Jade," Darren chewed out, every line in his face filled with anger as he pointed his finger in Kaeden's face.

Kaeden knocked the man's hand away. "Trust me, I did more than *think* about it."

Kaeden instantly regretted referring to Jade in that manner, but seconds later a solid punch landed against his nose, sending his glasses flying off into the street. Vaguely he heard a tire run over them, shattering the glass and crunching the frame. He stumbled back— but just a little bit, before he bent low and went charging at Darren's middle.

A fight was on.

* * *

A collective gasp went through the entire restaurant as everyone watched the men fall to the ground.

All of the Strong brothers made a move to step forward toward the door, but Kael calmly held up his hand. "Don't take all three to break up a fight," he said calmly.

Kade, knowing his role as the oldest, immediately headed for the door.

Kael turned his mouth downward as he watched Kaeden deliver Darren a vicious uppercut and then a right hook.

"Ooh," Kaleb and Kahron grunted, making ugly faces at the delivery of the blows.

Kade pulled the two men apart.

Kael took a deep sip of the glass of sweet tea the waitress sat in front of him. "Well, guess Kaeden just taught that fella to not start something he can't finish."

Kaeden watched over Kade's broad shoulder as Darren turned and stormed back to his truck. Soon the sound of tires squealing echoed around them loudly. "Asshole," he muttered, straightening his clothes. He looked up, and even without his glasses he could make out that everyone in the restaurant—and those bold enough to step outside—had their eyes on the scene that had just unfolded.

"Damn, I'm outta here," Kaeden said, reaching in his pocket for his keys as he walked over to his car.

Kade chuckled. "Can you drive without your glasses?"

"Yeah. I got my contacts in here."

"So, Darren found out about what happened between you and Jade?" Kade crossed his arms over his chest.

Kaeden shrugged. "I guess."

"Wanna talk about it?" Kade offered.

Kaeden shook his head as he laughed sarcastically. "That's the thing. There is nothing to talk about. Jade and I—no, correction—there is no Jade and I. Never really was."

"Shee-it. Enough for that man to want to whup you over," Kade quipped.

"Man, shut up," Kaeden said, giving his teasing brother a reluctant smile as he opened his car door and slid onto the butter-soft leather seats and started the engine. He winced as he reached for his case of contact lenses and put them in as quickly as he could.

"Hey," Kade called out.

Kaeden looked over at him, lowering the driver's-side window. "Huh?"

"What are you gonna tell Felecia about your glasses . . . and the bruise on your cheek?"

Kaeden leaned to the right to look up in the rearview mirror. Sure enough, there was a bleeding scrape across his cheek and a dried trickle of blood that had run from his nose.

"Jade must be one helluva woman," Kade joked.

Kaeden shot him a glare before he circled out of the dirt parking area. He still couldn't believe that he'd just fought a man over Jade—particularly when he had a girlfriend and all that he and Jade shared was one crazy night in the woods.

He was just passing Cyrus's one-pump gas station

and convenience store when Jade's yellow Jeep Wrangler whizzed past him. His eyes darted up to watch her in the rearview mirror.

What role did she play in all this? No one knew about that night. Did she tell her man to get him jealous or something along those childish lines?

Easing his foot onto the brakes and flipping on his left turn signal, Kaeden checked for oncoming traffic before making an illegal U-turn. He knew she was headed to her little cottage and he headed in that direction.

Kaeden pulled up into her yard just as Jade hopped out of the driver's seat. She turned and looked at him in surprise.

The sight of her made his heart race—even as he wished it didn't.

Kaeden was startled to see that her eyes were slightly puffy and reddish. Like she'd been crying. *Probably over her man. Did they break up?* he thought.

"Kaeden? What are you doing here?" she asked, her keys jiggling in her hands as she placed her hands on her wide hips in the strapless print maxi dress she wore.

"Were you crying?" he asked in concern, stepping out of the car to walk up to her.

Jade averted her eyes briefly before she shook her head. "Listen, what do you want, Kaeden?"

"For your man to give me ten feet at all times," he told her. "You know that fool just stepped to me at Donnie's."

Her eyes widened and then shifted to the reddish bruise on his cheek. "Did you two fight?" she asked, reaching out as if to touch his bruise, but then she pulled her hand back like she had second thoughts about it. "I'm so sorry."

Kaeden frowned. "First, stop looking at me like I got my behind whipped. Secondly, sorry for what?"

"Darren asked me about that night," she said quietly.

"And you told him."

"I wasn't going to lie to him—"

"Like you lied to me."

Jade's mouth fell open. "I never lied to you!" she exclaimed.

"You never told me you had a boyfriend," he volleyed back.

"Because I didn't. Darren and I were only dating when that night happened. Let me clue you both in, since you're both lost in the sauce, but dating some-one is not the same as being exclusive *or* sleeping with them."

Kaeden did a double take. "You never slept with old boy? Come on, miss me with the BS, Jade."

Jade stepped up closer to him. "Well, if it's not Mr. High and Mighty looking down his nose at someone. Puh-leeze. Miss me with your BS, Kaeden."

He hated that the sight of her eyes fiery with emo-tion made him want her even more. "What BS?"

She looked him up and down before rolling her eyes. "Shouldn't you be somewhere getting fitted for your tux or something?" she asked, sounding tired and annoyed all at once.

Kaeden frowned. "A tux? For what?"

Jade laughed a little as she looked up at him with the wetness of tears still clinging to her long lashes.

"The wedding," she snapped and then wiped her mouth with her hands.

"Whose wedding?" he asked, completely lost.

The look she gave him was incredulous. "Yours. Is it secret or something?" she asked, becoming just as confused as he appeared to be.

"So secret it's not true," he said.

"Whatever, Kaeden. You don't have to lie to me. Congratulations to you and Felecia."

Kaeden's frown deepened. "Did she tell you we were getting married?"

Jade shook her head as she shifted the sandals on her feet in the dirt. "No, I saw her getting fitted for her wedding dress."

Kaeden's stomach dropped. "Nah, you were mistaken. Trust and believe that."

Jade waved her hand. "Whatever. I know what I saw, and you don't have to lie to me," she said before she turned and walked into her house, soundly closing the door behind her.

Kaeden made a move to follow her and knock on the door, but he changed his mind. He had no right coming to Jade's house anyway. It was another bad choice on his part. He'd just fought a man—*her* man—over her, and if Felecia caught whiff of that *and* the fact that he went to Jade's house, then he was going to get a lot of headache over something he was fighting hard to put into the past.

Kaeden climbed back into his BMW and this time made his way to Walterboro without a chance of him turning back.

And the whole seeing Felecia in a wedding dress

had to be a mistake. Why on earth would she be doing that? She had been talking about her cousin's wedding that morning. Maybe whatever Jade saw was in reference to her cousin's wedding and Jade just misunderstood. Or maybe it wasn't a wedding dress but just a white evening gown. Or maybe she was the same size as her cousin and tried the dress on for her?

He ran over a hundred different explanations, and the more he wondered, the more improbable and far-fetched they became.

Regardless of what Jade saw, one thing he knew for sure: Kaeden Strong was *not* getting married.

Regardless of what Darren thought, Kaeden Strong was *not* involved with Jade Prince.

Regardless of what his mind tried to reason with him, Kaeden Strong knew that of the two, there was one thing he wanted more than the other.

Jade. And regardless of whether he was with Jade or not, as long as he had this hidden infatuation for Jade, he wasn't being fair at all to Felecia.

What had caused Jade's tears? His heart ached at the thought of her shedding one solitary tear. What was it about that woman that called out so deeply to him? Why couldn't he shake her? Sighing, he turned on his satellite radio and hoped the right song would come on to help him get lost in anything but his own reality.

Chapter 15

Jade was thoroughly embarrassed.

She still couldn't believe that Darren had started a fight with Kaeden and sparked the flame of gossip through the small town that the fight was over her. So on top of all the other drama, she was sure many people mistakenly thought she was dealing with both men making her a bona fide hoochie mama.

This last week had been filled with lots of side-eyes, whispers as she walked past, and bold people flat-out asking her about the fight.

Drama.

"What's wrong, Jade?"

She shifted her eyes back to her mother, who was sitting across the table from her in their favorite Charleston restaurant, California Dreaming.

"Nothing," she mumbled before she took a bite of her salad.

Deena took a sip of her glass of wine as she eyed her daughter over the rim. "There's a group of fellas across the room and they are looking this way. Don't look."

Jade looked anyway. She shot them a look that would discourage any and all thoughts of approaching their table. "I have enough drama regarding men. Last thing I need is to add to the mix, Mama," she said, turning her head to look at her mother.

Deena sat her fork down on her plate. "I heard about the fight," she said.

Oh great, Jade thought, avoiding her mother's assessing eyes.

"How is everything at the business? You know, everything with Darren?"

Jade shrugged as she pushed the food around on her plate. "He left me a note saying he was taking the week off since we didn't have any tours scheduled. I haven't seen him since their fight, and he won't answer my calls."

Deena reached across the table to lightly massage the top of Jade's hands. "There's only one good thing about a rumor floating around a small town."

Jade looked at her mother in question.

"It doesn't last long because someone else will be the topic of conversation real soon. Trust on that," she assured her with a soft smile.

"We'll see," Jade said, sounding sad.

"Oh no, you don't. You hold your head up, Jade Prince. That's your life, and you live it how you want and don't be ashamed. That's a definite no-no."

Jade just shrugged as she reached down to pull the top of her strapless dress up higher on her breasts.

"Just one thing, baby girl. In the woods?" Deena asked with a wink. "Now that's a new one on me."

Jade froze. "Who told you that?" she asked sharply.

Deena took a bite of her shrimp. "You didn't know that everyone's saying you and Kaeden slept together in the woods on the camping trip?"

Jade's heart thundered in her chest as she tightened her grip on her fork before she released it to clang loudly against her plate. "No. No, I didn't."

Deena leaned across the table. "So . . . did you?" she asked with a bright gleam of interest in her eyes.

"Mama," Jade snapped.

"What?" Deena asked with an air of innocence. "Listen, you can't control where passion takes a hold of you, and you shouldn't. Now, it took me almost twenty years to rediscover mine, and I don't want that for you. Life is too short and those Strong brothers are too fine. Humph, Lisha and Kael made some good-looking boys."

Kaeden.

Jade thought of him. She got those nervous stomach flutters like a high school crush. Who knew a square like Kaeden Strong would have her head so messed up?

"Do you like him, Jade?" Deena asked.

"Huh?" Jade said, pushing away a hot image of Kaeden's hard and curving length hanging away heavily from his lean frame.

"I said do you like him?" Deena repeated.

"Who?"

Deena sighed impatiently. "Kaeden Strong. Do you like Kaeden Strong?"

"I had sex with the man on a dirty ground in the woods. . . . I would say that's a yes." Jade instantly hated the sarcasm dripping from her voice toward her mother. "Sorry, Mama."

"So it *is* true. That's my girl. Seize the day! Hell, seize the—"

"Mama," Jade cut her off quickly, her eyes widening.

Deena just laughed before she took a small sip of her wine.

"Mama, I really can't explain it," Jade admitted with a lick of her lips. "I barely knew Kaeden, but in that moment it felt like there was nothing else in the world I would rather do than be with him, and I don't understand because we are so different, Mama."

Deena smiled softly at her daughter before she reached across the table again to clasp her hand.

"I mean, I was dating Darren and . . . and he wanted to sleep with me but I just kept putting it off and putting it off, but with Kaeden . . . with Kaeden, Mama, it was like the most natural thing even though it was nothing like me, but it felt right."

"That good, huh?" Deena joked.

Jade closed her eyes and got lost in the memories of that night. The heat. The electricity. The passion. The oneness. The completion. The fulfillment. The pure unadulterated satisfaction. "Yes," she admitted in a whisper, amazed at the tears that welled up in her eyes behind her closed lids.

"Maybe there is something there that is bigger than whatever differences there are between you two. Maybe you need to give in and stop fighting it. Shut off your head and listen to your heart."

Jade shook her head. "I'm not in love, Mama. That I know," she stressed emphatically.

"Listen to your soul, then."

Jade opened her eyes and looked across the table at her mother.

"What if this Mr. Seems to Be Wrong for You is actually Mr. Right for You, Jade?" Deena asked.

Jade thought of Felecia trying on the wedding dress and just shook her head. "He's Mr. Right for Someone Else," Jade said softly before picking up her neglected margarita to sip deeply.

Plus her mind was filled with another more pressing matter: Did Darren or Kaeden tell of the tryst in the woods?

That was one question she was going to get answered.

Kaeden adjusted his new glasses as he followed Felecia inside her apartment. The lingering scent of whatever Sunday dinner she'd cooked was in the air and his stomach growled in response. "I am starving," he said, glad that Felecia had cooked before going to church that morning.

"Did you enjoy the service?" she asked as she removed the heels matching her pale peach suit before she walked into the kitchen.

"It was good," he told, glad that he'd attended church with her.

"Good, I'll be sure to tell my daddy," she called out from the kitchen.

Kaeden rolled up the sleeves to his crisp French

blue shirt as he walked across the living room and down the short hall past her bedroom to the bathroom. He paused in his steps, frowned deeply, and then took a few steps back to stand at her doorway.

What the . . .

A flash of white had caught his eye, and he thought he saw the sparkly hem of a wedding dress just barely peeking out from the closet. But he had to make sure. And sure enough, there it was.

Kaeden pushed the bedroom door open wider and walked across the room to open the closet door. The sight of the wedding dress hanging there made him take a step back.

Of course, proper etiquette didn't mean going into someone's room uninvited and snooping, but Kaeden felt he had every right.

Felecia had lied to him.

When he told her about "someone" seeing her at the bridal boutique wearing a wedding gown, Felecia had laughed it off as ridiculous.

"Why would I be trying on a wedding dress?" she said. "Did they speak to me to be sure it was me?" Then, "Well I must have a twin, because I was not at the Bridal Boutique," she lied.

And there was no mistaken that what hung before him on the door was most definitely a bridal gown. "What the hell is going on?" he asked himself, just as his eyes fell on the open chest against the rear wall of the closet. Kaeden's eyes widened as his frown deepened. He stepped into the closet and used both arms to push back her clothing.

His jaw fell open at all of the wedding paraphernalia

he saw inside. Wedding favors, magazines, an aisle runner, hundreds of laminated clippings—even down to shoes that resembled glass slippers. He bent down to pick up a picture of a bride and groom with a cutout of his face attached to the groom's body and a cutout of her face attached to that of the bride. He dropped that and picked up an engraved invitation:

Reverend and Mrs. Roderick Craven
request the honor of your presence
at the marriage of their daughter
Felecia Annette

to

Kaeden Tyler Strong
son of
Mr. and Mrs. Kael Strong on
Saturday, the eighth of May
two thousand and ten
at six o'clock in the evening
Insert wedding location
Reception
immediately following the ceremony
Insert reception location

"Kaeden," Felecia called out from the living room.

He rose and turned to step out of the closet just as she stepped into the doorway of the bedroom. "What's this all about, Felecia?" he asked, waving his hand at the dress and the chest, not hiding how disturbed he was by it all.

She rushed over to the closet to pull Kaeden forward

enough to close the door soundly. "That's my cousin's wedding dress. She's keeping it here so her fiancé doesn't see it."

"Stop lying, Felecia," he told her, holding up the invitation.

She reached up and snatched it from him. "Why are you in here, anyway?" she snapped.

"Why are you planning a wedding?" he asked, staring down at her with incredulous eyes. "Listen, we are nowhere near being ready to get married. I'm not even sure we're working out and you're around here planning a wedding for us—or I guess for whomever. Do you want to get married that badly, Felecia?"

She arched a brow. "Don't say that," she told him.

"Say what?"

"That we're not working out," she yelled, tears filling her eyes.

Damn. Kaeden knew at that moment that his relationship with Felecia had to end: his continuing feelings for Jade, his knowledge that he'd turned to Felecia in his hurt because she was the anti-Jade, Felecia scheming to get them married and holding out the sex until she was married. All of it added up to mismatch that needed to end, ASAP. The process was not going to be easy. "Calm down, Felecia," he said to her, taken aback by her emotional response.

She closed her eyes, swiped away her fallen tears as she breathed in and out like she was trying to calm down. "Don't do this, Kaeden," she said softly.

"Listen, we want different things, and I knew for a while now that I shouldn't have started things back up with us, so I apologize. Okay?"

She balled the invitation up in her hand and flung it across the room to hit the wall. "We are meant to be together and you know it," she told him vehemently. "Why are you doing this?"

"Because I realize now that you want more out of this than I do, and that's not fair to you," he tried to reason with her as the tears filled her eyes again. Kaeden just said a silent thank-you that they'd never slept together.

"So you led me on?" she asked, her face pain stricken.

"You're the one who introduced yourself to my mother and ambushed me with your family and has a creepy wedding hope chest. No, I didn't lead you on, Felecia. I think maybe you saw what you wanted to see and not what was really going on."

She looked insulted as she took a step toward him. "You saying I'm crazy?"

Yes. Yes you are. "No, I don't think that at all," Kaeden lied, thinking he'd better make his way to the exit because he wasn't all the way sure Felecia wasn't about to flip.

He walked past her and made his way to the door.

"Where are you going? We're not done," she told him.

He opened the front door and paused to look back at her. "When you calm down and you're ready to talk about why I'm ending this, please call me, but yes, yes, we are over," he told her, knowing that it was hurting her and hating that, but knowing he had to do it. With one last wave he walked out the door and closed it firmly behind him.

* * *

Darren walked into his living room with three bottles of beer, handing them to his brother, Mikal, and his two first cousins as sports highlights played loudly on ESPN on the television. His cell phone vibrated on the table. He reached to pick it up but just smirked at Jade's number on the caller ID. "Now she calling your boy," he said, tossing the phone across the table to his brother. "Man, forget her."

"Maybe she wanna give it up to you in the woods," his brother joked.

"He can have my sloppy seconds. I got the best of the puddycat anyway," Darren lied, motioning his hands like he was slapping Jade's rear while he stroked her from behind.

His brother and cousins laughed, but inwardly Darren still seethed with anger for Jade. Anger and the need for a little payback.

Felecia sat in the middle of her darkness, surrounded by the cool darkness and damp from her own tears. She had messed up. She had ruined everything.

When Kaeden accepted her offer to go to her church with her, she had gotten so excited that she tried on her newly altered wedding gown and spent an hour going through her chest. She had to rush to get ready for church and hadn't carefully put everything away.

And Kaeden saw it. And Kaeden got scared. And Kaeden left.

Sniffling, she looked up through puffy eyes at the small bit of light coming through the door and illuminating her dream wedding dress. And the light glinted off the pearls and intricate beading, making it seem to glow and glisten in the darkness.

Mocking her.

Taunting her.

Na-na-na-na-na.

"Why, Lord? Whyyyyyyyy," Felecia wailed as she threw her head back and cried like she'd lost her best friend.

Chapter 16

Jade was waiting on Darren when he walked through the doors of their Wild-n-Out offices. She sat in his office and waited for him. When he strolled in and saw her sitting there he paused.

"So how are we going to handle this, Darren?" she asked. "Because *this* is not just about you and me, it's also about this business."

"You created *this*," he said sarcastically.

Jade allowed herself a ten count. "Listen, you and I are done. Truthfully, we never should've even tried to date."

Darren snorted in derision.

Jade felt her annoyance at him increase and the first bud of dislike bloom. "Do you think you and I can work and run a business together with all of this ridiculous animosity that you have?"

He locked his eyes on her. "So you want out?" he asked her.

Jade locked her eyes with his. "I am sorry if you feel betrayed and hurt. But that does not give you the right to talk to me disrespectfully in my face or behind my back. And the next time that it happens, you *will* buy out my share of this business and run it by your damn self."

Darren laughed. "Is that right?"

Jade rose from his chair and came around his cluttered desk. "I'm not playing, Darren. I'm trying to have patience because I understand that you are hurt."

"Listen, I could care less about what you do," he told her, easing past her to sit behind his desk.

"You had no right confronting Kaeden, and you had no right spreading my business all over town."

Darren looked up at her. "Never do anything that you're ashamed of," he advised her. "Are you ashamed of your one-nighter in the woods, Jade?"

"Are you jealous of it?" she flung back. "Are you mad because it wasn't you?"

His expression closed up. "Don't say anything to me unless it's work related."

"Then keep my name out of your mouth," she told him.

"Get out of my office."

"Gladly," she told him, turning to leave. This wasn't how she wanted the conversation between them to go down, but sometimes life was more about reaction than action. She paused at the doorway. "I'm so disappointed that you thought scandalizing my name was necessary. But I mean it, if you disrespect me again, I'm out."

He said nothing at all.

Jade just shook her head before she walked out and closed the door behind her. She grabbed her purse and keys, leaving the office to hop into her Jeep. She needed air. She needed to get away from Darren before she choked his neck like a chicken.

Jade slid on her shades and enjoyed the wind blowing her dangling earrings as she drove. She wished she had a tour to do that day, but things had slowed down a bit. Even though she'd put in a good workout at the gym that morning, Jade steered her Jeep in the direction of Dairyland. A banana split would not hurt her exercise regime, and it would make her forget her troubles.

As she pulled to the light she glanced over at Kaeden's office. "I really should apologize for Darren's behavior," she said aloud, hesitating for just a second before she checked the rearview mirror, reversed a bit, and then turned the Jeep onto the long driveway.

What if his girl/fiancée/whatever had heard the rumors? Maybe showing up really wasn't a good idea.

"Why am I here?" Jade wondered aloud as she looked through the windshield of her Jeep at the offices of Strong Accountings.

Because I want to see Kaeden.

She threw her Jeep into reverse just as she saw Kaeden's BMW make the turn onto the driveway. She slammed on her brakes with her eyes still locked on the outline of Kaeden's figure in his car. Her heart pounded wildly just to know he was near.

He steered his vehicle off the driveway and pulled up beside her before climbing out. Jade felt nervous as she shifted her eyes to watch him, thinking he looked handsome in his black shirt and black slacks.

The bruise on his cheek had darkened and her hand itched to touch it.

"Jade," he said, standing near her vehicle. "Something I can help you with?"

She peered into his handsome face through her shades. "Is Felecia here? I wanted to talk to you about . . . about the fight."

"She doesn't work here anymore," Kaeden said. "Well, we don't see each other anymore either. So . . ."

Jade knew her surprise showed on her face.

"What about the fight, Jade?" he asked.

"I just wanted to apologize for that. He was wrong to confront you and wrong to spread what happened that night in the woods all over town. I feel partly responsible and I wanted to say I'm sorry." Jade pushed her shades atop her hair.

Kaeden nodded. "I'm cool. Are you?"

Jade nodded as she tapped her manicured fingers against the steering wheel. "We broke up," she confessed, accepting the relief she felt at the thought.

"Is that why you were crying that day?"

Jade locked her eyes with him. "No, not at all. It was for the best."

Their eyes stayed locked for a countless length of time.

Kaeden nodded before he pointed to his gold watch. "I better get in and start my day. Thanks for stopping by."

Jade smiled. "Okay. Bye, Kaeden."

He turned and jogged up the steps, unaware that Jade's eyes were glued to his buttocks as she reversed down the drive.

Kaeden and Felecia were done? As done as she was with Darren?

Jade pushed her foot down on the brakes.

What if this Mr. Seems to Be Wrong for You is actually Mr. Right for You, Jade?

Jade gripped the steering wheel and shifted her foot to accelerate forward. She didn't hesitate. She didn't think. She didn't second-guess.

Jade pulled to a stop next to Kaeden's car and hopped out to run up the stairs and into the office. "Kaeden," she called out.

He walked to the outer office, a ledger and a pen in his hands. "What is it, Jade?" he asked with patience and lots of distance.

"That night, what happened between us—"

Kaeden held up his hand. "Just let it go, Jade."

She stepped forward. "That's just it. I can't let it go. If I could I would, Kaeden. But I can't let it go. I can't forget. I can't help feeling like it was the best ever."

Kaeden released a heavy breath as he watched her.

"You don't understand, Kaeden," she stressed. "Before that night I hadn't been intimate with anyone in over a year, but I forgot all of my restrictions, all of my inhibitions with you. I'm still trying to figure it all out, but what I do know is that once you touched me, it was over and there was no going back, Kaeden."

Kaeden stared at her, and something about the look in his eyes thrilled her.

Jade was going for it. Life was about risks, and when it came to Kaeden she was willing to take the risk. She was listening to her soul. "Okay, I lied," she confessed as she stepped up to stand before him.

Inwardly she smiled at the smug look on his face. "The only other thing I know for sure is I want to feel that way again."

Kaeden's eyes dropped to her lips and then back up to her eyes.

"Can you make me feel like that again, Kaeden?" she asked, rising on her toes as she lightly grasped his face with her hands.

"Hell yeah," he told her before he dropped his ledger and pen to bring his hands up to grasp her soft buttocks and press her body close to his.

She gasped just before he passionately captured her mouth with his. Being in his arms. Being kissed by him. Just being near him felt so right. Jade squeezed her eyes shut to keep them from filling with tears as she wrapped her arms around his neck and gave in to their passion.

Kaeden growled as he sucked her tongue. He bent his legs and lifted her up. She wrapped her legs around his waist with a purr in the back of her throat as Kaeden walked them over to the desk to press her body down atop the hard wood. Jade tugged the hem of his shirt from his pants and then tore at them, causing the buttons to fly and his shirt to fall open, exposing his chest to her eyes and her eager hands.

"Hurry, Kaeden. I need you," she whispered in complete honesty into the heat between them.

He looked down at her with his chest heaving, his eyes missing nothing. "What are we doing, Jade?" he asked.

Jade's eyes were glazed with desire. "Huh?" she asked.

"What is this? Another hit it and split it or what?" he asked, leaning down to place his hands on either side of her head. "See, I don't want to be confused or lost in the sauce like I was the last time or like Darren was."

Jade sat up on the desk. "So what do you want, Kaeden?"

"More than sexing the hell out of you on a desk, Jade. I want to take you on dates and spend time with you and get to know more about you than how good you are in bed."

Kaeden wanted to take the risk just like she did, and that excited Jade.

"I haven't been able to forget that night either, Jade," he admitted. "And I was mad at you because I woke up that morning wanting to get to know you better. I still want that."

"When and where?" Jade said without a thought or a moment of hesitation.

Kaeden smiled before he bent his head to plant a kiss to her lips. "Tonight. Dinner. I'll pick you up at six," he whispered against her lips before kissing her again.

"Sounds like a plan," she said, lifting her hands to lightly tease his nipples and stroke the flat silver hairs of his chest. "So does this have to wait until later?"

Kaeden nodded before he hugged her upper body close to his. "Yes."

Jade groaned in disappointment and Kaeden chuckled as he stepped back to look down at his shirt. "You want that thing bad, don't you?" he teased with a huge grin as he pointed at his ruined shirt.

"Hush," Jade said as she rose to her feet and smoothed her short and frayed jean skirt down over her thighs. "I better let you get back to work since you on a strike."

Kaeden's eyes took in the way the short skirt only emphasized the strength and the shape of her deep mocha legs.

Jade walked to the door, only now realizing someone could have walked in on them. "So we're really gone try this, huh?" she asked, opening the door and then turning to look at him.

"It's worth a try, right?" he asked.

"And the wedding's off?" she asked.

Kaeden shook his head like something was a shame. "I'll explain all that foolishness tonight."

"Then yes, it's worth the try," she told him softly before walking out of the office and closing the door behind her.

Kaeden smoothed down the lapels of his black linen blazer as he inspected his appearance in the mirror. He kept several changes of clothes in the unused and sparsely furnished bedroom above his office, and he was glad he didn't have to drive all the way to his house and back to pick up Jade.

He paused. He still couldn't believe it. He was taking Jade Prince out on their first date. And he felt as nervous as a teenager. Nervous but happy.

This was what he had wanted from the first moment he laid eyes on her and definitely after the first night he made love to her. This was almost more exciting than being intimate with her. For so long he'd wanted Jade Prince in his life—and not just in his bed.

He grabbed his car keys after he made sure his black silk shirt and distressed jeans were wrinkle free. He'd even skipped his beloved glasses and wore the dreaded contacts because he remembered her saying she favored him without the spectacles.

Glancing at his Gucci watch, Kaeden left the bedroom and jogged down the stairs. He quickly turned off the office lights and locked up before he made his way to his car.

As he drove down Highway 17 toward Holtsville, Kaeden wondered if they were making the right decision. They were so different, but one thing he agreed with Jade about was the connection they shared that night. He fully believed that it was like nothing either of them had ever shared.

Of course he still had questions:

Was she only interested in him now because Darren had ended things?

Had Darren ended things?

Was is true that she had been celibate for a year before that night, meaning she hadn't slept with Darren?

Was she truly looking for some good sex or something more?

Would a full-blown relationship between them work? That was the most important question of all.

Pulling into the front yard of Jade's cottage, Kaeden turned off his cell phone and left it in the console of his car. He hopped out and grabbed the bouquet of lilies he'd brought for her.

He had barely made it to the small stoop before the front door opened and the doorway was filled with

Jade. She completely took his breath away in the wide-leg peach pants she wore with a cream off-the-shoulder shirt and gold accessories. Her makeup was done, enough to enhance her beauty but not too much to make him feel like he needed to ID her. "You look good," he told her with pure appreciation dripping from his baritone voice.

"You too, Mr. Strong," she told him, reaching up to pop the collar of his shirt.

"Can I kiss you?" he asked as his eyes took in her full glossy lips curved into a smile.

Jade tilted her head and looked up at him. "Careful, they're like Lay's potato chips—you can't have just one," she teased in a soft voice.

Kaeden stepped up close to her and dropped the flowers onto the swing before he softly placed his hands on her face as he looked down into her eyes. His heart swelled as he looked at this woman he had admired from a distance for so long, and now here she was. "You know I could fall for you," he whispered against her lips before he lowered his head and captured her mouth for a kiss.

"Then let's fall together," she told him huskily, then brought her hands up to grab his lapels as she traced the outline of his mouth with her tongue before she opened her mouth wide and allowed his tongue to twirl with hers.

Kaeden shivered and felt goose bumps race over his tall frame as her hand massaged his neck beneath his collar. He shifted his mouth down to kiss her neck and he felt her shiver. "We have to stop this, Jade, or soon I won't be able to," he whispered fiercely in her ear as she eased one hand down between them to massage his lengthening erection.

"Maybe I don't want to, Kaeden."

He released a heavy breath as he tilted his head back and looked up at the darkening skies. "I thought we were gonna discover more than this physical thing between us?" he asked, not sounding confident himself.

Jade stepped back until she was standing just inside her living room. "I have a refrigerator full of food and drinks. I have a very comfortable couch for conversation and getting to know one another. And . . . I have the best bed ever for something we both want. Now, are you coming in?" she asked him.

Kaeden knew that once he stepped over that threshold, he would strip them of their clothes and try to bury himself deep within Jade. There was no reasoning beyond that threshold. He reached for her hand and pulled her back out onto the stoop even as his dick throbbed. "We both know there'll be some conversation—straight dirty, and some eating—but not the food in your fridge."

"Okay," she acquiesced as she pulled the door closed and turned to lock it.

Kaeden picked up the bouquet to give to her, and he liked the pleasure he saw in her eyes.

"They're beautiful, Kaeden." She looked up at him. "I can't remember the last time someone gave me flowers. Thank you."

She kissed his cheek sweetly before she walked past him. He watched the movement of her buttocks in her pants before she climbed into his BMW. He rushed over to close the door for her.

Chapter 17

Jade took another sip of her wine and watched over the rim of her glass as Kaeden watched her from across the table. They were having a good time. The small and intimate seafood restaurant was the perfect locale for a romantic dinner. The food was good. The flirting was fun.

"You do know I couldn't stand you the first few days of the camping trip?" she told him as she sat her wine goblet down onto the glass tabletop. "I wanted to wring your neck."

Kaeden laughed. "So what changed your mind?"

Jade shifted her eyes away and shrugged slightly. "I liked that you put your brother in check for me. His lame game was really working my nerves. You were my knight in shining armor."

Kaeden leaned back in his leather club chair as he played with his own glass of rum and Coke. "I was more mad that he had the balls to say something to you when I really wanted to," he admitted.

Jade placed her head in her hand. "Oh, you were feeling me the whole time, huh?"

Kaeden picked up his glass and took a sip. "I've been feeling you since the first time I laid eyes on you in church."

Jade looked at him in surprise. "Really?"

Kaeden nodded. "You fine as hell, Jade."

She smiled and scrunched up her nose at him. "Aww. Thank you . . . but why didn't you ask me out?"

Kaeden laughed. "You would've accepted?" He balked in disbelief.

Jade shook her head and smiled. "I just needed to see past the glasses and the suits and the way I thought you were so quiet and shy. But once I did, once I did, man, you got under my skin and I couldn't understand or explain it."

"Hey, I'm not Steve Urkel."

Jade felt like maybe she'd hurt his feelings, so she reached across the table and stroked his strong hand with her finger. "Remember in the end Steve got his girl."

Kaeden nodded. "And I got mine," he told her with confidence.

She nodded as she locked her eyes with his. "And she's happy about that," she promised him huskily.

Kaeden sat up and leaned forward to raise her hand and place a kiss on her wrist.

"So . . . what happened with you and Felecia?" she asked.

"We just didn't work out."

"And?" she asked, prodding him.

"Okay, that was her in the bridal boutique that day,"

he told her, as he released her hand and picked up his drink to take a deep sip. "Let's just say she was planning a wedding with yours truly as the groom and I knew nothing about it."

"Every woman has dreams of her wedding day, Kaeden," she said.

He frowned. Deeply. "Does every woman buy the wedding dress before they're even proposed to?"

"Okay, that *is* going overboard, but it had to be more than that, Kaeden."

"She wasn't you."

Jade's heart thundered. Kaeden was really showing up big-time. Everything he said and did was on point.

"She's highly pissed at me right now. I guess I could have ended things better, but the trunk of wedding crap freaked me out."

Jade frowned. "Wow, she really wants to marry you."

Kaeden shook his head. "I think she really wants to get married. Period."

"She looks like that marrying type. You know, the French roll hairdo, the skirt down past her knees, the Bible on the backseat of the car."

Kaeden laughed. "And what type are you, Jade Prince?"

"Actually, I'm the marrying type, but because of the way I look men try to group me in the 'just a hit it and split' type." Jade sat back in her chair and crossed her legs as she eyed him. "Now, be honest. When you were checking for a sister on the low, you ever thought about me meeting your mama *or* were you imagining what all this looks like without clothes?"

Kaeden cleared his throat and shifted in his seat.

"Mmm-hmm. See. Told you," she teased.

He laughed.

"And that's why I resisted getting physical with someone."

Kaeden wiped his mouth and hands with his napkin. "Seriously?" he asked, not even hiding the obvious doubt that he had.

"A lot of Darren's anger is not because I cheated on him—because I didn't. He's mad that you got something he's been working overtime to get," she drawled as she picked up her fork and resumed eating her shrimp scampi.

"Ouch," Kaeden said.

"I want you to understand that what happened between us is not the norm for me, Kaeden." A thought occurred to Jade. "You know, I should thank you for keeping me from being a hypocrite."

"How's that?"

"I'm always complaining about men wanting me just for my body and not caring for me as a person, and here I have this really great guy offering to take me out to dinner and all I wanted to do was jump him like a horny dog."

"It wasn't easy. That was one helluva invitation." Kaeden held up his hands. "You have to understand that you are fine as hell."

"But I am also smart, determined, passionate, loving, empathetic . . ."

Kaeden leaned forward. "Those are the things I want to learn about you. Sexing the hell out of you is the easy part, and I'm ready for the work of being in a relationship with you."

Jade met his stare with one of her own as she wondered if Kaeden Strong was absolutely too good to be true. "I'm ready too," she told him.

"Good."

"Great."

"Fantastic."

Jade looked up at the deep sound of Kaeden's voice and caught the light of desire in his eyes and she picked up one of her shrimp and sucked the garlic sauce from it. "Won-der-ful."

Kaeden's eyes fell down to watch the move.

Jade loved the way his facial expression became like that of a child awaiting a huge surprise. "We're going to learn a lot about each other, but there are things we already know," she told him huskily as she swirled the shrimp in the sauce on her plate and then proceeded to suck it again.

Kaeden swallowed past a lump in his throat. "I agree. I know that you love the outdoors and you're very athletic."

Jade nodded as she eased her foot from her sandal. "And I know that you and the outdoors don't mix."

Kaeden licked his lips. "And I know that you like wearing dresses and skirts."

"And you are all over suits and slacks." Jade slid her bare foot across until she pressed it against his leg.

Kaeden jumped in surprise. "We both go to the same church," Kaeden offered as Jade massaged him intimately with her toes.

"We *used* to go to the same church," she amended.

She smiled like an angel while she enjoyed the feel of him getting hard against the sole of her wandering foot. "We grew up in the same little town and we know each other's families."

Kaeden wondered whether, if Jade didn't stop, his dick would get hard enough to lift the edge of the table. "Can we go deeper?"

Jade swirled and sucked the shrimp. Again. "Ooh. I always like it deep."

"How deep?" he asked.

Jade ran her foot up and down the length of him. "About eleven . . . inches . . . deep."

Kaeden spread his legs wider beneath the table as he shook his head. "Eleven and *a half*," he corrected her with a gleam in his eyes.

The bud between Jade's legs throbbed and she shifted in her seat. Her body felt warm and flushed. Her nipples hardened and strained against the thin lace of her brassiere. She was slightly panting and she wasn't quite sure she wasn't ready to cum right there at their table. "Ooh," she purred with a lick of her lips as she leaned back a bit to fan herself with her hand.

Kaeden reached under the table and grabbed her foot to press against his hardness. "So we had the dinner and drink, right?"

Jade nodded eagerly. "Check."

"Conversation."

"Check."

"And now for dessert?" Kaeden asked in a low voice filled with hunger for her.

Jade turned in her seat and eyed their waitress, waving her over. "Check . . . please."

"Strip," Kaeden ordered from his spot on his couch in the dimly lit living room as he unzipped his pants and removed his lengthening erection.

Jade's eyes glazed over, loving that Kaeden was just as uninhibited sexually as she was. She kept her eyes locked on him stroking the length of his dick as she slowly undressed. First her pants. Then the shirt. Panties. And lastly the bra. She stood before him nude and proud as she reached down to grasp her breasts. She pushed the full globes high until she was able to lick her throbbing nipples with the tip of her tongue while she worked her hips in a sultry back-and-forth motion.

"Hell yeah, Jade. Bring that thing to me, girl."

She watched him hurry out of his clothes and drop down to sit on the floor with his back pressed against the sofa. "What you gone do with it?" she asked as she teased her own nipples, loving the pleasure she was giving herself and so anxious for the pleasure he would give her.

"Sit on my face," he ordered.

Jade laughed huskily as she pressed her knees onto the end of the sofa so that she was straddling his head with his open mouth blowing cool air against her throbbing core. She gripped the back of the couch as Kaeden grabbed her buttocks and sucked the whole of her core into his mouth. She rocked her hips and bit her bottom lip. Her legs quivered and her feet felt like they were held to the flames as he sucked her clit deeply.

Kaeden moaned at the smell and taste of her, enjoying the treat just as much as Jade obviously did.

When she jerked her hips away he was disappointed . . . until she turned around on her knees and then leaned down the length of his body until she slid his hard length into her mouth to suck deeply.

"Aaah," he cried out, her buttocks and core splayed out before him.

"That's called a switch," she informed him as she licked from the thick base of him to the throbbing warm tip.

Kaeden nodded before he turned his head and sucked her buttocks as she jiggled her cheeks against his face. "You better stop 'fore it cum, Jade," he warned her as his heart pounded wildly in his chest.

With a last fast and deep sucking motion of his tip, Jade worked her body the length of him and spread her legs wide on his lap before she raised her buttocks and then slowly eased her core down onto his dick.

Kaeden's mouth dropped open at the sight of their union and the feel of her on him, surrounding him, gliding up and down him, riding him. He bit his bottom lip as he slapped her cheeks soundly.

Jade paused her core on the tip, exposing the wet length of him to the air as she jiggled her buttocks and squeezed her walls before expertly dropping down in one swift and hard swoop down onto him.

Kaeden's heart stopped and he roughly grabbed her buttocks to ease some of his length out of her before he filled her with his seed and ended the ride that had just begun. This position he just could not stand.

"Switch," Jade called out before she rolled off his erection but then climbed onto his lap to ease down onto it again.

"How many of these switches are we going to have tonight?" he asked, almost breathless as she worked his dick like a piston with her walls.

"As many as you can stand."

Kaeden just let himself drift back as he gripped her hips and enjoyed the ride.

Jade sighed as Kaeden pushed her naked body up against the wall. She arched her back as he sucked her neck. Her body shivered. She raced her hands down his body to tightly grasp his buttocks, enjoying the feel of them. "Yes," she moaned into the heated air.

Kaeden lifted one of her legs high on his arm before he bent low and guided his dick up into her.

"Lord, you on my spot," she told him before she hotly licked his chin and bit as each thrust pressed her buttocks against the cool wall.

Kaeden stared into her eyes as he tilted her head up and kissed her passionately. "God, I love sexing you," he whispered into her open, panting mouth.

"Oh, it's good. It's good." Jade smiled before she sucked his mouth.

"I'm all up in it," he told her cockily.

"All of it, baby."

He buried his tongue in her mouth and they rocked against each other as the wall kept them both from falling to the floor. And they didn't rush it. It was a slow and steady grind complemented with deep kisses as their eyes stayed locked. Intense. Passionate. Fulfilling.

Kaeden dropped his head down on hers as his entire body went still.

Jade continued to move.

"No, I don't want to cum yet."

"Kaeden," she whispered into his ear.

"Huh?"

"Switch."

Jade sat down on the edge of the bed and spread her knees wide as Kaeden knelt down between them. She pressed her hands into the bed and leaned back as he lowered his head to capture one taut and throbbing nipple in his eager mouth as he probed her core, searching for the heat and wetness to quickly and deeply slide into.

They both cried out.

Jade at the hardness.

Kaeden at the tight heat.

Shivering, he began to flex his square buttocks with each thrust into her tightness. He enjoyed the sight of Jade's full chocolate globes lightly bouncing against her chest with her nipples pointing at him as he drove into her. Again and again and again.

"Uhmmmm," Jade moaned in sweet ecstasy as she leaned back to work her hips against his in a circular motion that was a sight to see and to feel.

Kaeden leaned back to watch his dick slickly slide

in and out. Her thick, hairless lips snuggled against him as her walls milked him, gripping and releasing perfectly. "Damn, Jade. Damn it," he cried out as his pulse raced and sweat covered his entire body.

"What?" she asked cockily as she looked up at him. "Good, ain't it?"

Kaeden gripped her thighs. "Damn right."

"Say it," she ordered.

"It's good, baby. Damn, it's good."

"It gets even better," she told him, leaning up to wrap her arms around his neck as they continued to mate in the most primal fashion.

"Jade."

"Hmmmm?"

"No more switching."

She leaned her head back and laughed. "No more?"

Kaeden wrapped his arms around her snugly and buried his face in the sweet hollow of her neck, allowing himself to get lost to time and place.

Jade wrapped her legs and arms around him just as tightly.

Back and forth they rocked, slow and steady, in perfect unison until they both soon were tensing and shivering with the sweet explosions of release.

Both felt complete.

Chapter 18

Jade eased Kaeden's arms from her body and slid from the bed. Stretching her nude frame, she tiptoed out of her bedroom and made her way into the kitchen where she fixed herself a glass of ice water. She felt exhausted and exhilarated all at once.

She and Kaeden had been inseparable the last few weeks, sharing steamy, sex-filled nights and dates showcasing more of Charleston than she had seen during her entire twenty-five years growing up in Holtsville. She smiled into her glass remembering the good times they had shared. The funny moments. The quiet and reflective moments. The sensual ones. All of them had made for a good time for the new couple.

Jade was finally beginning to believe that her mother was right that Kaeden was her Mr. Right and there was nothing wrong with that.

"I missed you in bed."

Jade turned. She smiled at Kaeden standing behind her in a pair of pajama bottoms that were slung low on his narrow hips, while he wiped his eyes with the back of his hands. "Needed some water. Want some?" she offered.

At his silence she looked over her shoulder at him. His eyes were running all over her nude body. When those eyes shifted up to her face they were filled with desire. Jade sat the glass down on the counter and covered her privates with her arms as best she could. "Oh no, Kaeden Strong, you know I have a camping trip I'm leaving for early in the morning. I need my rest," she told him.

Kaeden reached out and grabbed her to pull her close to his body. "Trust me, once I get done you won't have no choice *but* to sleep," he whispered near her ear before biting her playfully.

Jade tilted her head back as his dangerous mouth planted kisses along her neck. "I can't, Kaeden."

He gave her one final kiss to her collarbone and then soundly slapped her ass.

"Ow!" Jade exclaimed, rubbing her bottom as they made their way back to her bedroom.

"You don't mind me slapping that ass when I'm hitting it from the back." Kaeden climbed back into the bed.

"Well, I'm usually pretty preoccupied then." Jade snuggled close to Kaeden, laying her head on his chest, her arms across his abdomen, and her leg across his legs.

Her body fit his like a lock to a key.

Kaeden brought his hand up to massage her lower back and the deep curve above her buttocks. "Your body feels good, Jade."

She smiled like a cat stretching in the sun as she

looked up through the open window at the full moon seeming ready to burst through. "Do you have any regrets, Kaeden?" she asked him softly into the quiet of the night.

Kaeden nodded. "I have a few. Do you?"

Jade laughed huskily. "I have plenty."

"Share."

They had shared many a conversation like this over the last few weeks. Random questions. Reflective thoughts. Both the impetus for talks where they really got to know one another. "I wish my mother and I were as close as when I was a little girl," Jade admitted.

"Why do you think you're not close?"

"She's so busy catching up on her lost youth that she wants a hang-out partner and not a daughter." Jade's eyes saddened. "Have you seen my mother? She looks like my sister."

"Ain't that the truth," Kaeden drawled.

Jade pinched his side.

"Ow!"

They both laughed as they settled back against one another.

"Your turn," Jade prodded him.

"I always wondered why I'm the black sheep of my family," Kaeden said, the sadness in his voice revealing how deeply he meant the words.

Jade hugged him closer.

"It was real hard growing up and having to watch my brothers through the window while they played or worked the farm. I felt like the boy in the bubble," he joked, obviously trying to lighten the mood.

"Awwwwww," she said sympathetically.

Kaeden chuckled. "Hell, if I didn't have the silver hair and looks like Kahron I would think I was adopted or switched at birth."

Jade thought for a moment as she lightly stroked his abdomen. "Families are like puzzles, Kaeden, every piece is cut differently and every piece has its predestined spot . . . but when you put the pieces all together, they fit perfectly."

"That's deep." Kaeden placed a kiss to the top of her head.

Jade twirled her tongue around his nipple, the hairs tickling her tongue. "I can get all philosophical when I wanna."

Kaeden shivered. "If you don't stop that you're gonna get all this," he told her, lifting his chin in the direction of his dick tenting the sheet.

Jade laughed as she turned over in the bed to lie on her side. Kaeden immediately shifted his own body to spoon her from behind. She released a contented sigh as one of his warm hands settled on her breast. "No nipple action tonight," she told him with a yawn, having learned that he liked to fall asleep teasing her nipples.

Kaeden slid his hand down to her belly. "All I'd have to do is lift your leg and slide in. Just a little light one. We won't shake the bed or even break a sweat."

Jade had to admit that it sounded tempting—especially with his hardness pressed against her buttocks. But if she gave in she wouldn't be worth a quarter in the morning. So she closed her eyes and threw out a fake snore.

Kaeden chuckled. "Night, Jade."

"Good night."

Kaeden spent most of that weekend at his parents' missing Jade and avoiding as much of the outdoors as he could. He knew she was getting in today. He just wasn't sure what time to expect her. But as soon as he got the call he would walk out of church if he had to, to get to her. He was ready for his woman—*his* woman—to get home. Particularly from a trip where she might be the lone woman among a group of men. Jade in jeans and sweatshirt was just as tempting as a nude woman. There wasn't much she could do to hide her wide hips and full bosom.

Bzzzz.

A text. He grabbed his BlackBerry.

Almost to Holtsville. Meet me @ my house.

Kaeden smiled broadly as he rose to his feet. "This is good," he told the rest of the Strong bunch that were lounging in their Sunday finest on the porch. "But I gotta go."

"Must've been one helluva message," Kahron drawled as he led one of the ranch's ponies with Kadina and KJ nestled on its back.

Everyone laughed.

"Is Jade back from the trip?" his mother asked.

"Yes, ma'am," he answered as he walked down the stairs and made his way to his BMW.

"So you're going to miss church this morning?" Kael called to his son.

Kaeden looked up, surprised because his father usually didn't want to go to church himself. But his concern faded at the twinkle in his father's eyes. "Jade and I might come back later this afternoon," he told them before climbing into his vehicle.

They all waved him off as he reversed in an arc and then pulled off down the drive. The idea of bringing Jade around his family was spur of the moment but the more Kaeden sat with it, the more he liked the idea of it.

At first he worried Kaleb would hold a grudge because his brother was with the woman he briefly tried to pursue, but when Kaleb first heard the news he just shook Kaeden's hand and asked: "Sure you can handle all that?"

Kaeden had gripped his brother's hand tighter and replied: "Trust and believe that."

They laughed. It was done. Kaeden 1, Kaleb 0. When it came to Jade, anyway.

And Kaeden was happy with Jade.

The sound of a horn blaring made him shift his bespectacled eyes up to the rearview mirror. He smiled as the black Wild-n-Out van turned into the yard. Before she had even come to a stop, Kaeden was out of his car and ready to swoop her into his arms as soon as the driver's-side door opened.

"Hey, ba'y."

"Hey, sexy."

They smiled even as their lips touched.

"Miss me?" Jade asked as she wrapped her arms up around his neck.

"Yeah, I did," he told her with complete honesty as

his body reacted to being near her and having her in his arms.

"Good," she teased with a laugh.

Kaeden looked down into the smiling mocha face and he felt some powerful emotional clutch at his heart. "I could really fall for you, Jade Prince," he told her low in his throat.

Jade's smile faded as her eyes glimmered. "And I think I have already fallen for you a little bit," she told him.

Kaeden dropped his hands to her waist. "Just a little bit?" he joked.

Jade leaned back in his arms and winked. "Just a *lee* little bit."

Kaeden kissed her deeply with a hungry moan opening his heart and allowing himself to freely fall.

Jade held the sheet up with her arms to cover her nudity as she fed Kaeden fresh fruit from a glass bowl. "This was nice," she told him before biting into a bright red strawberry and then offering him a bite as well.

"You're welcome."

Jade leaned down and licked the trail of juice from the fruit that drizzled down his chin. "Now, why does that taste better than the actual fruit?"

"Must be all this chocolate," Kaeden mused, dropping the sheet to expose his chest.

Jade playfully plucked one of the lenses of his glasses. "Well, I loved my bubble bath and the breakfast in bed and the massage and the things that happened *after* the massage."

Kaeden reached over to rub light circles on her back with his fingertips. "I know you like to relax after an excursion."

Jade lifted the sheet to stretch her body out next to Kaeden's. "All I want to do right now is sleep, and then I'm going to make us dinner."

"Actually, I thought we could ride over to my parents' and eat there," he told her before he removed his glasses and set them on the nightstand. They both turned on their sides and snuggled close in their beloved spoon position. "But if you're tired, we don't have to go."

"No, let's go. I wanna go horseback riding."

Kaeden stiffened. *Please don't ask me to ride with you. Please don't ask me to ride with you.*

Jade's eyes popped open before she rolled onto her back. "Actually, I know your allergies get to you, but I think it would be cool if we rode together for a little while."

Kaeden knew that Jade made concessions for him all the time. She was an outdoors baby and they spent the majority of their time together indoors because of him. "Yeah, we can ride," he promised, a man of his word.

If he had to go to his allergist and get a dozen shots in his butt to take Jade horseback riding for an hour, then he would just have to do that.

Jade took a deep sip of her glass of cherry lemonade as she and Kaeden sat in his parents' kitchen eating fried chicken, cabbage, white rice, and huge spoonfuls of macaroni and cheese. "Oh my God, this is so good," she sighed, doing a little dance on her stool.

Kaeden laughed. "My mom and my sisters-in-law cook like this every Sunday," he bragged before taking a bite of a chicken thigh.

"I couldn't eat like this all the time. I would blow up like a double-wide mobile home."

Kaeden leaned back to eye her buttocks and her long shapely legs in the jean shorts she wore with studded flip-flops. "Nah, don't do that," he told her in appreciation.

"Y'all done eating?" Lisha Strong asked as she strolled into the kitchen.

"Yes, ma'am, everything was so good. My grand-daddy would love it," Jade said as Kaeden rose to pick up their plates.

"Take a plate for Esai," Lisha said, moving to the pantry to grab one of the hundreds of to-go containers they kept handy. "Him and Kael used to hunt with that Holtsville Hunting Club, and the wives took turns taking food out to their little clubhouse, so Esai's eaten plenty of my food."

Jade nodded as she watched the becoming woman ladle heaping servings of food into the Styrofoam container. "Thank you, Mrs. Strong," Jade said, hating that she sounded as nervous as she felt.

"Uhm-hmm. No problem. I'm just going to leave it in the fridge 'til y'all go."

Kaeden squeezed her shoulders comfortingly before he briefly kissed her neck and whispered, "Relax, Jade. She doesn't bite."

She smiled . . . until Garcelle, Bianca, and Kaitlyn strolled in. *Oh great, I'm about to be quizzed*, Jade thought, stiffening her back as Kaeden gave her one last wave and left the kitchen.

Of course Jade knew of the women—they all lived in the same small town and attended the same church—but Jade didn't know them personally. Jade knew she was an attractive woman, but watching this unholy trifecta was still intimidating.

Garcelle was a Beyoncé look-alike, curves and all.

Bianca was equally gorgeous with a stomach flat as a board—all hints of a baby bulge gone.

And Kaitlyn was tall and thin and willowy, with a head full of curly jet-black hair.

"Jade, would you like something to drink?" Garcelle asked, moving to the fridge.

"I have lemonade."

Bianca waved her hand. "Not that. We mean a real drink."

Kaitlyn sat four crystal wine goblets on the island. "Oh my God, Jade, Garcelle makes the *best* white sangria."

"Ooh," Jade sighed as she eyed the huge glass pitcher of white sangria filled with slices of oranges, peaches, green apples, and grapes. She filled each of the glasses halfway.

"Let the men have their ugly and nasty beer in a can, but we ladies sip on sangria." Lisha winked at Jade as she opened a bottle of Sprite and topped off each glass with a splash.

Jade accepted the goblet passed to her and immediately raised it to her lips.

"Oh, no, no, no, no, no," Mrs. Strong admonished. "First we toast to something good in our lives."

Bianca snuck her a look saying, *just smile and nod.* And so Jade smiled. And then Jade nodded.

"Now, I'll start." Mrs. Strong cleared her throat and raised her goblet high. "Here's to family. The most important thing to me."

Kaitlyn stopped checking her nails to pick up her own goblet. "Here's to Louis Vuitton and Gucci. Chocolate mani-pedis and stone massages. Ooh, I almost forgot—"

"Kaitlyn!" Mrs. Strong snapped.

"Remember the rules, Mama, no judging," Kaitlyn reminded her chidingly with a twinkle in her eyes.

Mrs. Strong rolled her eyes heavenward.

Bianca held up her glass next. "Here's to sisterhood."

"I'm thankful for Kade agreeing that we should start trying to make a baby brother or sister for Kadina," Garcelle added softly with a smile, her Spanish accent prominent.

All of the women, including Jade, sighed in pleasure.

"Well, I'm adding on that I am thankful for that," Lisha said with a wink at Garcelle.

"Enjoy the liquor while you can, Garcelle," Kaitlyn teased.

"Okay, Jade, sugar, what are you toasting?" Mrs. Strong asked her.

Surprised, Jade eyed each of them. "Me too, huh?"

"Uhm-hmm," they all said in unison.

"Okay, um, I am thankful for meeting Kaeden and

not letting our obvious differences keep us from getting to know each other better." Jade lifted her glass high into the air, filling in their circle.

Jade watched the camaraderie among the women. Lisha Strong seemed to be closer to her daughters-in-law than Jade felt to her own mother. And so far, Jade genuinely liked them all. They laughed together. They shared things. They loved one another. She'd thought they were going to grill her or rake her over the coals, but instead they had welcomed her into their midst.

"Cheers, ladies."

"Cheers."

Kaeden's throat was itching. His eyes were watery behind his spectacles. He wanted so badly to pull his inhaler from his pants pocket and suck for dear life on it.

But he didn't.

"Isn't this the most beautiful thing ever," Jade said in complete awe from atop her horse, looking out at the sun setting on the horizon. The sky was a myriad of vibrant colors with just a streak of darkness on the perimeter.

Kaeden shifted on his own horse and tried his best to concentrate on the view, but all he could think about was the long stretches of land that was kicking his allergies into overdrive.

"I just love the outdoors. I have to get it from my grandfather because my dad is all my GQ and my mom is . . . well, she's my mom."

Kaeden gripped the reins of his horse as he rubbed his tongue against his palate.

"Thank you for this, Kaeden, I really appreciate it," she told him. "So much so that I think that one good turn deserves another."

Kaeden felt Jade's hand on his thigh and for the first time since he met her he doubted he could focus enough to get hard. "Jade!"

Jade and both their horses jumped.

"Listen," he began, digging in his pocket for his inhaler, which he promptly used. "Making love to you in the middle of this hayfield is way too much to ask from your man right now."

"Awwww, baby, I'm sorry," Jade said consolingly as he removed his glasses and wiped his eyes. "Why didn't you say something?"

"Because you love the outdoors and I know you hate always being cooped up in the house," he told her in between puffs.

Jade leaned over and pressed a kiss to his shaven cheek. "Listen, we have to be real with each other, and if that means using your inhaler, then use it. If that means leaving something we're doing early, then we'll leave. Got it?"

Kaeden nodded as he shoved his inhaler back into his pocket. He smiled at her.

She laughed. "I swear, you are the weirdest *but* the sweetest man I've ever known, Kaeden Strong."

Kaeden slapped her rump and the horse's to send them ahead of him headed back to the ranch.

* * *

"It's over, Felecia, and I'm sorry if you're hurt, but you have to stop calling me."

Jade lay deathly still in the bed as she pretended to be asleep while she listened to Kaeden trying to talk low on his cell phone.

"Felecia, if you threaten to hurt yourself again, I'll have to call your father and clue him in." Kaeden sighed. "I didn't think you wanted that either."

Jade frowned. *Hurt herself. What the hell?*

"Felecia, another woman has nothing to do with this."

Jade started to sit up but she held herself in check.

"Felecia, we barely dated for a month. I think if you just come to grips with it being over, you will agree with me that we weren't working out."

Having had enough, Jade made a show of stirring in her sleep and sitting up in the middle of the bed.

Kaeden turned to look at her and blew her a kiss. "I gotta go, Felecia."

Jade was at least glad he didn't try and hide who he was talking to, but she was even more pleased when he finally ended the call. "So, Felecia's not taking the breakup well?" she asked.

Kaeden remained by the bedroom window, his figure outlined by the light of the moon. "I let the fact that you were seeing Darren push me into dating Felecia again."

"Again, huh?" Jade asked.

"And that's why I feel bad, because I knew we didn't click the first time and I really shouldn't have messed with that this time."

"So why did you?" Jade asked, watching him as

he set his phone on the nightstand and then got back in bed.

"I told you why."

"Oh," was all that Jade said as she pulled the sheet up around her breasts.

"Hell, even you said we made a cute couple," Kaeden told her as he flung the sheet over his body.

Jade lightly boxed his arm. "Don't play with me."

Kaeden chuckled before he reached out to wrap his arm tightly around her. "You and your girlfriend make a cute couple," he mimicked in a feminine voice.

Jade bit her bottom lip to keep from smiling. "Get off me."

He wrestled her down in the bed and then slid on top of her, grabbing both her wrists and pressing her arms above her head. "You don't want me to get off of you. You know you want me to get in you."

Jade shook her head. "Since you don't have on your glasses, Mr. Magoo, I know everything is blurry right now. I just shook my head no."

"Ha, ha, ha. Now you got jokes."

She smiled. "No more calls from Felecia, especially when you are fresh from my bed, Kaeden Strong," she told him just before she lifted her chin and offered it to him to kiss.

And he did plant a kiss there, and a few on her high cheekbones and then her neck and along her collarbone. "And if I ask you not to work alongside Darren all day every day in that little office?"

Jade arched her back, presenting the tips of her breasts to him. "I would tell you that I like a man who is secure and not ruled by jealousy."

Kaeden circled his tongue around one sweet chocolate tip and then the other. Jade shivered. He took another hot lick. "I would tell you I like the same from my woman."

Jade struggled a bit against his hold on her wrists as Kaeden sucked nearly half of her breast into his mouth. She gasped in pleasure and closed her eyes at the feel of sweet torture. "And how do I know Felecia's antics to get you back won't work?" she asked breathlessly as that now familiar heat between them began to rise like steam.

Kaeden planted a soft and tantalizing bite to the fleshy side of one brown mound before he looked at her. "You have men sniffing behind you all the time. How do I know one of them won't swoop you away from me like I swooped you from Darren?" Kaeden asked.

Jade was surprised to discover from the intensity of his eyes that Kaeden was serious. "Because you can trust me, Kaeden," she whispered to him. "You are all the man I need. You satisfy me. You complete me. You make me happy. And sometimes this all scares me because I have never felt this way about anyone. Not so fast and so strong. You were nothing like what I thought I wanted, and now you are everything I need."

Kaeden released her arms and laid his head down on her chest with his ear pressed just above her heart. "I have no idea where we're headed, but I do know that I am not ready to stop the ride."

Jade wrapped him tightly in her embrace, sure that he could hear the beat of her heart. She spread her legs open beneath him, snuggling him into the intimate vee of her legs.

No further words were spoken—or needed—as Kaeden shifted his body up, pressing his chest down upon her twin mounds as he maneuvered his hips upward to guide his hardening shaft deep inside her.

Jade closed her eyes and bit his shoulder.

Kaeden felt his dick harden and stretch inside her, filling her, cruising along her ridged and moist walls.

There in the center of the squeaking bed, their limbs tightly entwined, their bodies ultimately united, Kaeden and Jade made the most heated and emotionally intense love of all.

Chapter 19

Kaeden had to hire a replacement for Felecia. In the six weeks since their breakup he was catching pure hell trying to answer the phones and focus on his work.

Brrrrnnnngggg.

These days the very sound of a ringing phone irked his nerves. Roughly pushing his spectacles up his nose, he dropped his favorite Montblanc pen and snatched up the phone. "Strong Accountings," he said, trying to make his deep voice sound pleasant.

He immediately recognized Jade's husky laughter. "You never worked at McDonald's, did you?" she teased. "You're supposed to say, 'Strong Accountings. How may I help you, please?' See?"

Kaeden actually smiled. "Seeing how you know the drill so well, why don't you help your man out and come answer these phones?" he asked, only semi-joking.

"Oscar the Grouch is here today, so I don't see why

I can't zip over there and help you out—i.e., place an ad for a new receptionist."

"I would really appreciate that," he told her.

"On the way."

He hung up the phone and focused his attention on his work. Soon the chime on the front door sounded.

"It's just me, baby," Jade called back to him.

Moments later she appeared and Kaeden thought she looked refreshing in the white cotton flowing skirt and off-the-shoulder peasant blouse she wore with chunky silver-and-turquoise accessories. "That's pretty," he told her as she walked over to plant a kiss to his mouth.

"Thank you."

"Your boy still giving you the cold shoulder?" Kaeden asked, tapping his pen against his wooden desk.

Jade sighed. "If it's not work related, he has *nothing* to say to me."

"Do you care?" Kaeden snapped.

Jade eyed him in a scolding fashion. "It's just a really uncomfortable work environment, and I don't want to give up the business. You know how much I love it."

Kaeden nodded. "I know you do. Does he know we're together?"

Jade shifted her eyes from him. "Huh?" she asked innocently.

"Does he know, Jade?" Kaeden asked again in a hard voice.

"No . . . but we don't talk about personal things. He never asked. I never volunteered the info. It would just make us owning the business together way worse,

Kaeden." Jade came around to stand behind his chair. She pressed her fingers into his shoulders, massaging him. "Did you tell Felecia about us?"

Kaeden stiffened beneath her fingers.

Jade dug her fingers deeper into his shoulders. "But did *you* tell her?" she asked again.

Kaeden laughed as he shook off her pinching touch. "Okay, no."

Jade wrapped her arms around him from behind and planted a kiss on the top of his silver hair. "Just let me handle this my way, Kaeden. I promised that you can trust me, right?"

He leaned back against her. "Right."

"You and Felecia never did the nasty in here, did you?" Jade asked with a scowl.

"Felecia and I never did the nasty—as you say— she's saving herself until she's married."

Jade released him and walked back around the desk to look at him. "You never told me that," she said in mock accusation.

"You never asked," Kaeden said simply before shifting his glasses on his face and then turning to his laptop.

"Kaeden," Jade called out to him.

He looked up.

She twirled like Wonder Woman, causing her skirt to lift up like a parasol around her waist, exposing the black thong she wore. "I love this skirt. Do you?"

"Is that all you're wearing under there?" he asked, frowning in disapproval.

"What more do I need?" Jade asked, coming back

over to him to lift and then lower her skirt over his head and shoulders.

"Something that doesn't have your ass jiggling every which way for any man to see," he said. "You might as well have nothing on, Jade."

She promptly removed the thong and then tossed it atop the files and folders on his desk. "You know what, you're right," she told him.

"I'm serious, Jade, you shouldn't be in a skirt with nothing but a skimpy thong on—"

"But I don't have the skimpy thong on anymore, Kaeden. See?"

Kaeden shook his head, fighting the grin that wanted to spread across his face as his anger dissolved into nonexistence. He eyed her cleanly shaven and plump mound as he inhaled deeply of the scent of perfume on her thick thighs. Against his better judgment, he bent his head and sucked the mound before he lifted his hand to slip two stiff fingers up into her moist and tight being.

Jade's hips bucked and she trembled uncontrollably as his two fingers stroked her while his thumb massaged the throbbing bud that was the center of her passion.

Kaeden removed his fingers and sucked her juices away.

Jade removed the skirt and watched him. "Good?" she asked hotly with a lick of her lips.

"Damn good," Kaeden assured her.

Jade bent over. With eager hands she undid his belt buckle and zipper.

Kaeden spread his thighs wide and arched his hips

at the first feel of her warm hands on his shaft. And when she held the thick rod up straight and lowered her mouth onto him, Kaeden's buttocks clenched and his heart pounded wildly. He reached underneath her skirt to massage and slap her buttocks as she sucked him like there was nothing in the world she'd rather do.

It took him a minute to remember that they were in front of a bay of windows on the front of the house looking out onto the front yard and street. "Jade, let's lock up and go up to one of the bedrooms upstairs. Someone might see us through the window."

"So?" Jade said, releasing him as she climbed across his lap and settled her throbbing core down onto him in one vicious swoop. "Let 'em look. They might like it. They might learn something."

Kaeden's dick hardened at her boldness. She was his sexual equal. When it's on, it's on, and nothing else matters.

So he leaned back in his chair, grabbing her hips and sucking wildly at her breasts as he enjoyed the ride.

Felecia's eyes widened in surprise and then squinted in anger at the sight of Jade Prince's attention-seeking yellow Jeep Wrangler parked next to Kaeden's BMW. "How cozy," Felecia drawled sarcastically, assuming that the woman had finally returned to hire Kaeden as the accountant or business manager for her little business.

She pulled up and parked her car, checking her

appearance in the rearview mirror before she climbed out and walked up the stairs.

She wasn't ready to let Kaeden go yet. She still had hope that he would see that she was the woman for him. And she was so sure of this fact that she hadn't clued her family in that Kaeden had dumped her, saving on the embarrassment when he returned.

Felecia walked up onto the porch and her eyes immediately went to the set of bay windows of Kaeden's office. Wanting to see him busy at work, she walked to the window. Her mouth fell open at the sight of Jade riding Kaeden in his office chair.

He tilted his chin up and said something to her that made Jade ride him harder as she sucked the tongue he then offered to her.

Felecia let out a little wail, stepping back and pressing her back to the house as she clutched at her chest. She panted as she closed her eyes and tried to settle herself.

Felecia knew that a woman—some wild woman without morals and boundaries—*had* to have wooed Kaeden away from her. She *knew* it. So it was Jade "Miss 36–26–40" Prince.

Felecia forced herself to calm down. She forced herself to think.

The sins of the flesh were a strong temptation for a man. Hmph, she'd even had a few naughty dreams herself. So she decided she could forgive Kaeden, because it was very hard to stop a child from accepting candy that was freely offered, and men were like children when it came to sex (i.e., the forbidden fruit).

But she could not and would not compete with Jade

on this level. Sneaking one little look just to make sure they were still "busy," Felecia tiptoed across the porch and down the stairs. She hated to start her car but she reversed out of the yard so quickly she was glad there was no oncoming traffic.

Felecia knew she had to break up Kaeden and Jade. For that she knew she needed a little help. She knew just where to find it.

Felecia parked her car on the corner of Main Street and then climbed out to walk until she found the storefront she was looking for. Soon the colorful logo for Wild-n-Out Tours caught her eyes.

She walked in and her eyes immediately recognized the tall and handsome light-skinned man who walked out to greet her.

"Welcome to Wild-n-Out. I'm Darren. Can I help you?"

Felecia accepted the hand he offered. "Actually, Darren, I think we can help each other. I'm Kaeden Strong's ex and soon-to-be wife, with your help, I hope."

Darren eyed her from head to toe for a few quiet moments like he was sizing up her and the situation. "You just might be right. Come on into my office."

Hours later Jade was busy at the computer putting the finishing touches on the advertisement she drew up for a new receptionist for Kaeden. She was proud of herself because after their tryst she really wanted to take a quick nap. Instead they rushed upstairs and took a shower.

She was just about to fax the ad over to the local newspapers and find out how to post it with Job Service when the door opened. She smiled at the tall, wide, and solid man who walked in. "Welcome to Strong Accountings. Can I help you?"

He smiled like he'd won the lottery as his eyes took in her bare shoulders and the slight bit of cleavage showing. "Damn right you can help me. You replacing the other lady that worked here? What was her name? Felecia."

Jade forced a fake smile. "I'm just helping out today. Do you have an appointment?"

"Well, I'm Juba Lockhart. And your name, beautiful?"

"Nice to meet you, Mr. Lockhart. I'm Jade. Jade Prince," she told him, shifting her hand away when he reached down to touch her.

"So when can I take you out, Jade Prince?"

"Never."

Jade jumped in surprise at the sound of Kaeden's voice as he strolled into the outer office. She could tell from the tightness of his jaw that he was annoyed, and Jade felt her own anger rise. *Damn, give me a chance to check a Negro*, she thought as she watched the two men shake hands.

"Was I stepping on your toes, Kaeden?" Juba asked as his eyes shifted from Kaeden to Jade and then back again.

Kaeden nodded at him.

Juba laughed at him wolfishly. "You lucky dawg you."

Jade slapped her hand in exasperation against the

desk and rolled her eyes. "Hello, I'm sitting here, fellas," she told them.

"Yes, ma'am." Juba reached in the back pocket of the overalls he wore and handed Kaeden a folded manila envelope. "Just dropping off those titles. They're all signed and ready to be turned over."

Kaeden accepted the envelope. "Thanks, Juba."

The man gave Jade one more appreciative look before he chuckled and walked to the door. "No disrespect, ma'am, but he *is* one lucky dawg," he said before leaving.

Kaeden turned to walk back into his office.

"Um, Kaeden," Jade called out.

He turned back to her. "Yeah, baby?"

"I am capable of stopping an admirer in his tracks," she told him, not even looking at him as she turned back to the computer.

He said nothing else before he walked back into his office.

Kaeden was taking a break from his work with his chair turned to face the window. He was thinking about the jealousy he felt when he overheard Juba Lockhart flirting with Jade. Jealousy had made his entire body feel on fire with anger.

Only to himself would he admit that he felt like Jade was far out of his league and he was just waiting for her to discover that and leave him.

Releasing a heavy breath, he swiveled his chair, inching it forward to resume his bookkeeping duties. Jade hadn't spoken to him all day, and whenever he attempted to strike up a conversation, she straight short-talked him until he returned to his office.

Deciding to just give her time to cool off, Kaeden had stayed in his office and focused on work. Their bid for their farm equipment had finally been accepted and Kaeden was busy handling the transfer of funds and then the exchange of titles.

"No," Jade cried out.

Kaeden looked up and then immediately came from behind his desk to rush into the outer office. "Jade, what's wrong?" he asked, coming to see the alarmed expression on her face as the phone dropped from her hand.

"Can you take me to the hospital? My grandfather just had a heart attack."

"Of course. Let me lock up and we'll leave right now," Kaeden told her without any hesitation.

"Kaeden." Jade grabbed lightly at his wrist. "Thank you."

He pulled her forward and planted a consoling and loving kiss to the top of her short ebony curls as he massaged her back. "That's what I'm here for," he promised her.

Darren watched Felecia leave his office, his eyes dipping down to take in the up-and-down motion of her small but soft buttocks in the slacks she wore. Felecia had been a wealth of information.

She had just walked in on Jade giving up the good-ies in Kaeden's office. First the woods and now in front of an open window. "No-good trick," he swore, even as jealousy burned the pit of his stomach.

He was not going to sit back and let the two of them skip off to happiness while he was left looking the fool. Felecia would be useful in his need for revenge . . . particularly when he took great pleasure in telling Kaeden Strong *when* he slept with his ex.

"Payback is a bitch," he said aloud to himself.

Jade and Kaeden sat in the intensive care unit of Colleton Memorial Hospital. The TV played but neither focused on it. Jade's mind was on her grandfather and the stupid hospital policy that prevented them from seeing him any more than one hour every four hours.

Kaeden's mind was filled with concern for Jade. She hadn't spoken much since their arrival. Even as the doctor filled her in on her grandfather's stable condition, she hadn't said much.

"Do you want me to get you something to eat?" he asked her as she snuggled deeper against his side.

"Don't leave me."

He nodded and hugged her closer as he planted a warm kiss to her forehead.

They both looked up as hard footsteps echoed down the hall and then the doorway to the waiting room was suddenly filled with activity. Kaeden knew the tall and curvaceous woman with the waist-length weave, form-fitting jeans, blinged-out T-shirt, and stilettos was Jade's mother, Deena.

The two women looked like sisters.

"I got here as soon as I could," Deena said, moving to sit down beside Jade and placed a comforting hand—complete with inch-long acrylic nails—on her thigh.

"Thanks, Ma. I called Daddy and he's on his way, so please don't start, this is not about y'all or y'all marriage," Jade said wearily, her head still on Kaeden's shoulder.

"How's your grandfather?" Deena asked as she sat her large gold handbag on the empty chair beside her.

"He's stable now. It wasn't his heart. His sugar was too high. They finally got it down and they're waiting on a private room to move him," Jade told her mom.

They all fell silent.

"And you must be Kaeden," Deena said.

"Yes ma'am," he said, leaning forward slightly to offer Deena his hand.

She accepted it and sized him up. "Oh, okay. Okay," she said with a nod of her head. "I see it. I'm feeling the sexy nerd thing. All right."

He took that as her form of approval.

Jade released a very long and very heavy sigh.

Kaeden hugged her closer.

Unlike Deena, the appearance of Jade's father and stepmother was surprising. Suddenly they were there. A tall and handsome bald-headed man with a silver-flecked goatee and a beautiful woman who was obviously around Jade's age.

"Careful, Harrison, it might be past her bedtime," Deena drawled sarcastically.

"Mama," Jade snapped, sitting up.

"At least she's acting her age," Harrison drawled in

return, reaching back to take his wife's hand in his—a decidedly protective move.

"Daddy!" Jade snapped, turning in her chair to eye him.

"What?" he asked in all his over-fifty swagger in his silk shirt, linen shorts, and leather sandals. "This is my father laid up in the hospital, so why does my wife have to be accosted as soon as we walk in the room?"

"I could care less about you and my mini-me wannabe, you played-out eighties reject," Deena snapped as she jumped to her stilettoed feet.

Kaeden watched Jade's stepmother step back like she was afraid Deena was going to attack her. Beside him Jade dropped her head in her hands.

"The eighties? Careful, Deena, your age is showing," Harrison drawled before he twisted his gold watch on his arm and sat down across from Deena's seat.

His wife eyed Deena carefully as she eased by her and took the seat next to Harrison.

"Are you thirsty, baby? I think I could dig up one of Jade's old bottles for you," Deena threw over her shoulder before she reclaimed her seat.

"Pick with someone your own age, Deena. I'm sure there's a geriatric wing or something."

Deena hopped to her feet again and Harrison jumped to his until they were nose to nose arguing and name calling.

Jade stood to push them apart. "I'm sick of both of you. When did I become the dang on parent, because both of you acting childish," she snapped at them both before she stalked out of the waiting room.

The silence following her exit was awkward.

Kaeden gave them a smile and then hurried out of the room. Jade was standing at the end of the hall with her forehead pressed against the glass. Her shoulders shook and he knew she was crying.

He said absolutely nothing as he wrapped his arms around her from behind. It was like she was waiting for him because her body went weak as she turned to press her face into his neck. "Kaeden, you are my rock. My constant. When I'm with you I feel calm and I feel protected. I thank you so much for that. I thank you for being the one piece of sanity in my crazy-ass life," she whispered to him as her tears wet him.

"And I will be that for you as long as you let me, Jade," he whispered back to her, hoping to create a separate world for her in his arms. Kaeden placed comforting kisses along the side of her face.

Chapter 20

Jade didn't see her little cottage for two entire days while she waited for her grandfather to be released from the hospital. Everyone else came and went but she was the constant, sleeping on that awful pull-out armchair in his private room and just being there to watch television with him. Mostly she tried to keep his independent mind off going home before it was time.

Kaeden had brought her a change of clothes and kept her free of hospital food for dinner, coming to the hospital as soon as he closed the Strong Accountings offices. And she loved that he and her grandfather had gotten along so quickly and so well. Once she even fell asleep in her chair and woke up to find them still talking.

Kaeden had shown and proven that he was her rock. Just another layer to the man that she was finding to be quite addictive.

For the week following her grandfather's release, Jade had spent a lot of time at her grandfather's making sure he was sticking to his diet and taking his pills. Kaeden had been so patient with her and so supportive. He would come and spend time at her grandfather's with her. When her parents would show up to visit at the same time, he would play the buffer between them and fill one up with random conversation so that they didn't have time to argue with the other. And when she was exhausted from going on expeditions or tours and still rushing to her grandfather's, at night he would massage her down, cook her dinner, and just let her sleep in his arms.

Finally her grandfather had sent them all away, wanting his freedom and independence back.

That had been two weeks ago, but Jade clearly remembered a brief but very significant conversation they shared one evening on his porch.

"You love that boy, don't you?"

Jade was standing behind her grandfather and brushing his soft and curly shoulder-length hair. She paused. "I like him a lot," she offered before she went back to brushing the deep ebony waves.

"Humph. What's the difference? School an older man."

"Liking a man means we enjoy having fun together and I appreciate him as a person. I look forward to seeing him and hate to see him go. You know, stuff like that."

"And loving him?" Esai asked.

"For me, loving him means that I just can't imagine my life without him."

"Just that simple, huh?"

Jade nodded as she gathered his hair tightly

*with one hand and picked up a band with the
other. "Yup, just that simple," she answered as
she bound his hair.*

*"And you're not there yet, so you say, with
Kaeden?" Esai asked as he looked up at her.
"Right now in this moment, if you found out you
would never see him again, how does that make
you feel, Jade?"*

*Jade looked pensive as the truth slammed
home just like that. She would be lost without
Kaeden. Jade closed her eyes and licked her lips,
struggling for composure as she felt emotional
tears well up in her eyes.*

*"Listen, there's no time limit on love. Some-
times it's slow to build and sometimes it comes in
a rush, almost like the universe was just waiting
for that one man to find his one woman."*

Settled into the passenger seat of Kaeden's BMW,
she turned and looked at him. Was she truly having
that loving feeling for Kaeden? Was she that one
woman for this one man? Was that why that first night
between them was pure chemistry? *Do I love you,
Kaeden? It feels like I do*, she thought as her eyes caressed his handsome angular profile. *And better yet,
do you love me?*

"My grandfather likes you."

Kaeden looked over at her briefly, looking handsome and unusually casual in a T-shirt and jeans. "I
like him too. He's deep."

Jade laughed huskily. "Now, you know what happens when the word 'deep' is flung around," Jade said in a husky voice.

Kaeden shivered as Jade ran her hand along his thigh. "Actually, I have a busy day today . . . but let's meet up at Grilling and Chilling for lunch."

"How about we turn around, go back to your house, and reconnect *before* you go to work?" Jade asked as she undid his zipper and slid her hand inside to stroke him.

"You know once I get in I'm never in a rush to get out."

Jade playfully pouted.

Bzzzzzz.

Kaeden reached to his hip for his BlackBerry. He released an exasperated breath at the sight of Felecia's number. He sent the call straight to voice mail.

"Who was that?" Jade asked in curiosity as she looked down to see him lengthen in her hand.

"Felecia."

She released him.

His erection eased.

The mood was killed.

"Hey!" Kaeden said, looking down at his now-limp member lying there.

Jade waved her hand at him dismissively and shifted in her seat to look out the window.

"If I put him up, he's not coming out later," Kaeden warned her.

Jade looked over her shoulder at him and shrugged. "I'm not a jealous person, but I am really sick of Felecia, Kaeden. She called your house phone all night until we had to turn off the ringer, and I think I saw her drive through your subdivision this morning. You have a bona fide stalker."

"Imagine if I had gave her some," he quipped.

Jade cut her eyes at him. "Not funny."

"Listen, I don't want to be with Felecia."

"I know that. I believe that. I trust that. But I am still sick of her," Jade emphasized. "The way I feel is not jealousy or fear or insecurity, it is pure annoyance. Now either you handle it or I will. I mean it."

They fell quiet as they entered the main strip of Holtsville. When Kaeden slowed down at her turnoff, Jade waved her hand. "I'll just go into the office now. No need to drive two cars when you're staying with me tonight anyway. Plus I need to talk to Darren about something."

"Now *I'm* sick of him," Kaeden muttered as he adjusted slightly in his seat.

"Hell, so am I. I had no idea he would still be holding a grudge. He is really showing me a side of him that I didn't know was there, and I'm not sure I want to be in business with someone who is vindictive and mean."

As Kaeden came to a stop sign, they glanced over at each other at the same time. That made them laugh together, and the disjointed mood between them dissipated.

Kaeden slid his keys into his pocket as soon as he walked through the door of his offices. He was glad to get out of the sweltering summer heat and into the air-conditioning. It was a week before July, and the only respite from the heat was air-conditioning and a tall iced glass of sweet tea.

Kaeden jogged upstairs and rushed into the bedroom. He emerged not long after in a navy suit and a crisp French blue shirt that he decided to wear with the top two buttons undone.

As a black man who owned his own business, Kaeden always made sure to present a professional image. He catered to all businesses regardless of who owned them, and unfortunately he was well aware that he couldn't present himself in the same fashion as his white counterparts.

As he jogged down the wooden stairs, he was able to see the front door open and Darren walk in. His steps paused just a bit before he flexed his shoulders and continued on. "You have some nerve coming here," Kaeden said coldly as he entered the outer office. "What? You come to write another check your ass can't cash?"

"Actually, I thought about it and I owe you an apology," Darren said, sliding his hands into the pockets of his distressed denims. "I shouldn't have taken out my frustrations with Jade on you."

Kaeden crossed his arms over his chest as he eyed the man suspiciously from behind his glasses.

"I mean, if I ran around trying to fight every man Jade slept around with . . ." Darren shrugged.

"Don't disrespect her like that," Kaeden warned, fighting the urge to knock the hell out of the man again.

Darren held up his hands. "No disrespect. Just truth. I feel like a fool for trusting her and over and over again when she was lying to me. Man, Jade is a player. Men are constantly trying to get at her, and all that attention is hard for a woman like Jade to ignore. Don't let her make a fool out of you like she did me."

Kaeden pierced Darren with his eyes. "You two never slept together."

Darren looked shocked. "Come on, man, is that what she told you?"

Kaeden said nothing.

"You really think you're the only man Jade is messing around with?" Darren asked, shaking his head like it was a shame.

Kaeden wiped his mouth with his hand.

"Come on, she cheated on me with you, so you think she not gone do the same to you?"

Kaeden walked to the door. "Listen, man, I heard enough of this."

Darren nodded as he turned on his heel and walked to the door himself. "I used to be caught up in her just like you, and regardless of what she tells you, she can't be trusted. She's real good with the whole 'I can't stand jealousy in my man' kick. Just another way to keep you off her trail."

Kaeden opened the door wider as his jaw clenched.

Darren stepped through the door. "Oh, and um, I'm sure only someone who's been that close knows about the mole." He threw that over his shoulder before he walked out the door.

Kaeden slammed the door shut. The mole was on the inner lip of Jade's intimacy. *That* would have to be one helluva guess.

He walked into his office and dropped down into

the chair behind his desk. He focused his eyes on the rows of trees on both sides of the driveway as he fought the urge to call and confront Jade.

The seeds of doubt had been planted.

Jade looked up from her laptop as Darren strolled into the Wild-n-Out office.

"Hi, Jade," he said in a friendly voice as he strolled past her office and walked into his.

Jade arched a brow and leaned back in her chair, completely shocked by his sudden change in demeanor. She was pondering the cause for the niceties when he appeared at her doorway. "Listen, I just want to apologize to you for the way I've been acting. First and foremost, I should have put the business and our friendship first. I didn't do that."

Jade turned her lips down as she rocked in her ergonomic chair and looked at him. "I appreciate your apology, Darren. It has been really hard working with you and I considered selling my share to you and leaving it alone, but I hoped we would be able to get back to business."

"I'll tell you what, let's go catch some lunch," he offered. "A peace offering on my behalf."

"Rain check? I already have lunch plans," she said.

Darren nodded. "With Kaeden?"

Jade started to be vague for the greater good, but maybe the greatest good was being 100 percent honest. "Yes," she answered him softly.

"I guess the better man won."

Jade locked her eyes with his. "There wasn't a competition. I'm a woman, not a prize or a trophy."

Darren held up his hands. "I better head to my office before I say something and wreck our big make-up scene."

Jade gave him a genuine smile. "That sounds like a plan."

He patted her door frame with his hand twice before he turned and walked back to his own office.

Jade picked up her office phone and dialed Kaeden's office line and then his cell phone. She frowned when she didn't get an answer on either one. They did have plans to eat lunch.

She grabbed her purse and walked outside to the street to see if she spotted his car. Nothing. Grabbing her cell phone, she dialed his cell and office numbers again with no luck.

Come on, Kaeden. Where are you?

She was just turning to walk back into the office when she spotted his BMW turn the corner and head up the one-way street. Jade smiled as she stepped off the sidewalk just as the car pulled to a stop beside her. She opened the car door and climbed inside. "Hey, baby, I've been calling your phone," she told him as she slipped her seat belt on.

Kaeden said nothing.

Jade looked at him. She frowned a little at his silence and the hard cut of his jaw. "What's wrong?"

"Nothing," he told her shortly.

"Look, if you're in a bad mood you could've left me at work 'til you cool off, calm down, or get over it," Jade told him, annoyed at his behavior.

Kaeden said nothing as he drove.

It took Jade a minute to realize he was not headed to their favorite lunchtime restaurant but instead was headed down Highway 17 toward Holtsville. "Where are you taking me?"

"Home to get your car . . . unless Darren was going to take you home?" he said sarcastically.

"What the hell are you talking about? And why do I need my Jeep when you're coming to my house anyway?" Jade asked as she turned in her seat to face him.

"I'm not coming to your house. I'm headed home. I have a lot on my mind right now," he told her coldly.

Jade hated the fear she felt at Kaeden's attitude. "Like what?" she asked.

He shook his head. "I really don't feel like talking to you right now, Jade."

That stung her deeply. "Like. What," she stressed, even as she felt like the rug was being pulled from underneath her.

Kaeden just sped up like he was really anxious to get away from her.

Jade looked at him like she didn't know him. Her heart pounded and she felt ill because she was so clueless to the cause for his obvious anger. Clueless and helpless.

Turning forward in her seat, she sat there stunned.

Kaeden suddenly turned in the parking lot of a gas station. He turned angry eyes on her. "I thought you told me you never slept with Darren."

Jade whirled to stare at him. "What?"

"If you never slept with Darren, then how does he know about your mole?"

"Where is all this coming from?" she asked him.

"All of what?"

"All of these lies?"

Kaeden locked his eyes on her. "Are they lies?"

Jade's jaw literally dropped. "Kaeden, are you kidding me right now?"

"You slept with me on the first night while you was dating him," he fed into the silence.

"And I told you that I never slept with Darren. I told you that he's mad because I didn't. And I told you that you could trust me the same way I trust you, always up on the phone trying to console Felecia the Fruit Loop."

Kaeden banged his fist against the steering wheel. "I have every right to get to the bottom of this. I'm not trying to let you play me out, Jade."

Jade eyed him sarcastically even as one angry and hurt tear raced down her cheek. "So you think I'm a ho, Kaeden?" she asked him coldly as she roughly swiped away the tear with the side of her hand. "You think I'm banging you and somebody else? Huh? You think I'm some insecure, insipid, foolish little girl who finds her self-esteem between a man's thighs? Huh? Kaeden. That's what you *think* of me."

Kaeden shifted down deeper into his seat. "I don't know what to think."

"Well, guess what, Kaeden. You should."

"So you saying you can't even fathom why I would have trust issues with you?" Kaeden asked.

Jade laughed bitterly. "I think you forgot you were

right there with me enjoying that night in the woods, Kaeden. So what assumptions should I make about you?"

"Did you sleep with Darren or not?"

Jade turned her head and squared her eyes with his. "Why be with a slut you don't trust?" she asked him.

"I didn't call you a slut."

"I sure don't hear you calling me an angel." Jade shook her head in disbelief. "I think we both need a little space right now. Take me home."

"Jade—"

"Take. Me. Home."

Kaeden checked for oncoming traffic before he pulled out of the lot and back onto Highway 17. And they rode in the worst possible silence.

As he neared her cottage, Jade slid her hand on the door, ready to get the hell away from him as soon as the car stopped in her yard. "Hurry up and get me home," she told him in a tight and angry voice as tears threatened to fall.

When he did pull into her yard, he shut off the car.

Jade eyed him like he was straight crazy. "I don't know what you shutting off for, Kaeden. Go get comfy with your accusations and your insecurities—"

"Insecurities?"

"That's right. Your insecurities." Jade climbed out of the car and then slammed the door before she walked over to her car.

She felt insulted.

She felt betrayed.

She felt disrespected.

She felt hurt.

She never thought Kaeden would bring all of that into her world. Never.

"Jade, let's talk."

She shook her head. "No, Kaeden. Go to hell, or better yet, go talk some to Darren and let him fill your gullible ass up with more lies," she told him over her shoulder before she climbed into her Jeep.

He climbed out of his car and walked over to stand at her door. "Where are you going?"

Jade licked her lips before she turned and looked at him. "What? Scared I'm going to get my back blown out?" she asked snidely.

"That's uncalled for, Jade."

"*That's* uncalled for?" Jade eyed Kaeden. "I can't help the way I look or how men react to it, but I can help the way I conduct myself and I can help the people I let into my life and into my bed."

"Why do you act like you don't at least understand where I'm coming from on this?"

"I'm lost, Kaeden. What do you want from me? Do you think if you keep asking me the same question the answer will change? Do you want to argue this out and sex this out . . . until something else I do strikes up your jealousy? I don't do the make-up break-up cycle."

Jade cranked up her Jeep.

Kaeden eyed her. "It's funny how you've flipped this whole thing to make me the bad guy."

Sadness and disappointment weighed Jade's shoulders down. "Because of the way we began and because you're so ready to believe the worst of me, you're forever going to be wondering if I'm lying to you or if

I'm cheating on you," she said sadly. "Doesn't sound like a fun relationship for either of us. I can't. I won't. I refuse."

"So what are you saying?"

"I'm saying that this relationship is over, Kaeden. I want you to move your vehicle so that I can leave. I'm saying you should work on building your view of yourself up so that there is no room to tear your woman down."

Kaeden stepped back from her vehicle. "This is how you want it?"

Jade shrugged even as her heart broke. "This is how it is," she told him as she circled the front yard and drove between Kaeden's rear bumper and the road.

She stopped.

He turned to watch her.

"Why is it so hard for you to believe that you *were* enough man for me?" she called out to him before she accelerated down the road, wanting to be free of his presence before the tears fell.

Chapter 21

Kaeden's feelings were taking him on an emotional roller coaster and he could definitely blame some of it on the alcohol. As soon as he left Jade's cottage he headed back to his office and fell right into the bottle of cognac he kept in his mini-bar. "Shit," he swore, realizing that Jade might be out of his life for good.

That didn't sit well with him, but neither did the idea of Jade lying to him. Not once had she answered how Darren knew about something so intimate as the flat mole on the inside of the lips of her femininity.

Images of Darren and Jade, naked and thrusting, plagued him.

Maybe their breakup was for the best.

Sitting at his desk, he poured another drink and tossed it back, wincing as it burned a hot trail against the back of his throat before settling like liquid fire in his stomach.

"Hi, Kaeden."

He looked up over the rim of his glass at Felecia standing in the doorway of his office. He held out his hand. "Give me my office keys, Felecia," he said in a bored and tired voice before he tipped his head back to take another sip.

Something dropped in his extended hand, but he frowned at the soft and silky texture. He knew it before he looked and he sighed heavily. Sure enough, Felecia stood before him naked as the day she was born with her dress draped over his hand.

"Make love to me, Kaeden," she said in a mock-sultry voice that came off like she had a horrible cold.

Sitting his glass down on his desk, Kaeden rose and walked over to her, his eyes giving her a slow once-over. "Not bad, by the way," he began before he shook out her dress and wrapped it around her. "But you know this is not what you want to do."

"Yes, I do," she told him emphatically as she flung the dress away and jumped up on him to wrap her arms and legs around him.

Kaeden just stood there and wiped his mouth with his hand. When she moaned loudly and planted wet kisses on his neck, he grabbed her arms and pried her off his body. "Enough, Felecia," he said roughly.

She stumbled back from him and covered her face with her hands.

Kaeden bent down, picked up her dress, and covered her nudity . . . again. "Sit down, Felecia," he ordered her before he turned, grabbed another snifter, and poured her a drink.

"I don't drink," she told him as she put the wrap dress back on correctly and tied it securely.

"You don't have sex either, but tonight you were in for a change . . . so drink up." Kaeden dropped back down in his seat behind his desk. "Enough is enough, Felecia."

She smoothed her mussed hair as she took the seat and the offered drink. "What?"

"I have a lot going on right now and not much time to spare," Kaeden began. "There is more to you than being someone's wife. You are a smart and attractive woman, but your demeanor comes off desperate and clingy at times, and I'm here to tell you that it scares men away."

Felecia crossed her legs and stiffened her back in a dignified manner—like she hadn't just jumped butt naked onto him. "I don't know what you mean."

"Yes, you do." Kaeden eyed her as he placed his head in his hands atop the desk.

"You're drunk."

"Yes, I am. And you're desperate."

Felecia looked offended.

"When you have no reason to be," he added. "You were willing to throw away all of your convictions to sleep with me to try and get me to get back with you. And I could have hit it and still quit it, Felecia. You setting yourself up to be used. Think about what I just said."

Felecia shifted her eyes away from him and took a sip of the drink. She frowned and gagged comically at the taste.

"Burn that wedding trunk thing you have. Sell that wedding dress and go focus on living life. I bet the man of your dreams—the one that's meant for you—will come along, but you can't just pick somebody and try to make them love you or want you or marry you.

"Felecia, you and I will never get back together. I will never marry you. You are not the one for me and

I am not the one for you. Don't call me and I won't call you. I promise."

She slammed the glass down on the desk and rose to her feet to walk out of the office. She returned moments later to drop his office keys onto his desk. "It's your loss, Kaeden Strong," she told him.

Kaeden nodded as he leaned back in his chair and poured another drink. He thought about the drama swirling in his relationship with Jade and nodded solemnly. "You're probably right."

Felecia gave him one last long look before she turned and walked out of his office—and Kaeden hoped out of his life for good.

Jade was lucky she didn't get a speeding ticket when she made her way back to Walterboro. She parked and stormed into the Wild-n-Out office. She slammed the door behind her and it quivered on its hinges.

Darren walked out of his office and looked at her in surprise. "Something wrong, Jade?" he asked smugly.

And she saw red.

"You jealous hearted, evil, soulless, nutless, horny, lying son of a no good bitch," she spat in her anger, her eyes blazing with the angry fire burning in her belly.

And he laughed. He laughed in her face.

"You think my life is a joke?" she asked him as she advanced on him.

"You didn't take my feeling serious, so why should I give a damn about yours?" he told her coldly, his face suddenly etched in stone.

Jade poked her finger into his chest. "You know damn well I never slept with you."

Darren said nothing and continued to look at her with a smugness that made her want to grab his head and then knee his groin so hard that she made his privates into a vagina.

"You're pathetic," she said, pushing past him to walk into her office, grab a box, and chuck her laptop and personal items into it.

Darren just stood there watching her like he was enjoying the show.

Jade had enough. Darren with his revenge and Kaeden with his jealousy could both to hell. It took two trips to load her things, and each time she had to brush past Darren standing there with his arms crossed over his chest, watching her as if she was going to steal something. Well, she had a detailed inventory list complete with serial numbers if he tried it with her.

Standing at the door, Jade turned and gave Darren a withering look, pointedly stopping at his crotch. "All of this because I wouldn't give you any? A business and friendship ruined because you wanting to get five *little* inches wet. Sad. So sad."

"To hell with you," he screamed.

It was Jade's turn to have the last laugh as she walked out on Darren and their business.

Kaeden winced as the telephone on his desk rang loudly. Groaning from the awful hangover he was trying to live through, he reached for the phone.

"Strong Accountings," he said, in as clear a voice as he could muster.

"Kaeden, it's me . . . it's Jade."

He sat up straighter in the chair, and that caused the pounding in his head to intensify.

Last night had felt so awkward without speaking to or seeing Jade. Spending the night in a drunken stupor upstairs in a sheetless bed hadn't helped either.

"Just listen," she ordered softly. "Darren knows about my mole because I told him and a few other people about it during a stupid game of Truth or Dare."

Kaeden removed his glasses as his eyes squinted in thought.

"I was dating Darren when you and I slept together. We were not in a relationship and I had every right as a grown woman to date and to sleep with whomever I want."

"Jade—"

"No, let me finish."

Kaeden leaned back in his chair and closed his eyes as he gripped the phone tightly while he pressed it to his face.

"I'm telling you this because I don't want this to end with you thinking that I did you wrong—because I *didn't*. We had this amazing thing. This connection. It was special, Kaeden, and I hope it wasn't one of a kind because I want to feel that way again with someone who loves and appreciates me. I want you to know that you messed up a good thing, Kaeden Strong, over not just a lie by a man filled with revenge but because of your own issues."

He heard the tears in her voice and his heart literally ached.

"I want it clear that we are through because I refuse to be with a man that doesn't trust me. I refuse to be in a relationship clouded with doubt and filled with foolishness. I am way too together for that. So this is goodbye, Kaeden."

Long after Jade hung up the phone, Kaeden sat there with the phone still pressed to his face. His mind was filled with a million different things.

"I'm not trying to let you play me out, Jade."

"We had this amazing thing. This connection. It was special, Kaeden . . ."

He leaned forward to hang up the receiver and replaced his glasses before he turned in his chair to look out at the traffic whizzing past.

"You think I'm some insecure, insipid, foolish little girl who finds her self-esteem between a man's thighs? Huh? Kaeden. That's what you think of me."

He frowned.

"I think you forgot you were right there with me enjoying that night in the woods, Kaeden. So what assumptions should I make about you?"

His frown deepened.

"Go get comfy with your accusations and your insecurities—"

"Why is it so hard for you to believe that you were enough man for me?"

Kaeden shook his head in disbelief at that one.

"I'm saying that this relationship is over, Kaeden."

And that one? Well it seemed like it echoed inside his head and his heart for infinity.

* * *

Felecia sat in the middle of her bed with her legs crossed looking at the wedding gown she *would* wear one day. She was meant to be a bride—a wife. She was meant to have the happily ever after. And she would have it.

Since it wouldn't be Kaeden, she was more than capable of setting her sights on someone else . . . and she had someone in mind.

Felecia picked up her cordless phone and dialed the cell phone number he gave her. She smiled when she thought of the handsome fair-skinned man who made her pulse race every time she laid eyes on him.

"Hello."

Felecia smiled. "Just checking up on you."

"I'm fine. They're broken up just the way I wanted. How 'bout you?"

She shrugged. "Darren, I just decided not to go through with it," she lied.

No need for him or anyone else to know Kaeden turned down her goodies served up to him on a platter.

"To hell with that clown, anyway," Darren told her.

"To hell with that Jezebel, right?"

"Right."

Felecia climbed down off her bed and lifted her wedding dress from the door hanger. "Actually, I was thinking that maybe you and I could grab a bite to eat . . . and console each other for being done wrong by our lousy exes," she told him as she held the dress up to her body and twisted and turned to study her reflection.

"That sounds like a good idea."

"And, Darren, what was your last name again?" she asked as she held the dress to her body with her fore-arm and twirled around the room.

"Jon. Why?"

Mrs. Felecia Jon, she thought with satisfaction. "Um, no reason," she said.

Jade used a tablespoon to dig out a big scoop of Ben & Jerry's Chocolate Macadamia ice cream. The entire pint was ninety grams of fat and she knew it meant plenty of extra miles on the treadmill, but so be it. She needed it.

Just as she was settling in with the idea that she could love Kaeden—really love him—now they were over.

Jade eased another creamy spoonful into her mouth. She was resolved to the fact that her first instincts about Kaeden Strong had been right. They were too different to work, and incredible sex or not, she wished she hadn't even brought Kaeden into her life. Because now that he was out of her life, she knew it was going to take some time to get over him.

Lots of time.

Chapter 22

Three weeks later

"Okay, baby girl, enough is enough. It is time for an intervention."

Jade looked up as Deena picked up the remote and turned the television off with a click. "You make me sound a crackhead," Jade drawled before she dug her tablespoon into the pint of Ben & Jerry's Chocolate Macadamia ice cream.

"At least a crackhead doesn't put on ten pounds in two weeks," Deena said.

Jade looked comically offended.

Deena strolled over on her gold heels and snatched the pint of ice cream away.

Jade jumped to her feet in her plaid-footed pajamas. "I have no job, no business, and no man," she said emphatically before she stuck out her hand. "Now give me the ice cream."

Deena felt like she was squaring off in a ring. She quickly kicked off her stilettos as she kept her eyes locked on her daughter and her hand locked around the carton. "Why are you sitting around here doing this to yourself when *you* broke it off with *him*?"

"Mama, please give me my ice cream?" Jade asked calmly as she took a step toward her.

Deena took two steps back. "A moment on the lips and a lifetime on the hips."

Jade released a heavy breath. "It's just ice cream."

"So why are you acting like it's crack?"

Jade threw her hands up in the air. "What's with you and the crack fixation today?"

Deena eyed Jade before she took off across the room and slammed the ice cream in the trash just as Jade took off behind her.

"Wow, old lady, you're faster than you look," Jade drawled.

Deena laughed. "Sex is like exercise, and trust me, your mama *stays* in shape."

Jade pretended to gag herself as she made her way back to her couch. "Oh good God, Mama, please!"

Deena walked over to the sofa, sitting down and settling her daughter's covered feet in her lap. "Hey, your granddaddy called me and he's worried you're all cooped in this house and moping around behind Kaeden."

Jade shifted her eyes to her mama. "I miss him," she admitted.

Deena patted Jade's leg. "Do you want him back?"

Jade shook her head. Then she nodded. Then she shrugged.

"But you miss him?" Deena asked.

Jade nodded. "But I don't miss the jealousy thing.

It's a big issue for me and you know it. I've been there and I've done that. He would really have to prove to me that he's dealt with his issues and he can trust me."

"So in the meanwhile, you're going to sit around here and live in a funk." Deena sniffed the air and held her nose. "Smelling like funk."

"I don't stink. I wash."

"Good. Just checking." Deena looked relieved.

Jade dug down deeper on the couch. "I'm fine. I promise."

"Well, I need you to get up and find a cute outfit to put on," Deena said, rising to her feet. "We're going out."

Jade snuggled down even deeper on the couch. "I'll pass."

Deena waved her hand dismissively. "Whenever I'm in town you and I hang out. There's nothing that changed because Mr. Lover Lover has been put on pause. Up and at 'em."

Jade eyed her mother and she knew it was give in quick or be harassed until she gave in. Without another word, Jade rolled off the couch and made her way to her bedroom thinking of what to wear. Who knew what her mother had planned.

She tied her hair with a silk scarf before she turned on the shower spray and waited to climb in once the steam swirled up to the ceiling. She sighed in pleasure at the feel of the water pulsating against her skin.

As she closed her eyes and leaned forward enough to wet her face and not her hair, Jade thought the sound of the water hitting the wall and the tub and the shower curtain sounded just like a waterfall.

She shivered at the memory of the first night she'd shared herself with Kaeden. The sound of the waterfall in the distance had been the serenade to their passion. Passion like she had never known and often wondered if she would ever feel again.

Swarmed by sudden emotions and afraid that her face would be wet from more than just the water spray, Jade rushed through the rest of the shower. She rubbed her body down with baby oil before she patted herself dry with a soft towel.

Maybe a night out was just what she needed.

After pulling on a thong and lacy bra, Jade reached for a pair of her favorite jeans. She frowned when she couldn't pull them any higher than her thighs. She had put on weight! "Oh, hell to the no . . ."

Jade valiantly tried to pull up and then zip the jeans. She lay down and pulled. She stood up and jumped. She sucked in and tried to zip.

"Still want the Ben and Jerry's ice cream?" Deena drawled.

Jade turned to find her tall and shapely mother leaning in the doorway of her bedroom. "Oh, hush."

Jade flew backward onto the bed and kicked her feet high up in the air as she peeled the now-offending jeans off. As she ignored her mother's smug and pretty face, Jade promised herself a couple of things. One: She was going to have a good time tonight. Two: It was good-bye to Ben & Jerry and hello to the gym.

Kaeden slammed his fist against his desk as an image of Jade and some faceless man having sex flashed before him. Closing his eyes, he wiped his hands over his mouth. Kaeden tossed the remote onto the leather ottoman serving as the coffee table in his living room. He stretched his tall frame on the sofa, trying very hard to think of anything else but Jade.

Three whole weeks.

He missed her.

Throughout the day he was preoccupied with thoughts of what Jade was doing. And with whom. And the thought of another man with her tore him up on the inside.

"What's up, stranger?"

Kaeden looked up and his face shaped with surprise to see Kade strolling into his office. "What's up, bubba?"

"Nothing much," Kade said before he folded his tall frame into one of the chairs in front of Kaeden's desk. "I had some errands to run in town and I'd thought I'd come check up on you."

Kaeden felt guilty. In the time following the breakup, he had pulled away from his family and buried himself in work. "Just been real busy."

"No Strong is too busy for family," Kade told him. "You have to stop letting this thing with Jade kick your ass. Talk to us about it. Talk to me about it. I'm here."

Kaeden locked eyes with his brother through his spectacles. He released a heavy breath as he shrugged a shoulder and leaned back in his chair. "I know we didn't have a lot in common, but I really felt like what we had was going to last."

"So what happened?"

"Bunch of nonsense and lies that I fell for from her ex and . . . she claims I was too jealous."

"Were you?"

Kaeden thought back to little things he'd done in their relationship. The phone calls just to see where she was. Feeling threatened whenever he saw her just talking to a man. Not wanting to let her out of his eyesight or wanting her to go places where a lot of men were.

These were things he *thought* he'd never revealed to Jade or to anyone else. Maybe he hadn't held his feelings as close to his chest as he thought, especially when he went off on her behind Darren's lie.

"Let me ask you something," Kaeden said, shifting in his seat to lean forward on his desk.

"Go."

"Garcelle is beautiful, and no offense, but her body is . . ." Kaeden used his hands to mimic an hourglass.

Kade smiled broadly. "That's my baby," he said.

Kaeden slapped his hand down on his desk, causing papers to flutter. "See, I couldn't take another man telling me about Jade's body. I would . . . would wanna break your neck," he told his brother emphatically.

"You're my brother and I wouldn't let you be disrespectful about my wife, but you didn't say anything to make me wanna toss your young ass from that chair."

"When we were together, I felt like there was always somebody waiting to step in and take my place with her," Kaeden confessed. "It felt like I had to keep her close so some knucklehead didn't get in her ear, and I always had suspicions that she was cheating on me."

"Was she?"

"No. Yes. Hell, I don't know."

"So you don't trust her?"

"That night in the woods really messes with me because she *was* dating that dude Darren. So no, I guess I don't trust her," Kaeden said as he shook his head. "And that's a big issue for her."

"Sounds like an even bigger issue for you, little brother," Kade told him.

"How do you and Kahron do it? How you can be so laid back with these fine-ass women walking around, living life, with men probably flirting and trying to get at them?"

Kade smiled. "Because I have the utmost faith that I am handling my business as a man, and not just in the bedroom. Emotionally. Financially. Mentally. Socially. I'm a good man and I'm good to my wife. Listen, it boils down to me trusting my wife and me being secure in myself. I'm sure Kahron feels the same way."

"So I'm insecure?" Kaeden balked.

Kade held up his hands. "You don't have a reason to be insecure, but hey, are you?"

Kaeden shifted his eyes away.

"Listen, little brother, and this might be hard for you to hear . . . but if you can't trust Jade and have faith that you are giving her everything she needs from a man, then there's no need for you to get back together."

Kaeden fell silent.

"Listen, Jade is ten. That we know. Now it's time for you to work on realizing you're a ten too. Jade is not slumming by being with you. She's not doing you a favor. She got one hell of a catch—just like you did.

Until you deal with that, you two are gonna have nothing but drama."

"Look here, Dr. Phil," Kaeden joked, trying to lighten the mood.

Kade laughed.

"I appreciate always looking out for me. Hell, for all of us. You are the best big brother ever," Kaeden told him with honesty.

Kade shrugged. "It's what I do," he said, rising to his feet.

"And Kaeden—"

"Don't worry, this is between just me and you," he threw over his shoulder before he walked out of the office.

Kaeden knew Kade was right. His brother's comments had echoed Jade's own question of why he didn't feel he was enough for her. He didn't want to be that dude around town acting a straight fool because of his jealousy. As much as he missed and wanted Jade, maybe it was time for him to take some time and get his head on straight.

Chapter 23

Ten months later

"Here you go, Mr. Strong."

Kaeden looked and smiled at Mrs. Hoover as she handed him a stack of incoming mail. "Thank you," he told his new receptionist/secretary before she turned and walked back out to the outer office.

She was a short and thin sixty-year-old woman who had been happily married to the same man for the last forty years. Everything about her had seemed drama-free for Kaeden when he interviewed her a month ago, and so far his instincts had been right. With Mrs. Hoover came a dependable employee and lots of coffee with freshly made bakery products.

He glanced at the clock over the fireplace. He had to call it an early day if he was going to make it to the wedding on time. And there was *no* way he was going to miss it.

Scratching his new five o'clock shadow, Kaeden tried his best to stay focused on his short list of things to do. He was just selecting files to load into his Coach briefcase when Mrs. Hoover knocked on the door and stuck her head in.

"You better get going," she told him. "Weatherman is calling for rain. I hope it doesn't ruin your friend's wedding."

Kaeden paused at the term "friend" but didn't bother to explain otherwise as he slid the files and his laptop into his briefcase. He hurried into his suit jacket. "Yeah, I'm headed out now. Thanks."

"I'll lock up, and you have fun," she called behind him after he strode past her and out the door.

He made a move to adjust his glasses but then remembered that he no longer wore glasses or contacts since he had the Lasik surgery last year. Turning up the radio, Kaeden settled in for the forty-five-minute ride to downtown Charleston.

It actually felt good to leave the office early. With the expansion of his business, it seemed like he hadn't been home before nine in ages. He was considering bringing on a junior accountant to assist with his bulging workload.

Bzzzz.

Kaeden picked up his BlackBerry from the passenger seat.

"Hey, Kade."

"No, this is Garcelle."

He smiled at the sound of his sister-in-law's voice. "Hey, you calling to tell me my new niece or nephew has arrived?"

Garcelle laughed. "No, not for two more months, Kaeden. We're throwing some meat on the grill and we want you to come before you head home. I'm making quesadillas on the grill."

Kaeden's stomach growled at the thought of Garcelle's quesadillas. "I have a wedding to go to in Charleston, but I'm not going to the reception so I'll be there."

"Who's getting married?"

Kaeden laughed. "I'll tell you about it later."

"Is Taja with you?"

"No, Taja and I broke up couple of weeks ago. I'm going alone."

"Oh good grief, Kaeden, another one bites the dust," Garcelle said, her accent prominent.

Kaeden laughed.

"What was wrong with this one? You know what, never mind, we'll talk when you get here."

Kaeden tossed the BlackBerry onto the seat as he made the left turn onto the parking lot of the church. He put on the tailored jacket to his gray lightweight summer suit and smoothed it out as he made his way toward the brick steps of the towering church.

He laughed a little as he thought of Garcelle's reaction to his breakup with his most recent girlfriend, Taja. During the last few months, his dating life had become the running joke among his family. He finally decided to start to date again, but as soon as he would find one it didn't take long to find something— anything—wrong with her . . . and soon she was out of there.

He hadn't had much luck in the love department ever since his breakup with—

"Hi, Kaeden."

He froze. *Damn if that didn't sound like . . .*

"Jade," Kaeden said as he turned around and spotted her standing there. His heart hammered so loudly in his chest that he was almost deafened by it. He was speechless.

He hadn't seen her in months, and she was still just as beautiful.

Her chocolate skin gleamed. Her hair was cut into a shoulder-length bob with long asymmetrical bangs. Her makeup made her eyes and lips glow. And the silver strapless satin dress she wore emphasized her shape and her long legs below the knee-length hem.

She smiled at him and gave him a little wave.

Kaeden had to check himself to recover. "Hey, whassup," he said, sounding casual even though his heart beat so quickly and his whole body felt more alive than ever. "It's good to see you."

She stuck her long and slender sequined clutch under her arm as she stepped up to stand before him. "It's good to see you too, Mr. Strong," she said in that husky voice of hers, and she looked up at him.

"This is an odd place to run into each other," he told her as he pushed his hands into his pockets.

Jade laughed. "That's an understatement . . . but I couldn't miss it."

Kaeden laughed. "Me either," he admitted.

"You look different. Good. I mean . . . great. But different. I like the beard."

Kaeden grinned as he ran his hand over it. "Well, you know, what can I say," he said in the worst imitation of J.J. from *Good Times*.

"And no more glasses," she said with an approving nod.

"Lasik," he told her.

They fell silent as they stood there in the parking lot. Both looked around at anything but each other, and when their eyes did happen to lock they both laughed nervously.

"So, um, no date?" Kaeden asked.

"No, nope, no date," Jade admitted as she used a hand to swipe her hair behind her ear. "You?"

"Nah." Kaeden shook his head before he offered her his arm. "Want to enjoy the show together?"

Jade slipped her arm through his. "Oooh, this should make it even more interesting."

They walked into the crowded church together and sat on one of the pews in the rear.

"Those two deserve each other," Jade muttered under her breath.

"Tell me about it," Kaeden drawled.

They both shook their heads as Darren lifted the veil and planted a kiss on Felecia's smiling lips.

"Lawd, they gone have some crazy babies," Jade quipped as they rose to their feet.

Kaeden laughed.

Jade glanced over at him, and the nervous anxiety she felt since she saw him in the parking lot only increased. The man was finer than ever with his five o'clock shadow and minus the glasses. The color of his suit fit his caramel complexion and the silvery flecks in his low-cut fade. And there was more of an air of confidence about him that Jade could not deny.

Feeling that familiar breathlessness, Jade licked her

lips. "I should do like J.J. and trip 'em up," Jade joked as Darren and Felecia made their way up the aisle to an up-tempo song.

The couple were so caught up in each other that neither even noticed Kaeden and Jade standing in the pews.

After the bridal party made their way down the aisle, the wedding goers started to file out the church. Jade and Kaeden waited until the church was nearly empty. "Were you going to the reception?" Jade asked him as they stepped into the aisle.

"Nooo. Nah. Nah." Kaeden laughed as he looked around at the massive amounts of floral decorations. "When I got the invite I just felt like I had to see it to believe it."

"Me too. Me too." Jade nodded. "You know, I think they think that it would bother us."

Kaeden shoved his hands into his pockets as he looked down at her. "Those two can have each other. Trust and believe that."

They fell silent as they stood at the end of the altar, their feet pressing into the petals on the runner, the scent of flowers teasing their noses.

Jade glimpsed at him and those familiar stirrings were awakened. "I better get going," she said softly as she stooped down to scoop up a handful of petals.

"Yeah, me too."

Jade tossed the petals up into the air just as she stepped up to press her hand to Kaeden's chest and then lightly kiss his cheek as the petals rained down upon them. "It was good seeing you, Kaeden," she whispered in his ear.

"You too," he whispered back.

They stepped apart slowly and made their way up the aisle side by side. As they reached the open double doors, they both turned and looked down the length of the artfully decorated aisle at the altar.

With one last shared look they left the church and went their separate ways.

Kaeden took a sip of his light beer as he watched his parents doing the shag while Kade grilled steaks on the brick patio in his and Garcelle's backyard. His brothers and Garcelle's dad were losing horribly in a poker game with a pregnant and round Garcelle. As always, his sister Kaitlyn was off on some out-of-town adventure with her friends. And Bianca was inside putting KJ and Kadina to sleep. Or at least she was until she walked out the back door.

"Hey, brother-in-law, why are you over here by yourself?" she asked as she came to stand beside his chair.

"Got a lot on my mind," he admitted, taking another swig of his beer.

"I heard we can add Taja to the pile."

He looked up at Bianca, her diamond hoop earrings flashing as she shook her head.

"You know, after you and Jade didn't work out, it took you a long time to start dating again, and we all were glad because we could tell that you were hurting." Bianca stepped down on the porch and took a seat next to Kaeden's feet. "But you know what, you're not fooling me or anyone else."

Kaeden shifted his Kenneth Coles as he cut his eyes over at her. "What do you mean?"

"You still want Jade and you know it."

Kaeden silently took another swig of his beer.

"And all these women you dating don't have a chance against that." Bianca eyed him. "I thought the whole Felecia thing you told us all about had cured you of that."

Kaeden shook his head. "Not the same thing at all."

"Kinda . . . sorta . . . maybe. Nope, you know what? Definitely."

Kaeden chuckled as he held the bottle from his mouth. "It's funny that you mentioned Jade. She was at the wedding too."

"Oooh! The plot thickens." Bianca leaned back a bit and fanned herself.

Kaeden laughed at her. "She look good too. Real good."

"She still stay in Holtsville? I never see her at church anymore."

Kaeden sat his empty bottle next to his feet. "Yeah, she eventually switched churches after we broke up."

"Whatever happened with you two?" Bianca asked, knocking her shoulder against his knee. "We all really thought she was the one for you."

Kaeden's eyes clouded over and he clearly remembered everything that led to their downfall a year ago. "I messed up. I was a jealous ass and she wasn't having it. Took some time and it was a hard pill to swallow, but I realized she was right. My jealousy would've had us fighting and carrying on all the time."

Bianca nodded in thought. "You know . . . there are

many reasons why people get eaten up with jealousy. The solution is to find out why we're jealous and work through it. Did you ever do that?" Bianca asked.

Kaeden shrugged. "I was mad at her for a little bit after the breakup. By the time I got my act together, I felt like she had moved on with her life. I barely saw her. I was dating again. Our lives just were on two different tracks . . . *again*."

Bianca nudged his leg again. "How was it seeing her today?"

Kaeden smiled. "It was a'ight. You know, no biggie."

Bianca arched a brow and leaned back to cast him a disbelieving eye.

A vision of Jade smiling up at him tugged at his heart, but Kaeden pushed it away. "Seeing her again messed my head up for a little bit, but it's back on straight again."

Bianca acted like she wanted to say something, but she stopped herself. Instead she just patted his knee before she rose and walked away. "Pride goeth before the fall, brother-in-law," she told him over her shoulder before she walked away.

Kaeden released a deep breath, lost in his thoughts.

Jade's brain was working overtime as she put her body through an intense workout on her home treadmill. Sweat was pouring off her body and her pulse was racing. Her muscles ached but she felt good. She felt exhilarated. She'd almost exercised all thoughts of Kaeden out of her brain.

At the thought of him she lightly pounded her fist against the handlebar in frustration as she ran faster. Seeing him had left her filled up with thoughts of nothing but Kaeden, Kaeden, Kaeden.

Thinking of Kaeden.

Yearning and wanting . . . Kaeden.

And she was sick of it.

It had been nice seeing him at the wedding, but if she had known that that one moment in time would leave her absorbed into him again, then she would have climbed back into her Jeep and never spoken to him at all.

In the last few months, she had gotten back into dating, she enjoyed her new job, everything about her life was stable. Everything was just fine.

She didn't want to go back to the place she was in after their breakup. It had taken her a month to lose the weight she'd gained from her days on the couch sucking down Ben & Jerry's Chocolate Macadamia ice cream like it was nobody's business.

Jade breathed heavily after she hopped off the treadmill. She reached for the bottle of ice water on the table as she looked out the living room window. The skies were darkening as she took a sip. It had rained nearly every day that week, making any local outdoor adventures nearly impossible. Jade was definitely feeling stir-crazy, especially being left to her thoughts.

Wanting to grab some fresh air before the rain, Jade grabbed her journal and left the cottage to sit down on the small stoop. The journal was one of the new additions to her life after the end of her personal relationship with Kaeden and her business relationship with

Darren. She had stopped trying to find the answer to all her frustrations inside the bottom of an ice cream bowl. So she axed the spoon and reached for a pen.

Eventually Darren bought out her share of the business. Jade put the money in her savings and went to work for a larger adventure tour company that kept her away from home on the weekends. And that had been ideal because she didn't want to run into Kaeden. She wanted that time to get over him once and for all.

And Kaeden. In time she'd gotten over him. Every day she missed him and loved him a little bit less. Every day her journal entries became more about reclaiming her own happiness and not dwelling in the sadness created by their breakup. And she had been a wreck in the weeks following their split.

It took her longer to get over him than she had actually been with him. Crazy. Jade opened her journal and bit her bottom lip as she made her newest entry . . .

Dear Me,

Saw Kaeden today for the first time in a long time. Okay, truth? I never expected him to show up to the wedding. Hell, I wasn't even sure I would go. Those two fools made our lives miserable but I just felt like I had to see it to believe it. ☺

Kaeden looked good too. Loving the whole beard thing. He seemed more confident. Had more swagger. It is definitely a good look for my ex-boo!

Jade bit the tip of her pen, so clearly remembering how that chemistry between them was still there. She wrote on . . .

Today was good for us because at least I know we could be friendly.

We had felt comfortable together. It was like all the months had evaporated into nothing . . . and that is scary.

Jade closed her eyes and thought back to the amazing moments they had shared. It had seemed the start of something epic. Something real. Something lasting.

Where did they go all wrong?

Ultimately it didn't matter because there was no going back. They both had moved on.

Brrrnnng.

Jade jumped at the sound of her cordless phone ringing beside her. She laughed at herself before she picked it up and answered. "Scary black girl," she said jokingly, having already seen her mother's number on the caller ID. They hadn't spoken since the wedding.

Deena laughed. "Please. I don't think anything gets to you."

"I don't know. I saw Kaeden today and that got to me." Jade looked up to the turbulent skies.

"Wooow. Okay. So how long before the panties dropped?"

Jade rolled her eyes. "Mama, please, I saw him at a wedding."

"You *went* to that wedding of your ex and Kaeden's ex?" Deena exclaimed in surprise.

"*Anyway* . . . he was there looking finer than ever, Mama. Oh my God." Jade shook her head.

"Gave you fever, huh?" Deena teased.

Jade smiled. "Yeah, and it opened some doors that I wish stayed closed."

"Was he alone or was he with someone?"

"He was alone, and I didn't ask if he was seeing somebody. I wouldn't doubt it. He has all this new swagger, like he getting punany thrown at him left and right."

"Sounding a little jealous," Deena said.

Jade looked up again as a slow mist began to fall. She held her free hand out and let the water spray on her hand. "And I am *sooo* wrong for that."

"Hey, listen, since Kaeden is looking so yummy to you, why don't you call him up and go take a bite?"

"Mama!" Jade exclaimed.

"What?" she asked innocently.

Jade laughed. "Oh, Mama, you are one of a kind."

"Well, I'll be in town this weekend, and we'll go down to Savannah like we always do and shop. Let's just blow my whole alimony check from your father."

Jade just shook her head. "I will see you this weekend," she told her as thunder rolled across the skies like furious drums. "I gotta go. Bye, Ma."

She hit the button to hang up the phone. For a long time she stared at it, fighting the urge to call Kaeden. Frustrated at herself, Jade fought the urge to fling the phone across the yard.

"Damn," she swore.

Chapter 24

Jade climbed to her feet to go into the house. After locking up, she took a quick shower and pulled on a cotton nightshirt. Jade turned off all the lights in her little cottage and climbed into bed. For a long while she lay there watching the storm clouds that threatened a heavy rain as she fought to push thoughts of Kaeden away.

But that was hard. Very hard.

Kaeden Strong had been firmly placed in her past, but one rare moment of curiosity over someone else's business had sent their paths spiraling together.

Jade flung her sheets back as she flopped over onto her stomach. "Damn," she swore as she closed her eyes and visions of Kaeden flashed like a slideshow.

Kaeden laughing.

Kaeden sneaking to use his inhaler.

Kaeden trying to endure the outdoors for her.

Kaeden naked and hard with a smile that said, "Come and get it."

Kaeden's expression when she made him cum.

Rolling over onto her back, Jade childishly kicked her foot against the mattress in frustration.

In those weeks after their breakup she had forced herself not to call Kaeden and tell him to bring it on back to her—and the fact that she had to fight not to call him made her will not to cave even stronger. The issue of jealousy had been an important one to her. She'd been there and done that, wasn't doing it again. She'd taken a stand.

The thing was, her stand had left her . . . standing alone.

But it had been hard to get over him, and it took time just like she thought it would. And now just one half hour in his presence and she was feigning again for the man and his loving.

Fate was bitter and ugly sometimes.

Jade saw headlights flash against her bedroom wall as someone turned into her yard. Thinking something was wrong with her grandfather, she jumped out of bed and hurried to the front door to swing it open.

Her heart stopped to see Kaeden climbing out of his BMW. She stepped down onto her little stoop and pulled her door closed behind herself. "Hey, Kaeden." Her voice reflected her confusion even as her entire body came alive at the very sight of him. She crossed her arms over her chest to cover her hardening nipples, which protruded through the thin cotton.

He put his hands in his pockets and walked over to stand by her stoop. "I like your hair like that. It's really pretty on you," he told her.

Jade swallowed her heart back down. "You came

here just to tell me that?" she asked him with the hint of a smile at her lips.

"Do you know one year ago this month we went on that camping trip?" he asked her.

"I'd forgotten that."

"I haven't."

A wave of some emotion floated over Jade's body and she felt weak. She moved to sit down on the stoop, afraid her knees would give out beneath her. "Kaeden, what's this all about?"

Kaeden cleared his throat as he looked down at her with those intense eyes and long lashes. "You know, I never apologized to you for the way I acted just before . . . before we broke up."

Jade waved her hand. "There's no need reliving the past because it is what it is, you know?"

"I was a fool."

Jade looked up at him with soft eyes. "You know what, Kaeden? Yes, you were, but again, it's all in the past. We both made it through. It's okay."

"But it's not okay because . . . because I haven't stopped missing you or wanting you, Jade," he said in his deep voice.

"Kaeden, don't," she pleaded softly.

He pulled his hands from his pockets and squatted down before her. "Don't what? Don't tell you that I need you, because I do. Don't fight for you like I should have done months ago, because I *have* to."

Jade closed her eyes and let her head fall back as tears swelled up.

"The day we had that argument in your yard and you pulled off in your Jeep, you asked me a question."

Kaeden placed his hands on her legs. "Why is it so hard for you to believe that you were enough man for me?"

Jade remembered it well.

"For so long I had a thing for you, Jade. Your beauty and that body had my head gone. I never dreamed that a woman like you could—or would be—mine. To me you were on a pedestal. Unreachable. Unattainable. Only in my dreams. But then the dream became a reality."

Jade's eyes searched his, and she felt herself falling all over again.

"But I kept on thinking you was too fine for me and that some other man—a better man, in your eyes— would come along and help you realize that you should do better. My jealousy was stupid fear, and in the end I pushed you away. Not another man, but me. Just me."

"Kaeden, that's crazy. Plenty of men tried and failed. I didn't want anyone but you. Only you. Didn't you get it? Only you," she stressed as emotional tears fell down her cheeks. "I was just as happy to have you as you were to have me."

He lifted his hand and brushed her tears away with his thumb. "I'm sorry for the way I handled you. I'm sorry that I didn't trust you. I'm sorry that I lost you, Jade."

She shook his all too warm and electrifying hands away to rise to her feet, needing space. She couldn't think straight with him so close. "I accept your apology, and you know we're cool," she said, trying and failing to sound casual and lighthearted.

Kaeden rose to his feet, nodding in understanding. "I'm a different man now, Jade," he told her. "I'm not that little nerd who felt like I wasn't your equal. And I'm ready—more than ready—to be the man that you need and want. I've had plenty of time to get my act together, and I want you back. I want what has been missing from my life."

Jade felt overwhelmed. "I can't do this right now, Kaeden. I can't. I can't." She turned and entered the house, securely closing and locking the door behind her. She pressed her back to the door as her heart pounded.

Kaeden couldn't just expect her to take him back just like that after nearly a year apart. What did he expect her to do, run into his arms and scream "Take me"?

She looked out the window just as he turned and walked back to his car.

Jade's hand literally itched to reach out and stop him. Hold him. Feel him. Touch him.

But she didn't.

She couldn't.

And so she wrapped her arms around her own body as she watched him climb into his vehicle and reverse out of her yard and her life once more.

Kaeden was disappointed, but he wasn't ashamed or regretful. He'd made a valiant effort to fight for Jade and there was nothing wrong with that. Jade Prince would forever be the love of his life, but now he felt like they had the closure they both needed so that they could move on with life.

Kaeden slowed down as he made a right turn onto a nearly secluded dirt road that would give him a short-cut to his side of Holtsville. He looked up in his rearview mirror as a pair of headlights flashed on and off behind him. He frowned when the person also started to lay on their horn. "What the . . ."

The vehicle sped up and he saw a flash of bright yellow. "Jade?"

The thunder and lightning intensified as he slowed down and pulled off the road. She pulled off as well.

Kaeden climbed out of his vehicle and watched as Jade did the same. She ran to him and before he knew it she was in his arms, snuggling her face in his neck with her heart beating as wildly as his. "Kaeden. Kaeden. Kaeden. Why did it take you so long?" she asked in a whisper against his cheek.

The skies opened up and rain poured down upon them.

Neither cared.

Kaeden wrapped his arms around her and hugged her close to his body, enjoying the sweet feel of her again. "I thought you didn't want me back, Jade."

She leaned back in his arms. "Kaeden, I waited for you," she hollered to him to top the sound of rain pelting against the empty dirt road, their vehicles, and the neighboring trees.

Kaeden lowered his head and hungrily pressed his mouth to Jade's. The taste of the rain mingled with their kiss as Jade sucked his tongue into her mouth with a deep, guttural moan that was filled with her undying need for him.

Kaeden turned them and pressed Jade's body to the

side of his car, bringing his hands up to twist in the wet tangles of her hair as he ground his hardening length against her belly. "I need you right now," he whispered into her mouth.

Jade released him long enough to peel her nightshirt up and inched her plastered thong down her hips and legs to carelessly fling over the car and into the trees.

Kaeden unbuttoned and unzipped his pants, roughly shoving them and his boxers down below his buttocks as Jade arched her back, exposing the sight of the wet sheer material clinging to her breasts. Licking his lips with a sexy bite, he dove his head in and captured one taut nipple in his mouth, circling it with his tongue.

They both shivered as the rain continued to pelt down upon them, only intensifying their passion and fueling their fever. Jade's fingers dug into his shoulders as he spread her legs and thrust his hips upward to unite them hotly.

Their mating was primal, without inhibition and based on instinct.

Kaeden delivered a wicked series of fast, furious, and deep thrusts that were made slick by the rain pouring down his body. Filled with a desire that made him almost mad, Kaeden stepped back, freeing his dick from her wet heat, and twisted Jade over onto her stomach. He used his hand to press her down on the hood as he nudged her lips open with his tip and then united them again and again and again. He felt like he couldn't get enough of her as he continued his thrusts and bent down to suck at the rainwater drizzling down her back.

Jade gasped hotly, pounding her fist lightly against

the hood as she used her hips to match him grind for grind. She closed her eyes and allowed herself to become familiar again with their matched ardor.

They fell in sync just like that.

That chemistry between them was there, as strong as ever.

The passion and fervor they created together was unmatched.

Needing to feel his arms around her again, Jade wiggled him free from her core and turned. Kaeden lifted one of her long and shapely legs over his arm before he bent his knees to fill her swiftly.

Jade met his thrusts with wicked motions of her hips that made her buttocks lightly slap against the car as she lowered her hands to tightly grasp his buttocks like she wanted to pull more of his hardness and strength into her. She enjoyed the feel of his buttocks clenching and releasing with every thrust that spread her tightness and made room for his girth.

The mood shifted between them as Kaeden brought his mouth up to lock with hers again. Their union went from fast and furious to a slow and sensual rocking motion that was fluid. They both felt electrified as the hunger created from nearly a year apart quickly pushed them both to the brink of ecstasy.

Jade tilted her head back against the roof of the hood and she let the rain pour down on her face, throat, and chest as she enjoyed the in-and-out of Kaeden's rod against her walls. She moaned as she bit her bottom lip and allowed waves of pleasure and ful-fillment to course over her body. She allowed the tears to fall as white-hot spasms burst inside her core and shimmied over her body so that she felt like she was floating. She felt so complete in his arms. She could only sigh in the complete moment of ultimate fulfillment, and she knew that no man could give that to her like Kaeden.

Kaeden pressed his face in Jade's cleavage as his loins hardened just before his body jerked, spilling his seed deep within her. He winced in pleasure as he came again and again until his body was weak and shivering against hers. Until he was quivering and spent. Kaeden felt overwhelmed from their reunion . . . but in truth, they had only just begun.

"Are we doing the right thing?" Jade asked Kaeden as they lay entwined together in the middle of her bed.

"It feels right," Kaeden assured her.

"Yes, yes, it does," Jade agreed as she looked up through the open window at the rain falling.

She sighed as she enjoyed the feel of his hands lightly massaging circles in the dip where her back arched into her full buttocks. That morning when she arose she never imagined she would end the night with Kaeden in her bed and in her life. She had so many thoughts fluttering in and out of her head, but the one constant was the love she knew she had for this man. A love that withstood a breakup and almost one full year apart.

She had gotten over Kaeden but she had never forgotten him. There were many times she filled her journals with silly random thoughts of him. Memories. Anecdotes. Wishes. Regrets.

Jade fell silent.

"Thoughts?" he asked.

Jade lifted her head, pressing her chin lightly against his hard chest as she looked at him. "I think we should state clearly what it is we're getting into and what it is we want and expect from each other."

Kaeden felt his nature rising as his hand settled on the curve of her buttocks, but he pushed his needs away because this was a part of the healing. "I want you, Jade Prince. I want a committed relationship. I want to spend time with you but also understand that I like to hang out with my brothers. I want sex on demand and—"

Jade pinched the side of his buttocks.

Kaeden chuckled. "Just kidding. Listen, I want the kind of woman that I can build something with. Someone that I have this amazing connection with. Someone that will one day be my wife and bear my children. Someone I can grow old with. I believe that you are that woman, Jade. Only you."

Jade pressed a kiss to his chin. "And I want someone who can trust me and know that I could only step outside of something I normally wouldn't do because I felt this amazing chemistry like nothing I've ever known before. I want someone to respect me and honor me and have my back. I don't want you to see any other women. I want just me and you against the world. I want to feel the way you made me feel that first night all the time. And I want you to also respect that I love being with you but sometimes I like my space as well. Please know that while you are my man,

I will never disrespect you or lie to you or play you. I want you. That's all. That's it."

Kaeden's eyes searched hers and his heart swelled as she inched up his body to press her mouth to his. "If the way we feel has lasted even when we were apart, then it has to be the realest shit ever, Jade," he told her with emotion.

She nodded. "It was meant to be. The only thing that can destroy it is us . . . so let's not do it. You are all the man I need, and I wish I could make you feel what I feel when you touch me or just look at me or make love to me. Nobody can compete with that. Nobody can take that away from me."

"I told you before that I am a different man, Jade. I'm not that man who doesn't understand that I can be all you need. That I am your equal. That you and I were meant to be and nobody can touch that."

Jade smiled. "Oh, it's me and you against the world, baby," she told him with swagger.

With a moan of pleasure they shared a passionate kiss that made that familiar heat between them rise. Jade shifted her body so that she was straddling his narrow hips, his broadening erection pressing up with strength against her bud. She ground her hips, moving up and down the length of him in a sinful back-and-forth motion as she sucked his tongue deep into her mouth.

"Damn, I love you, Jade," he moaned against her cheek.

Jade froze and jerked her head back to look down at him. Sitting up, her breasts swaying as she did, Jade locked her eyes on him. "What did you say?" she asked him huskily.

"I said I love you. What's wrong?" he asked, grasping her wide hips.

"That's the first time you ever said it, you know," she reminded him gently before a huge smile spread across her face.

"It's not the first time I felt it," he told her huskily. "I love you, Jade Prince."

"Awwwww," she sighed.

Kaeden looked up expectantly.

"Don't think I'm Felecia," she began with a smile. "But today at the wedding, when we were standing at the end of the aisle, it felt like that would have been us getting married if we stayed together."

"I felt that way too, Jade," Kaeden admitted in a deep voice filled with emotion as he held her tighter against his chest.

"So yes, I love you, or there is no other way I could even picture spending the rest of my life with you."

"Say it again."

"I love you," she said softly with a playful tilt to her voice as he pulled her back down.

"And again."

"I love you. I love you, I love you, I love you," she told him. "Is that enough?"

Kaeden's eyes became serious. "I could never get enough."

"Me either."

They kissed, and it was filled with passion and promise.

Epilogue

Six months later

Jade sealed the last box with tape and then sat back on her heels with a sigh. Her little cottage didn't look like her little cottage anymore. She sighed sadly at the emptiness and could have sworn it echoed.

She was thrilled about moving in with Kaeden, she just hated giving up the place. She had spent many a happy hour within the little cottage, but she was going to create many more happy memories with the man she loved. That she knew.

They had both lived up to their promises to make the second time around their best time. Whether at his house or her cottage, they had spent every single night in the same bed together. Moving in together had seemed like the natural progression forward. Today was the start of a new chapter for them.

So why doesn't it feel all the way right? she wondered.

As Kaeden and his brothers noisily carried the rem-

nants of her independent living out the door and onto
the moving truck, Jade stood and wiped her hands on
the sides of her fitted jeans.

"Something wrong, Jade?" Mrs. Strong asked.

Jade pressed a smile to her pretty face as she found
Kaeden's mother, Kaitlyn, Garcelle, and Bianca
watching her. "No, moving is just a little stressful,
that's all."

"Tell me about it. When I moved all my stuff from
Atlanta, I thought I would never get everything organ-
ized," Bianca said, pausing in labeling the boxes.

Jade looked out the window at Kaeden as he talked
with his brothers, his father, and her grandfather. Her
heart swelled with love for him.

"We're doing the right thing," she told herself.
"We are."

Jade couldn't shake her reservations, but she kept a
smile on her face as the last of the boxes were loaded
onto the truck. Tonight she would officially be shack-
ing with the man she loved. "I have some sandwiches
and lemonade inside the kitchen," she told everyone as
Kaeden pulled the rear door of the truck down. "And
thank you all for helping me. I really appreciate it."

Kahron pushed his shades atop his head and
winked. "No problem. You're family."

Not legally, she thought with a strained smile as
everyone piled into the cottage.

"You okay?" Kaeden asked as he pulled her close to
him to press a kiss to her cheek.

"Yeah, I'm fine, baby," she told him. "You go ahead.
I'll be right in."

He soundly slapped her rear before he strode up the path and into the cottage.

"Stop this, Jade. He asked you to move in and you excitedly said yes, and now that the day of reckoning has arrived you can't weird out on the man." Jade kicked a rock. "So be happy, Jade. This is a big step. He loves me. We're doing this."

Jade turned and walked inside the cottage. She paused at the doorway to find Kaeden on his knee with everyone standing behind him. Her eyes dropped to the engagement ring he held in his hand. She gasped and touched her hand to her chest.

"Jade Prince, you are the one for me and I don't doubt that in the least. You make me a better person. You've made a better man."

She smiled as several of the ladies sighed in pleasure.

"I knew about a month ago that I was dying to see just how pretty you would look in a wedding gown walking down the aisle to me."

Jade stepped forward until she was standing before him.

"So when we leave here, I want you to know we are headed to our home where we will build a life together and make babies together and grow old together."

Jade reached down and touched her hands to the sides of his face.

"Marry me, Jade."

"I love you sooo much, Kaeden," she told him in a whisper as she blinked away tears.

He stood and wrapped one arm around her waist to pull her body close to his. He planted a dozen kisses on her mouth before deepening it with a moan.

"Um, is that a yes?" Kaitlyn asked dryly.

Jade laughed as she broke the kiss and looked over his broad shoulders at them. "It's a definite yes," she told them emphatically.

Everyone applauded in happiness for the couple.

Kaeden reached for her hand and slid the weighty three-carat solitaire onto her finger.

They stared at each other for the longest time, just lost in their own little world.

"So I guess you won't be moping around here anymore, Jade," Garcelle teased, even as she wiped tears from her own eyes.

"Or kicking rocks," Esai teased as he stepped forward to kiss her cheek.

"Or talking to yourself," Kahron added.

Jade eyed them all, finally feeling like everything was just right as Kaeden pulled her close for one of many kisses to come.

Hello all,

Another Strong family sibling has fallen in love, and I must admit that I am having a ball bringing love into their lives.

Jade and Kaeden are the epitome of opposites attracting, but once they got beyond their differences, they discovered a love that is meant to be. Destiny. Fate. Chemistry. The one. All of that. It's nothing but the pure goodness that we all search for . . . and many have found. Sigh. Ain't love grand? I love it. *Love* it. Ow!

So, my romance-loving people, three Strong siblings down and two more to go. Next up is Kaleb, and you will never guess who is going to wrangle this playboy cowboy. It takes one playa to know another . . . and to slow down another. The ultimate cougar on the prowl, Deena Rockwell, and the playboy rancher, Kaleb Strong, are going to discover that they are just what the other has been searching for. That's right, a sizzling May/December romance. Y'all ready? ☺

Best,
N.

Connect With Niobia

Web sites:	www.niobiabryant.com
	www.meeshamink.com
E-mails:	niobia_bryant@yahoo.com
	meeshamink@yahoo.com
MySpace:	www.myspace.com/niobiawrites
	www.myspace.com/meeshamink
Facebook:	http://www.facebook.com/InfiniteInk
	(for Niobia Bryant & Meesha Mink)
Shelfari:	www.shelfari.com/Unlimited_Ink
Twitter:	www.twitter.com/InfiniteInk

If you enjoyed *Give Me Fever*, don't miss

Lessons from a Younger Lover
by Zuri Day

Available now wherever books are sold

Turn the page for an excerpt from
Lessons from a Younger Lover . . .

There were two things Gwen Smith never thought she'd do. She never thought she'd move back to her rinky-dink hometown of Sienna, California, and she never thought she'd come back as a forty-year-old divorcée. Yet here she sat in the middle seat of a crowded plane, at the age where some said life began, trying to figure out how the boring and predictable one she'd known sixty short days ago had changed so quickly.

The first hitch in the giddyup wasn't a total surprise. Her mother's dementia had become increasingly worse following the death of Gwen's father, Harold, two years ago. Her parents had been married forty-four years. It was a tough adjustment. At the funeral, Gwen told her husband that she knew the time would come when her mother's welfare would become her responsibility. That she thought Joe would be by her side at this crucial time, and wasn't, was the fact she hadn't seen coming.

But it was true nonetheless. Joe had announced his

desire to divorce and packed his bags the same evening. Two months later she was still reeling from that okeydoke. But she couldn't think about that now. Gwen had to focus on one crisis at a time, and at the moment, her mother was the priority.

"Ladies and gentlemen, the captain has turned on the seat-belt sign, indicating our final descent into Los Angeles. Please make sure your seat belts are securely fastened and your seats and tray tables are in their upright and locked . . ."

Gwen stretched as well as she could between two stout men and tried to remove the crook from her neck. Still, she was grateful she'd fallen asleep. Shut-eye had been all too elusive these past few weeks, when ongoing worries and raging thoughts had kept true rest at bay. Fragments of a dream flitted across her wakened mind as they landed and she reached into the overhead bin for her carry-on luggage. Gwen didn't know if she wanted to remember it or not. Lately, her dreams had been replaced by nightmares that happened when her eyes were wide open.

"Gwen! Over here, girl! Gwen!"

Gwen smiled as a familiar voice pierced the crowd roaming the LAX baggage claim area. She turned and waved so that the short, buxom woman, wearing fuchsia cutoffs and a yellow halter top straining for control would know that she, God, and everyone within a five-mile radius had heard her.

"Gwendolyn!" Chantay exclaimed, enunciating each syllable for full effect as she reached up and hugged her childhood friend. "Girl, let me look at you!"

"You just saw me last year, Tay."

"That visit went by in a fog. You know the deal."

Gwen did, and wished she didn't. Her last time home was not a fond memory.

Chantay stepped back, put her hands on her hips, and began shaking her head so hard her waist-length braids sprayed the waiting passengers surrounding them. "What are we going to do with your rail-thin behind? You couldn't find enough deep-dish pizzas to eat in Chicago? No barbecue or chicken and waffle joints to put some meat on your bones?"

Gwen took the jab good-naturedly. Her five-foot-seven, size-six body had caused her heftier friend chagrin for years. No matter that Gwen had never mastered how to show off her physique, put on makeup, or fix her hair. The fact that she could eat everything, including the kitchen sink, and still not gain a pound was a stick in Chantay's craw.

Chantay enveloped her friend in a big bear hug. "You look good, girl. A day late and a dollar short on style with that curlicue hair straight out of *A Different World*, but overall . . . you look good!"

Gwen's laugh was genuine for the first time in weeks. "You don't look half bad yourself. And opinionated as always, I see."

"Honey, if you want a feel-good moment, watch *Oprah*. I'm going to tell you the truth even if it's ugly. And speaking of the 'u' word, those *Leave It to Beaver* pedal pushers—"

"Forget you, Tay! C'mon, that's my luggage coming around."

A half hour later, Gwen settled back in Chantay's Ford Explorer as they merged into highway traffic for the two-hour drive to Sienna. The air conditioner was a welcome change to the ninety-degree July heat.

"I still can't believe you're here."

"Me either."

"You know you've got to give me the full scoop. First, I never thought you'd ever get married, and if you did, you'd never, *ever* get divorced!"

"Obviously life wasn't following your script," Gwen muttered sarcastically.

"Oh, don't get your panties in a bunch, sistah, you know what I'm saying, and I'm not the only one. Who did everyone vote the least likely to, uh, get married?"

"I believe the exact description in the high school yearbook read 'would die an old maid.'"

"Well, I was trying to save you the embarrassment of quoting it verbatim, but . . . who was it?"

They both knew the answer was Gwen. But rather than help make the point, Gwen answered the question with one of her own. "Who did they say would probably have ten kids?"

"Hmph. That's because those nuckas didn't know that fornicate does not equal procreate. After being stuck with raising one *accident* and another *oops* by myself, I had my tubes tied. I told the doctor who did the procedure that if a 'baby, I pulled out' number three showed up in my pee sample, his would be the name on the father line. So believe me, if there's a sperm bad enough to get past the Boy Scout knot he tied, then that's a baby who deserves to be born."

Gwen looked out the window, thought about Chantay's two daughters, and watched the world whirl by while Chantay pushed past seventy and flew down the surprisingly light 405 freeway. While Chantay had often said she didn't want kids, Gwen had always looked forward to motherhood. She was still looking, but couldn't see any bassinet or baby bed because a divorce petition was blocking the view.

Chantay scanned for various stations on the radio before turning it off altogether. "Why are you making me drag the details out of you?" she whined, exasperation evident in her voice. "What happened between you and Joe?"

The name of Gwen's soon-to-be former husband elicited a frown. "You mean *Joey*?"

"Who the hell is that?"

"That's what he calls himself now."

"I call him 'bastard,' but I digress. What happened?"

Gwen sighed, sat up, and spoke truth straight out. "He met somebody else."

"You have got to be kidding. Corny-ass Joe Smith, the computer nerd who could barely pull the garter off at y'all's wedding?"

"That would be him."

"What fool did he find to listen to his tired lines?"

"You mean besides me?"

"Girl, I didn't mean that personally. Joe has some good points. He seems to know his way around a computer better than anybody."

"That's one."

"We've got ninety minutes of driving left. I'll think of something else."

Gwen laughed, appreciative of the levity Chantay brought to a sad situation.

"So . . . who is she?"

"Her name is Mitzi, she's twenty-two and works in his office. They both like motorcycles, Miller Lite, and poker. He tattooed her name on his arm and moved into her studio apartment last month. But I don't want to talk about him right now."

"Whoa, chick! You're sure going to have to talk about him later . . . *and* her. That was way too much information to leave me hanging. But I can wait a minute, and in the meantime change the subject to somebody you can talk about—Adam 'oh, oh, oh, oh' Johnson!"

"Chantay, you are too silly! I haven't thought about that line since we left high school." Gwen, Chantay, and a couple other misfits used to substitute his first name in Ready for the World's hit, "Oh Sheila." Chantay would hum it as he passed in the halls and the other girls would break into hysterical laughter, making them all look like fools.

"That is the single welcome surprise I've had these past few weeks—that Adam is the principal at Sienna. Can you believe it?" Gwen said.

"No, because I never thought a brothah with that much weight in his lower head would have any brains in his upper one."

"Well, there's that, but even more, the fact that he's back living in our hometown. After being such a standout at Texas A and M and going on to play for the Cowboys? I guess a lot happened to him since he was sidelined with an injury and forced to retire early."

"I can't believe his wife would agree to move back to such a Podunk town. She looks too hoity-toity for Smallville, but I only saw her one time on TV," Chantay said.

"They're divorced."

"What? Girl, stop!"

"Yep, he told me that when we talked. He was nice actually, not the cocky, arrogant Adam I remember. He wouldn't admit it, but I know he's the reason why my getting this post is, to use his words, 'in the bag.'"

"Don't give him too much credit, Gwen. You're a first-rate teacher, and it's not like our town has to beat off qualified educators with sticks."

"Maybe, but the way everything happened . . . I'm just happy to know I have a job secured, or at least I will after my interview next week. Mama has some money saved up, but that's all going into her assisted living expenses. I still need to support myself, and pay half the mortgage on the condo until it's sold."

"How's Miss Lorraine doing?"

Gwen shrugged. "Mama's about the same, I guess."

"Isn't she a bit young for what the doctors say is happening to her?"

"From what I've learned, not really. The disease usually comes with aging, but can actually occur at any time, from a variety of causes. It's usually given a different name when it occurs in someone, say, under fifty-five. But whatever the title, the results are the same—a long-term decline in cognitive function."

"Just be glad she's still here," Chantay replied. "You can always hug her, whether she knows you or not."

"Oh, she recognizes everybody, and remembers more than she lets on, I'm thinking. But I hear what you're saying, Chantay, and I'm grateful."

They were silent a moment before Chantay changed the subject. "Joe's a lowlife. He could have stayed in the condo and split the rent with the fool he's sleeping with until somebody bought it. He's just an asshole."

"That would have been too much like right. But it is what it is. Don't get me re-pissed about it."

Chantay started humming "Oh Sheila." "Wouldn't it be ironic if you moved back to town and snagged its star player after all these years? Now, we'll have to give your dated butt a makeover, but by the time I'm done with you . . . you'll move over all those other silicone-stuffed heifas in town."

"I wonder who else from our class still lives there."

"Girl, it don't even matter. Keep your eye on the prize." Chantay shot another sideways look at her friend. "Um-hmm. If it's Adam Johnson you want—trust, I can help you get him."

Gwen had thought about Adam, and what a nice balm he might be for the hurt Joe had caused her. Not that she'd get into anything serious right away. It would be months before the divorce came up on the back-logged Illinois court docket and was finalized. But since speaking to Adam, she'd fantasized a time or two about the heartthrob she remembered: tall, lanky, chocolate, strong, with bedroom eyes and a Jheri curl that brushed his shoulders. She never dreamed she'd get another chance with someone like Adam. But as she'd learned all too painfully in the past few months—life was full of surprises.